unMASKeD

JERRY B. JENKINS
TIM LAHAYE

with CHRIS FABRY

TYNDALE HOUSE PUBLISHERS, INC.
WHEATON, ILLINOIS

Visit areUthirsty.com

Visit Tyndale's exciting Web site at www.tyndale.com

TYNDALE is a registered trademark of Tyndale House Publishers, Inc.

Tyndale's quill logo is a trademark of Tyndale House Publishers, Inc.

Discover the latest Left Behind news at www.leftbehind.com

Unmasked is a special edition compilation of the following Left Behind: The Kids titles:

#26: *The Beast Arises* copyright © 2003 by Jerry B. Jenkins and Tim LaHaye. All rights reserved.

#27: *Wildfire!* copyright © 2003 by Jerry B. Jenkins and Tim LaHaye. All rights reserved.

#28: *The Mark of the Beast* copyright © 2003 by Jerry B. Jenkins and Tim LaHaye. All rights reserved.

Cover photograph copyright © by Dynamic Graphics. All rights reserved.

Left Behind is a registered trademark of Tyndale House Publishers, Inc.

Published in association with the literary agency of Alive Communications, Inc., 7680 Goddard Street, Suite 200, Colorado Springs, CO 80920.

Scripture quotations are taken from the *Holy Bible*, New Living Translation, copyright © 1996. Used by permission of Tyndale House Publishers, Inc., Wheaton, Illinois 60189. All rights reserved.

Some Scripture taken from the New King James Version. Copyright © 1979, 1980, 1982 by Thomas Nelson, Inc. Used by permission. All rights reserved.

Designed by Jackie Noe

Library of Congress Cataloging-in-Publication Data

Unmasked / Jerry B. Jenkins, Tim LaHaye with Chris Fabry.
    p. cm.
  ISBN 1-4143-0269-X (hc)
[1. End of the world—Fiction. 2. Christian life—Fiction.] I. LaHaye, Tim F. II Fabry, Chris, date. III. Jenkins, Jerry B. The beast arises. IV. Jenkins, Jerry B. Wildfire. V. Jenkins, Jerry B. Mark of the beast.
  PZ7.J4138Up 2005
  [Fic]—dc22   2004015565

Printed in the United States of America

10 09 08 07 06 05
 9   8   7   6   5   4   3   2   1

1

JUDD ran after Kasim, losing sight of him in the crowd. He hated leaving the Wailing Wall, but he couldn't let Kasim get away again. Judd had to convince him to abandon his assassination plot.

The streets were filled with vendors and drunken people still celebrating the witnesses' deaths. He elbowed his way through a crowd watching a television and jumped to see over the crowd. Kasim turned a corner and ran away.

A man pointed at the television and laughed. "Look at that. Three days and they're still dead."

The screaming vocals of Z-Van and The Four Horsemen drowned the crowd's laughter. Judd rounded the corner as Kasim disappeared into a group on the side of the street. A banner over a music store ahead read "Meet Z-Van today!" For a hundred Nicks, fans could receive a signed copy of The Four Horsemen's latest recording.

A woman screamed and ran from a bar, both hands

over her mouth. She knelt on the sidewalk. A middle-aged man followed her outside, pale and shaking. "They're alive!"

Judd ran to the bar as people streamed out, toppling chairs and tables. Judd pushed his way to the window and saw Eli and Moishe—alive! The two witnesses struggled to their feet, their chests heaving, their faces turned toward the sky.

Judd clenched his fists. "Yes!"

The street was alive now, people rushing back and forth, not believing the news. People near the music store darted out of line and rushed toward alleys. Others seemed confused. A window smashed and several people reached through and grabbed recordings. A rumor spread through the throng that Eli and Moishe were on their way to the main stage.

"That means they'll come straight through here!" someone said.

A few laughed, not believing the reports. "Those two have been dead three days," a man yelled. "They're not going anywhere."

A voice so loud Judd thought it had come from the speakers a few feet away said, "COME UP HERE!" The sun peeked through snow-white clouds, and the rays cast beautiful colors over the crowd.

"Look there!" a woman screeched.

Just above the buildings, Eli and Moishe rose like human hot-air balloons. People gasped and fell to their knees. The man who had laughed at the witnesses grabbed his chest and fell backward, knocking others to the ground.

Eli and Moishe were soon enveloped in white, the cloud picking up speed until it became a speck in the sky. Judd breathed a prayer of thanks.

When he opened his eyes, only a few people stood. Most lay flat, crying, moaning, begging God not to kill them. One person moved over the prostrate bodies toward the music store. It was Kasim.

Judd called to him, but as Kasim ducked inside the store, the street shattered. People flew in the air like missiles and crashed through windows. A woman was tossed into a tree and grabbed a branch. She held on a few seconds, then plunged to the ground.

"Earthquake!" people shouted as the street opened in front of them. Vendors' carts tipped, spilling contents into the great cracks. Several hundred people plunged into the chasm, screaming as they fell.

Judd crawled toward a hydrant, but another shock wave knocked it over and water shot into the air. Judd scrambled for something to hold on to as freezing rain-drops smashed onto his head. He threw up his hands to shield his face as the sky turned black. A car sped toward him, careening out of control. It hit a gash in the earth, flipped upside down, and skidded on its top until it dropped into the newly opened hole.

Glass and metal exploded as nearby buildings collapsed. Judd watched a tall building teeter and fall. People tried to get out of the way, but they were crushed.

The violent shaking ended, and Judd marveled at how quickly things had been destroyed. Trees lay in the street. Buildings leaned or were flattened. Judd remembered

3

how long the wrath of the Lamb earthquake had lasted and was glad this one had lasted only a few seconds.

The dark sky gave way to sunshine again, which cast an eerie, green light on the horror around him. As he carefully walked toward the building Kasim had entered, Judd heard a weak voice behind him. "Please help me."

People hurried past, pushing Judd to the ground. When he stood, he noticed someone's hand at the edge of the crevasse. He walked a few steps, then fell to his knees and crawled. To his shock, the hand wasn't attached.

"Over here," a woman said.

A few feet away, teetering on the edge of the crater, a car lay upside down. A woman hung out of the door, her leg wedged between the seat and the car's frame.

"Don't move!" Judd said. He scooted along, careful not to jostle the earth nearby. Steam rose from the engine, and liquid dripped near the woman's head.

"Is it going to catch fire?" the woman said.

"Don't talk. Stay still."

Other than the hissing of the steam and a few people moaning and crying, the entire area had been quieted by the massive quake. There was no more celebrating or dancing. Those who could walk hurried away.

Judd looked for a chain or some rope but couldn't find any. Bits of rock and asphalt trickled into the chasm, and he knew he had to work quickly. "Raise your hands and I'll grab you!"

The woman gingerly put up an arm, and Judd reached for her hand. When she lifted the other, Judd turned away. Her left hand was gone.

The car shifted in the crumbling earth, and Judd struggled to maintain his footing.

"I don't want to die!" the woman said.

Judd slipped and fell back, and the car tipped forward. For a moment he thought it would settle, but the door creaked and closed as the car plunged into the hole, silencing the woman's screams.

Judd rolled onto his back and put his hands over his face. How much death and suffering could the world take? Shouts from nearby brought him back to reality. He stood and rushed inside the music store to look for Kasim.

Lionel fought back tears as he ran. He had just seen Eli and Moishe rise from the dead. Their bodies had been shattered by Nicolae Carpathia and had decomposed since they were murdered, but now they were whole again. The once happy crowd was terrified.

After the witnesses had risen into a cloud, the earth shook so violently that Lionel struggled to stay on his feet. A few blocks away buildings crashed, and Lionel heard the sickening crunch of metal and glass.

People who had danced around Moishe and Eli now fled the scene in panic. A light post fell on a woman and crushed her.

Mr. Stein quickly gathered the believers. "Many will die today. We must help those who are trapped." They split into four groups and rushed toward the area that had been most severely hit.

Sam Goldberg ran next to Lionel. "Do you think anyone saw Eli and Moishe on television?"

"Wouldn't doubt it," Lionel said. "It's the biggest story of the Gala, but I'll bet Carpathia cans the replay."

"Do you think they'll still have the closing ceremony tonight?"

"Carpathia doesn't let a little death and destruction stop his party."

As Lionel and the others neared the death zone, they met hundreds of dazed and wounded people. Some helped friends and family members, but most walked by themselves, crying.

Huge cracks split the street, and many cars had fallen inside. Someone screamed, and Lionel and Sam walked into an apartment building. A woman pounded on an elevator, yelling for her husband. "He went for our camera, and I heard a crash!" The woman broke down, and Sam tried to comfort her.

Lionel punched the elevator button, but the power was off. He found a sharp tool and pried open the doors. The shaft was filled with dust. He found a flashlight in a first-floor office and looked down the shaft. Snapped cables lay on top of the mangled elevator car.

"Anybody hear me down there?" Lionel shouted. His voice echoed, but no one responded.

Lionel waited a few moments for the dust to clear, then climbed down a ladder built into the shaft. He held the flashlight under his arm as he pried open the top of the elevator. He pointed the flashlight into the hole and gasped. Three people lay dead, their bodies twisted in horrible positions. One man clutched a bloodstained camera.

"Do you see him?" the woman shouted.

Lionel climbed back up. "I'm sorry, ma'am. You don't want to—"

The woman grabbed the flashlight and pushed Lionel away. Lionel and Sam went outside as the woman screamed for her husband.

In the distance a Global Community public-address truck drove through the streets. "Attention, citizens! Volunteers are needed immediately to help with relief efforts. Closing ceremonies will take place tonight as planned. Religious fanatics have stolen the bodies of the preachers. Do not fall for fairy tales of their disappearing. Repeat: Closing ceremonies will take place tonight as planned."

Lionel and Sam looked at each other and shook their heads. They walked farther toward the earthquake zone, wondering what they would find in the rubble.

Vicki and the others at the Wisconsin hideout were fascinated by the live shot of Eli and Moishe rising into the cloud. As announcers at the scene searched for words, cameras shook and fell over. Mark rushed to the computer and composed a message to kids around the world.

Don't be surprised. God predicted it would happen. The Bible also predicts that a tenth of those living in Jerusa-

lem will die because of this quake. The Global Commu-
nity will probably make up something to explain Eli and
Moishe rising from the dead, but there is no doubt that
God is greater than a thousand Carpathias. Keep watch-
ing. There may be more surprises tonight.

As Vicki watched the news out of Jerusalem, she
wondered about Judd, Lionel, and the others. After the
live shot of Eli and Moishe, the GC said nothing about
their resurrection.

"Will any believers die in this quake?" Shelly said.

"I'm not sure," Vicki said. "I think these judgments
are mainly to get the attention of unbelievers, but Loretta
and Donny Moore and Ryan and a bunch of other believers died in the wrath of the Lamb earthquake."

Vicki noticed Darrion sitting alone. "You were talking
about how you brought some friends up here, and you're
still feeling guilty about it. You want to talk some more?"

Darrion shook her head. "Wait till this is over. I need
time to think."

Vicki put an arm around Darrion and looked at the
television. Sirens blared and emergency crews struggled to
get into the ravaged area. Vicki leaned forward as someone who looked like Judd ran past a reporter. She closed
her eyes and prayed.

———————————

Judd forced his way inside the nearly collapsed doorway
and put a handkerchief over his mouth and nose. It took
a few moments to see through the dust. Bodies lay

trapped beneath tons of rubble, and Judd wondered if he should leave.

Judd yelled Kasim's name, and someone called from the back of the building. He climbed over cash registers, stacks of music recordings, chairs, and speakers that had been set up for the special event. Most people had gotten out of the building, but he saw a few who hadn't. Some had been crushed by falling glass, others under cement. "Hang on, I'm coming!"

Sirens wailed in the distance as Judd moved debris and found a hallway that led to the back. The collapsed ceiling stopped him.

"Back here," someone yelled.

"Stay where you are. I've got to find another way." Judd forced open a restroom door and climbed onto the sink. The ceiling hadn't fallen here, so he lifted tiles and found enough space to crawl through. But what if the building shifted?

"Help!"

Judd pulled himself up and inched through the narrow passage, pushing with his feet and crawling arm over arm. Something rumbled, and Judd put his hands over his head, thinking it was an aftershock. The ceiling held, and Judd kept crawling until he made it through.

He found himself on the other side of the collapse in what looked like a small lunchroom. A refrigerator lay on its side, the door open and food scattered on the floor. A microwave lay next to it, along with silverware and broken dishes.

The back door had been smashed by a concrete block.

Someone was trapped underneath. Judd found the person's arm and felt for a pulse. Nothing. He crawled to the other side and saw Kasim, facedown, dead.

Judd sat back and shook his head. First Nada had been killed, now Kasim. He stood to leave when something moved behind him and a man said, "Are you going to help me or not?"

Judd went inside and saw a foot sticking out from under a smashed table. He cleared chairs away and found a man wearing a leather jacket and designer jeans pinned beneath it. Sunglasses lay a few feet away, unbroken.

"Better get me out before the whole thing comes down," the man said.

"Wait. I know you."

"Yeah, yeah, I'm Z-Van. But I'll be just another dead singer if I don't get out of here. Are you going to help me?"

2

JUDD stared at Z-Van. He was the lead singer for The Four Horsemen, a man who spat in God's face every time he sang. Young people worshiped him, dressed like him, memorized his lyrics, and imitated his twisted lifestyle.

Judd glanced out the back door. Why did God allow this man to live and Kasim to die? Judd thought.

"Get this stuff off me!"

Judd tried to lift the table, but it wouldn't budge. He checked Z-Van's legs for bleeding. "I have to get something. Hang on."

"Don't leave me!" Z-Van yelled, but Judd scampered outside and found a piece of lumber and wedged it under the table. It moved a few inches.

"Pull yourself out," Judd said.

Z-Van screamed in pain, but he couldn't move his legs.

11

Judd let the weight settle. He bent to catch his breath and put his hands on his knees. "How did you get the name Z-Van?"

"Look, I'll give you an autograph after you get me out of here."

"I don't want your autograph."

Z-Van shrugged. "Sounded hip at the time. Anything's better than Myron."

"Your real name's Myron? What's your last name?"

"I'll tell you that when my legs are out from under this table." Z-Van looked around the room. "I'm thirsty. Anything to drink around here?"

Judd turned on the faucet and dirty water trickled out.

"No way I'm drinking that stuff."

Judd rummaged through the refrigerator and found a bottle of water. Z-Van drank it and threw the empty bottle in the corner. "I shouldn't have agreed to this gig. The promoter said it was good publicity."

"Most people got out through the front, right?"

"It was awful. Building starts shaking, things flying off the walls, people screaming, climbing over each other. The owner took me the back way and—"

"What's wrong?"

Z-Van tried to sit up. "The owner was right beside me when this came down."

Judd crawled behind the table and noticed a man's shoe sticking out of the rubble. Z-Van shuddered and tried to move away. "I have to get out of here. Just do what you have to."

Judd walked out the back and heard a GC public-address truck in the distance asking for volunteers. He had to find someone to help him pull Z-Van out.

Vicki and the others watched the news reports the rest of the morning. Many areas of Jerusalem had hardly any damage, while the east side looked like a bomb had exploded. Cameras captured collapsed apartment buildings and roads that had become chunks of upturned asphalt and mud.

The death toll was first announced in the hundreds, but only a few minutes later estimates climbed into the thousands. Leon Fortunato hastily called a press conference and spread out a sheet of paper in front of him. He pursed his lips and grimaced.

"I have just come from a meeting with Potentate Carpathia about the situation on the east side. First, let me say that all delegates to the Gala should still attend the final ceremony tonight. It will be abbreviated.

"The potentate is involved in the search-and-rescue operation, but he asked that I extend his heartfelt condolences to all who have suffered loss."

"I'll bet he's involved," Conrad said. "The guy's probably watching from his hotel."

Fortunato quoted Carpathia as saying, "'Reconstruction begins immediately. We will not be defeated by one defeat. The character of a people is revealed by its reaction to tragedy. We shall rise because we are the Global Community.

"'There is tremendous morale-building value in our

coming together as planned. Music and dancing will not be appropriate, but we shall stand together, encourage each other, and dedicate ourselves anew to the ideals we hold dear.' "

Fortunato folded the paper and looked at the camera. "Let me add a personal word. It would be most encouraging to Potentate Carpathia if you were to attend in overwhelming numbers. We will commemorate the dead and the valor of those involved in the rescue effort, and the healing process will begin."

When Fortunato finished, Mark reported that thousands had logged on to the kids' Web site in the past hour. Vicki asked if there was any news from Judd or Lionel, and Mark shook his head.

Lionel pointed to a street in shambles, and Sam followed him into the death zone. Rescue workers hadn't reached the collapsed buildings yet, so Lionel and Sam searched for anyone they could help.

A man with blood streaming down his face limped along. Lionel reached out to help, but the man pulled away. Smoke rose from a few fires that had started. Lionel knew that if gas lines ignited, the whole block could explode.

From across the street came a familiar voice. "Lionel! Sam! Help!"

Lionel ran toward Judd and embraced him. "I thought you were dead."

"Close," Judd said.

"Did you find Kasim?"

Judd nodded. "He didn't make it."

"What?" Lionel said. He leaned against the roots of an upturned tree and ran a hand through his hair.

"There's no time to mourn now," Judd said. "There's a guy trapped in back."

Judd led them through the front of the building and into the narrow passage in the ceiling. "If we get him out from under the rubble, we'll have to find another way to get him to one of the rescue trucks."

"Who is it?" Lionel said.

"See for yourself."

Lionel knelt near Z-Van, and his mouth formed an O.

"Good, you found somebody to help," Z-Van said. "Hurry up!"

Sam ran to find another way out while Judd and Lionel worked on Z-Van. Lionel lifted the table a few inches while Judd tried to pull the man away from the debris. Judd almost had him out when the board snapped and the table fell on Z-Van's feet with a sickening crunch. The singer screamed in pain. Lionel put his fingers under the table and lifted with all his might until Judd pulled Z-Van away.

Lionel collapsed, wheezing and coughing. Z-Van's boots were covered with dust and his legs were twisted. They tried to make him comfortable, but the pain was so great that Z-Van moaned and cried.

Judd waved Lionel to the back door and showed him Kasim's body.

"Doesn't seem fair, does it?" Lionel said.

"That's what I thought. What should we do about Kasim's body?"

"No way we're getting it out of here by ourselves. Let's get this guy out of here and go tell Kasim's parents."

Sam rushed back, excited about finding a way to the street. Lionel rummaged through debris and found a board big enough to use as a stretcher. There was so much rubble that the three had to stop several times before reaching the street. Judd waved at a rescue truck, but it was already full.

"Tell them who I am!" Z-Van shouted.

"I don't think they care," Lionel said.

"Let's take him back to the General's house," Sam said. "He'll know a doctor."

"Take the key from my pocket," Z-Van moaned. "I have painkillers in my hotel room."

Judd took the key and noticed it was from the same hotel Carpathia and his potentates were using. Judd asked Sam to phone the General's driver and meet them a few streets outside the quake zone.

Judd and Lionel carried Z-Van to the meeting place. By the time they made it, Sam was there and Z-Van had passed out.

"The driver is on his way," Sam said. "General Zimmerman says they will have a bed ready and he's calling a doctor he knows."

"Good," Judd said, slipping the key back into Z-Van's pocket. "I don't want to go to that hotel room. We probably wouldn't be able to get by security anyway."

"What about Kasim's parents?" Lionel said as the limousine pulled up.

"Let's get this guy to Zimmerman's; then we'll find them."

Lionel noticed people walking toward the closing ceremony site and shook his head. "I can't believe they're going through with it."

"You know Carpathia," Judd said. "They'll throw this party even though millions have died. What's a few more thousand to them?"

Judd was surprised to find General Zimmerman's home almost empty. Mr. Stein and the other witnesses were still at the earthquake site helping victims.

Sam, Lionel, and Judd carried Z-Van into the house and placed him on a bed. He awoke and screamed for his pills. General Zimmerman ushered an older man into the room and led Judd and the others into the living room.

"The doctor is a neighbor a few houses away. He is not a believer . . . yet." The General smiled. "He is very good. He will help the young man."

Judd explained who Z-Van was and where they had found him. When he gave the news about Kasim, the General looked troubled. "We should find his parents quickly. They are helping with the rescue operation."

The General left the room to make a phone call to Mr. Stein while Judd flipped on the latest news. Aerial shots of Jerusalem showed that about a tenth of the Holy City had been destroyed.

"Early estimates of the dead have been changed," a reporter said. "It now appears, according to Global

Community sources, that the death toll could rise to as many as seven thousand by tomorrow morning."

"And they're still going ahead with the closing ceremony," Lionel said. "Unbelievable."

"One other note," the reporter continued. "One of the most popular performers at the Gala, Z-Van of The Four Horsemen, was making an appearance in the quake zone at the time of the disaster and is feared dead."

"Should we tell them he's all right?" Sam said.

"Not yet," Judd said. "We don't want the GC coming here."

General Zimmerman returned and said Mr. Stein had lost contact with Kasim's parents. Judd called Yitzhak's house, but there was no answer.

"What about Kasim's apartment?" Lionel said.

"I don't think they know where it is, but I'll check," Judd said. "You and Sam go back and look for them in the death zone."

Before Judd left, he checked Z-Van. The doctor reported that he was resting comfortably. "We won't know about his legs until I take him to my office for X-rays. We're going there now."

Judd told General Zimmerman their plan and the man nodded. "Take my cell phone and let me know if you find Kasim's parents. Will you be going near the Gala?"

"Kasim's apartment is located near the main stage."

"Be careful, and see if you can spot my friend Chaim Rosenzweig."

"I thought he was sick."

"He's made a miraculous recovery! He'll be in a

wheelchair, but I'm told he will sit on the main stage behind Carpathia!"

Judd walked into the street just as the sun moved from behind a cloud. The orange glow made the old city look beautiful—and yet, Judd knew this was another tragic day. They had lost another believer and friend, and thousands lay crushed under the rubble only a short distance away.

Judd thought about the Gala. Would this be the night Carpathia was killed? Would the brilliant Chaim Rosenzweig keep turning from God and follow Carpathia? And what if Judd found Jamal and Lina, Kasim's parents? How could he tell them of the death of their only son? Judd thought of Z-Van. He wanted to talk to the man about the truth, but he seemed so far away from God.

The sun warmed Judd as he walked closer to Kasim's place. People in the streets weren't dancing or drinking now. They soberly moved toward the man they thought had answers to their problems.

But Judd knew something they didn't. According to the Bible, Satan himself would soon inhabit Carpathia.

3

JUDD squeezed through the massive crowd and followed a couple into Kasim's building. The apartment wasn't locked and Judd walked in, hoping to find Kasim's parents. They weren't there.

Judd closed the door and sat in front of the window. Using Kasim's binoculars, he saw the ornate stage with a row of chairs set up behind the lectern. A man in a wheelchair was taken to the right just below the stage.

That must be Dr. Rosenzweig, Judd thought. He wondered if any of the members of the adult Tribulation Force were in the audience. But who could tell? A sea of people waited patiently for their leader.

A guard searched Dr. Rosenzweig. Then four men lifted the chair to the stage and rolled him to his place at the end of the row. Dr. Rosenzweig playfully drove the motorized wheelchair back and forth across the stage. The crowd, which had been quiet, began to respond to the old man, smiling and laughing.

Lionel and Sam searched for Mr. Stein, but hundreds of rescuers were in the streets looking for survivors. GC helicopters buzzed the tops of buildings, and on every corner emergency vehicles waited for the injured. Lionel overheard a radio transmission from a hospital saying it was closed to new patients. A nearby school had been set up as a temporary morgue.

Sam waved at one of the Jewish believers staying at General Zimmerman's house, and the man approached. "I believe God placed us here at this critical time," the man said. "I have prayed with three people since the earthquake."

As the sun set, Lionel and Sam returned to the music store to check on Kasim's body. No one had discovered him, so Lionel and Sam found two pieces of metal and began to dig. By nightfall they had pulled Kasim's body away from the rubble and wrapped it in a tablecloth Sam found inside.

"You're Jewish," Lionel said. "Don't you have a problem touching a dead body?"

"This is my brother in Christ," Sam said. "I want to make sure his parents are able to say good-bye."

Lionel and Sam carried Kasim's body a few blocks, avoiding GC personnel. General Zimmerman's driver met them and returned to the General's house.

"But we still have to find his parents," Sam said.

Judd watched the potentates climb the stage steps and shake hands with each other. The mood was somber, no

music or even an opening prayer. The huge lighting
system bathed the plaza in white light.

Judd scanned the crowd with the binoculars, searching for Kasim's parents. The gathering looked even bigger
than opening night.

Finally, Leon Fortunato and Nicolae Carpathia
mounted the stairs, surrounded by security guards.
When the crowd recognized them, they applauded
politely. Leon had each of the potentates stand as he
introduced them. Then he let Carpathia introduce the
final guest.

Vicki and the others in Wisconsin had watched the earthquake coverage all day and waited for word from Judd or
Lionel. When Nicolae Carpathia finally stood to quiet the
crowd, several kids groaned.

"Let me add my deep thanks to that of our supreme
commander's and also my sympathies to you who have
suffered," Carpathia began. "Many in the music world
mourn tonight because of the death of one of the leading
entertainers of our day."

A picture of Z-Van appeared on the huge screens
around the plaza and the crowd was silent, except for
some who cried and wiped away tears. After a moment of
silence, Carpathia continued. "I will not keep you long,
because I know many of you need to return to your
homelands and are concerned about transportation.
Flights are going from both airports, though there are, of
course, delays.

"Now before my remarks, let me introduce my guest of honor. He was to have been here Monday, but he was overtaken by an untimely stroke. It gives me great pleasure to announce the miraculous rallying of this great man, enough so that he joins us tonight in his wheelchair, with wonderful prospects for complete recovery. Ladies and gentlemen of the Global Community, a statesman, a scientist, a loyal citizen, and my dear friend, the distinguished Dr. Chaim Rosenzweig!"

Vicki shook her head as the crowd erupted. "You'd think somebody as smart as Dr. Rosenzweig wouldn't believe Carpathia's lies."

Judd had a perfect view of Dr. Rosenzweig as Nicolae held up the man's good arm in a gesture of victory. The crowd cheered on.

Finally, Nicolae returned to the podium and spoke somberly. "Fellow citizens, in the very young history of our one-world government, we have stood shoulder to shoulder against great odds, as we do tonight.

"I had planned a speech to send us back to our homes with renewed vigor and a rededication to Global Community ideals. Tragedy has made that talk unnecessary. We have proven again that we are a people of purpose and ideals, of servanthood and good deeds."

Three potentates behind Carpathia stood. The other seven rose slowly and clapped. Carpathia turned as the crowd picked up the applause.

That's strange, Judd thought.

The potentates sat and Carpathia hesitated. He turned and jokingly said, "Do not do that to me."

Judd jumped from his seat, aware that something was about to happen. He bolted from the room, binoculars dangling from his neck, and ran down the stairs. He had to get to the stage.

Vicki and the others wondered what was going on as Carpathia smiled and laughed. The camera switched to the potentates, three of whom stood again and applauded, as if trying to score points with Nicolae. The audience chuckled and applauded again.

"Look, Dr. Rosenzweig's doing his wheelchair routine again," Conrad said.

It was true. Rosenzweig wheeled himself toward Leon Fortunato as the crowd continued clapping. The camera panned the crowd. Everyone was on their feet now, raising their hands, shouting, and jumping.

"I wish we could cut to Vicki B. right now," Mark said.

Vicki nodded. "I'd love a chance to speak to this crowd."

Suddenly, an explosion rocked the festivities, and the camera went out of control. The kids all sat forward, trying to see what had happened.

Judd raced for the stage, but people stood shoulder to shoulder. Security guards had cleared people from trees surrounding the plaza, but Judd took a chance and put one foot on a tree trunk and jumped as high as he could, barely reaching the lowest branch. He pulled himself up and sat, trying to orient himself. One of the speaker stands was only ten feet away, so Judd could hear every breath from Carpathia.

Judd put the binoculars to his eyes just as a guard below shouted at him. Judd ignored the man and saw that he had a perfect view of the stage from the same angle as before.

"I said come down from there now, or—"

A gunshot exploded to Judd's right. The lectern shattered, and the huge curtain behind Carpathia ripped away. Judd turned to see who had fired the shot, but something silver caught his eye at the back of the stage. At first, Judd thought it was Chaim Rosenzweig's wheelchair, but as he looked closer, he saw Chaim holding a sword.

Carpathia reeled from the shot, stumbled, and fell backward toward Chaim. Judd gasped as Dr. Rosenzweig lifted the sword to meet the potentate. The blade plunged into his head, and Carpathia's hands shot to his chin. Chaim twisted the handle of the sword and let go. The potentate rolled to the stage floor and Chaim steered to the left, away from the body.

Judd kept his eyes on the platform as chaos broke out all around him. Dr. Rosenzweig seemed puzzled, like he was having another stroke. The other potentates scurried off the back of the stage and jumped to the ground.

The crowd screamed and ran away. Some at the front ducked under the stage. Others ran for safety and trampled those who were slower. A few climbed up the tree Judd was in and sat on other branches.

Dr. Rosenzweig moved his wheelchair to the rear of the stage and rolled out of the chair. To Judd's amazement, he tossed his blanket over the side, threw his feet over the edge, and disappeared behind the stage.

How did he do that? Judd thought.

Judd focused on Carpathia. The most powerful man on the face of the earth lay in a pool of blood. From the nearby speaker tower, Judd heard Carpathia gasp and speak a few words. "But I thought . . . I thought . . . I did everything you asked," he choked.

Leon Fortunato leaned over Carpathia's body, fell upon the potentate's chest, and pulled his body up into an embrace. The audio cut out as Leon rocked Carpathia back and forth. Judd looked closely and thought he saw Carpathia's lips move again. The nearby speaker crackled, and Judd heard the man say, "Father, forgive them, for they know not what they do."

Fortunato wailed, "Don't die, Excellency! We need you! The world needs you! *I* need you!"

People stampeded the plaza in a human tidal wave. Judd noticed a scaffold swaying as people ran by. Three stories up, the giant speakers leaned under the stress of the torrent. Suddenly, a ten-foot-square speaker box teetered. Judd instinctively shouted, but no one heard him. The speaker snapped its moorings and fell, landing on a woman. A man tried to drag her body from under the smashed speaker, but people around him pushed him out of the way and the crowd kept running.

Vicki shuddered as she and the others watched the replay of the assassination. The news anchors were almost speechless as they replayed video showing the lectern splintering and the curtain taking the impact of the bullet. Carpathia fell and the dignitaries onstage scurried away.

"I didn't think it was supposed to be a gunshot," Conrad said.

"Tsion thought it would be a sword," Mark said. "Guess he was wrong."

Lionel and Sam arrived at the Gala seconds after the shot had been fired. As thousands screamed and fled the scene of the assassination, Lionel and Sam inched toward the stage, unaware of what had happened.

As they came closer, Lionel saw Carpathia on the platform, his wrists drawn under his chin, his eyes shut. Blood trickled from his mouth and ears and he shook violently.

Leon Fortunato screamed, "Oh, he's gone! He's gone! Someone do something."

A helicopter landed and emergency medical personnel hopped out. Some rushed to Carpathia, while others tended to those who had been trampled in the plaza and to a woman who had been crushed by a falling speaker.

Emergency workers tried to help Carpathia, but it looked like gallons of blood had pooled from his wound. Lionel noticed Mac McCullum making his way up the steps.

Fortunato screamed and pushed his way between the medical personnel. He knelt in Nicolae's blood and buried his face in the man's lifeless chest. Another man gently pulled Leon away from the body, and the two talked for a moment.

GC guards surrounded the stage, holding high-powered weapons. Lionel tugged on Sam's arm and the two left.

"Who do you think did it?" Sam said.

"Doesn't matter," Lionel said. "They'll come after followers of Ben-Judah with a vengeance."

When Judd finally made it back to General Zimmerman's home, he found Lionel and Sam in the entryway. They took him aside and told him what they had done with Kasim's body.

"Kasim's mom and dad just got here," Lionel said. "They're waiting in the meeting room."

Judd found the two sitting, Mr. Stein kneeling before them in prayer. "Do they know?" Judd whispered to Lionel.

"Not yet."

When Mr. Stein had finished his prayer, Judd sat beside them and told them the whole story. Jamal and Lina asked to see Kasim's body, and Lionel showed them.

Judd wept with Kasim's surviving family members, thinking of Nada and all his other friends who had died. He longed for the Glorious Appearing of Christ, but he knew that was three and a half years away.

4

JUDD found something to eat and watched the news coverage at General Zimmerman's house. He was exhausted but couldn't sleep. He asked about Z-Van and learned the man had hairline fractures in both legs and feet.

"The doctor sedated him and put casts on," Lionel said. "He's asleep in one of the guest rooms."

"Does anyone know he's alive?"

"He told the doctor he didn't want anyone to know. Said he wanted to see how the media would cover his death."

Judd shook his head. "All those people killed in the earthquake and this guy thinks about publicity."

A grieving Supreme Commander Leon Fortunato appeared at a live news conference. He had changed from his bloodstained clothes and looked sad.

"As the news media has already reported, I now

confirm the death of our beloved leader and guide. We shall carry on in the courageous spirit of our founder and moral anchor, Potentate Nicolae Carpathia. The cause of death will remain confidential until the investigation is complete. But you may rest assured the guilty party will be brought to justice."

"They don't know who did it," Judd said.

"You mean who shot him?" Lionel said.

"He wasn't shot. It was a sword, just like Tsion said." Judd explained what he had seen to Lionel.

Lionel said, "But Dr. Rosenzweig has been very ill. How could he have done such a thing and escaped?"

"He must have been faking it," Judd said.

A news anchor said the body of the slain potentate would lie in state in the New Babylon palace before entombment Sunday. Judd looked at Lionel and swallowed hard. "When do you think it will happen?"

Lionel pursed his lips. "Sometime in the next two days. And then Carpathia is going to be even more evil than he has been, if that's possible."

Sam ran into the room and tapped Judd's shoulder. "Z-Van's awake. He wants to see you."

———————————

As the assassination coverage continued, Vicki gathered everyone. Some of the kids knew as much as Vicki, but Janie and Melinda were new to the Bible.

Janie scratched her head. "You guys really think Carpathia is coming back from the dead?"

"Tsion Ben-Judah thinks so," Vicki said, grabbing a

Bible. "Everyone was surprised about Eli and Moishe, but listen to this." She turned to Revelation 11. " 'But after three and a half days, the spirit of life from God entered them, and they stood up! And terror struck all who were staring at them. Then a loud voice shouted from heaven, "Come up here!" And they rose to heaven in a cloud as their enemies watched.' "

"Does it say anything about the earthquake?" Janie said.

"It says an earthquake will destroy a tenth of the city."

"Wow," Janie said. "So it says Carpathia is going to come back from the dead too?"

"Revelation talks about the beast—and we think that's Carpathia—receiving a mortal wound. He later ascends from the bottomless pit, so we think that means he'll come back to life."

"Couldn't he just indwell Fortunato?" Mark said.

"Yeah, but Satan loves to counterfeit what God does." Vicki pointed to the television. "And you can bet, if Carpathia does come back to life, they'll have the replay going 24/7."

"Wait," Conrad said. "Dr. Ben-Judah was wrong about his sword prediction. The reports say he was shot."

"I don't have a good answer for that," Vicki said.

"When he comes back to life, will he be the same guy or somebody different?" Melinda said.

"His body will be the same, and I assume his voice will be too, but there will be a big difference inside because of the indwelling."

Melinda scowled. "What does *indwelling* mean?"

Mark raised a hand. "It'll be the same bus, different driver."

"I still don't get it," Janie said.

"*Indwell* means to live inside," Vicki said. "Satan is going to live inside Nicolae's body."

Janie shivered and rubbed her arms. "You mean, like possession? I saw a scary movie once about a kid who talked in weird voices."

"Same thing," Vicki said, "only this is the ultimate possession."

Vicki glanced at the television and saw a group of children marching toward a picture of Nicolae Carpathia.

"It's video from one of those staged rallies," Mark said.

The children, most of whom were two to three years old, were dressed in cute GC outfits. When they reached the platform, they saluted and sang a short song of praise to Carpathia. Several laid flowers below the picture. Vicki turned up the volume as the children knelt and began a prayer. "Our Father in New Babylon, Carpathia be your name. Your kingdom come, your will be done. . . ."

Vicki shook her head and hit the mute button.

Shelly said, "I can't believe they brainwashed little kids like that."

"It's going to get worse," Vicki said. "Satan is drawing as many followers as he can. God is extending mercy to anyone who will follow him. It's a huge battle."

"Did people before the Rapture believe all this would happen?" Conrad said. "Nobody ever talked to me about it."

"I don't know," Vicki said. "The point is, we have to do everything we can to help people know the truth."

"Back to this indwelling thing," Melinda said. "When's it going to happen?"

"The Bible doesn't say. But I know a lot more people are going to believe Carpathia's lies after it does."

The television blared as Judd sat by Z-Van's bed. Pillows propped the man's legs, and he winced when Judd put a hand on the bed.

Judd wanted to tell the truth about God, but he could put their group in danger if Z-Van told the authorities what was going on in General Zimmerman's home.

Z-Van broke the silence. "Real bummer about what happened to the big guy, huh? I'd like to get my hands on whoever fired the gun."

Judd nodded. "How are you feeling?"

"Like I've still got a thousand pounds on my legs." Z-Van turned down the volume on another replay of the assassination. "I want to thank you—you and your friends. I can be pretty demanding; that's what my band members say. You did a good thing for me, and I want to return the favor."

"You don't need to—"

"I know, but if you hadn't come along, I might still be there."

"Somebody from your band would have found you."

Z-Van laughed. "Those guys were probably partying."

Judd changed the subject. "You never told me your real last name."

"Is that what you want?"

"I told you, I don't want anything for helping you."

Z-Van took a sip of ice water and pushed hair from his face. "Vanzangler. Myron Vanzangler. You call me Myron in front of your friends and I'll kick you with these casts."

Judd smiled. "So you switched the Z and the *van* around and became Z-Van?"

"Something like that." Z-Van grabbed a cigarette, lit it, and blew smoke toward the ceiling.

"Lionel said you didn't want anyone to know you were alive."

"Lionel—is that the black kid?"

Judd nodded.

"Where are you guys from?"

"A suburb of Chicago."

"You're a long way from home." Z-Van cursed, grabbed a pencil, and scratched underneath his cast. "I figure I'll pull a McCartney. Back in the 1960s, they put out records and stories that the guy was dead when he wasn't. Great promotion. Sales shot up and everybody wondered what happened. I'll do the same thing, and the Global Community will help."

"How?"

"I lay low for a few days, figure out a good time to come back from the dead, and voila, I'm bigger than ever."

"If that's the way you want to play it," Judd said.

"You don't think it will work?"

"Maybe it will. But what if your fans get ticked? You're fooling them."

"How would you play it?"

Judd thought a moment. "Tell them the truth. Fast. You were trapped in the earthquake, you got help, and as soon as you're better you'll be back onstage."

Z-Van shook his head. "No pizzazz. You gotta be more creative." He closed his eyes. "Okay, how about this? I stay gone for a year, work on some songs and let my legs heal; then I come back with a tour that'll rock their socks."

"I still think your fans will be upset. Somebody's going to see you, and the media will plaster your face all over the news."

Z-Van scratched his chin. "Hand me the phone."

Judd gave it to him and Z-Van dialed a number. "Westin Jakes's room?" He paused. "Wes, it's me. . . . No, just listen. I don't want anybody to know, all right? . . . Yeah, I figured you'd try. Where's the plane? . . . Good. Meet me there—" Z-Van put his hand over the phone. "What day is it?"

"It's past midnight . . . Saturday morning."

"Okay, have the plane ready early this afternoon. . . . No, don't file a flight plan; this is a secret. . . . Yeah, I'll have somebody with me, but not from the band."

Z-Van talked a few moments more, then hung up. "Wes is the only one I trust out of the bunch. He said he'd have the plane ready for us."

"Us?"

"Yeah, you need a ride back home, right? That's the least I can do for somebody who saved my life."

"But—"

"We'll talk tomorrow. Let me get some sleep."

Judd's mind reeled as he joined the others. Could God be providing a way home through this ungodly man?

New believers lined the walls of the meeting room and spilled into the hall. Mr. Stein called for quiet as Judd found Sam and Lionel and whispered what Z-Van had said to him.

Mr. Stein prayed, then said, "I believe we are in grave danger. If any of you wish to leave, now is the time."

"Why are we in danger?" a man in a long robe said.

"With the death of Nicolae Carpathia, the Global Community will have every reason to go after their enemies. I believe they will come after followers of Tsion Ben-Judah. It could mean imprisonment or perhaps our lives."

"What will you do?" another man asked.

"I met many of you at the earthquake site. It was there that you acknowledged the true God of heaven and his only Son, Jesus, the Messiah."

Men and women raised hands and shouted praise to God. Some fell to their knees and worshiped.

Mr. Stein allowed them a few minutes, then continued. "As you can see, these new believers have a great passion for the God who delivered them. I think they will be used by him in the next few days."

A young man whose clothes had been torn spoke. "I would give my life to proclaim the news that Jesus is the true Potentate. I want my family and friends who are still alive to hear the truth!"

Others shouted in agreement and praised God. General Zimmerman went through the crowd, explaining to newcomers where they could sleep.

Mr. Stein told the group about Z-Van's condition. A few murmured and Mr. Stein held up a hand. "We will pray that God would bring this man to the truth."

A noise outside startled the gathering. Judd ran to the front door and threw it open. Rolling bullhorns blasted a police report to the neighborhood in various languages. After a few moments of French, and then what must have been Italian, the announcment was finally made in English.

"Attention, citizens and all Global Community personnel! Be on the lookout for American Rayford Steele, former GC employee wanted in connection with the conspiracy to assassinate Potentate Nicolae Carpathia. May be in disguise. May be armed. Considered dangerous. Qualified pilot. Any information about his whereabouts will be rewarded by the Global Community. . . ."

Judd couldn't believe it. Rayford Steele didn't kill Carpathia, but the GC was charging him with the crime. Someone turned up the sound on the television, and Rayford's official GC photo flashed on the screen.

The news anchor smiled. "This should end any doubt about the ability of the Global Community to track down the killer. I repeat, fingerprints on the weapon found near the stage where Potentate Carpathia was shot and killed tonight are those of former Global Community employee Rayford Steele. Our sources tell us that from the different camera angles they have, Rayford

Steele fired on the Potentate and sent the world into a state of mourning."

The anchor questioned a GC crime expert and asked if the shooting might be a conspiracy. "Our source tells us Steele is a committed Judah-ite," the expert said. "At this point, anything is possible."

Judd got everyone's attention and told them the details of what he witnessed there and who had really killed Nicolae Carpathia.

"So it was a sword," Mr. Stein said, "just as Tsion predicted."

Someone shouted from the kitchen area, and everyone ran to the back of the house. Judd pushed his way through and gasped. Chaim Rosenzweig's house was engulfed in flames.

5

JUDD and the others rushed to the Rosenzweig estate, but it was too late. Flames licked at every level of the home and out the windows. Soon, the beautiful house would be nothing but charred rubble.

Global Community officers kept people back. A television crew set up nearby and prepared to go live.

"Behind me you see the estate of international statesman and beloved Israeli inventor, Dr. Chaim Rosenzweig," the young reporter said. "Dr. Rosenzweig was on the stage tonight as a special guest of Potentate Carpathia. Authorities fear that after the assassination of His Excellency, Rosenzweig returned here and was killed in this fire, along with his staff."

"What?" Judd said to Lionel. "How could they know that?"

"A Global Community source who asked not to be named gave us information that there are a number of bodies inside, and that there is no possibility of getting them out until the fire has been brought under control."

Judd shook his head and walked back to the General's house. He took Lionel and Sam aside. "Okay, help me figure this out. Rosenzweig kills Carpathia. The GC had to have seen it on the video. They torch his house and kill him, but then they accuse Rayford Steele of killing Carpathia. Why?"

"Maybe they think they can get two people with one assassination," Sam said. "Whether Steele fired the shot or not, they accuse him and all believers will be suspect."

"Do you really think Captain Steele fired the shot?" Lionel said.

Judd was distracted by the television news, which again showed Rayford Steele's picture and aired his voice. "This man may be in disguise," the anchor said. "He is considered armed and extremely dangerous. If you see him, contact your local GC post. Again, this man, Rayford Steele, is believed to be the lone assassin, the lone gunman who shot and killed Nicolae Carpathia Friday night. Global Community Security and Intelligence forces found his fingerprints on what is believed to be the murder weapon, a powerful handgun known as a Saber."

Mr. Stein turned the sound down as the others came back. Judd asked if he thought Dr. Rosenzweig could have prayed before he was killed in the fire.

Mr. Stein shook his head. "I hope he did. Now, let us pray for the protection of our brother Rayford Steele."

Lionel met with Judd the next morning after sending an e-mail to Vicki and the others back home. He explained all that had happened and asked the kids to pray about their return to the States.

"How did you sleep?" Lionel said.

"I thought about Z-Van's offer all night."

"You think I could come?"

"That's the only way I would go," Judd said, "but I don't know. This guy's life is so messed up. He's into himself and the Global Community. If he finds out who we are, he'll probably turn us in."

"He might listen. You don't get trapped under that much rubble and not think about God."

"Or we could just keep quiet." Judd looked in the other room. "What about Sam?"

"He's been with Mr. Stein a lot. He might want to stay here, but let's ask him if he wants to go to the States with us."

Vicki relayed Lionel's message, and the kids were astonished at what Judd and Lionel had seen. Everyone grieved the loss of Kasim and watched reports of the mounting death toll in Jerusalem. Nearly seven thousand had died according to the GC CNN reports. Mark took Lionel's e-mail, cut references to Chaim Rosenzweig and other people, and composed an "eyewitness report" from Jerusalem.

Vicki knew readers of the kids' Web site expected timely reporting. The response to Mark's article came immediately.

Thank you for preparing us, one girl wrote from Cleveland. *I've been watching the coverage nonstop and trying to tell my friends what's about to happen, but they don't believe me. Your article convinced one friend and she just prayed with me. Keep up the good work.*

Hundreds of messages came in all evening, and Vicki alternated between the television and the computer. Late that evening the kids agreed to take turns watching TV to make sure they didn't miss Carpathia's resurrection. Mark and Conrad took the first shift.

Vicki fell asleep quickly and was awakened after midnight by Darrion. "We're up."

Vicki poured them both a cup of coffee and they sat on the floor, afraid they would fall asleep on the couch. Vicki always loved the smell of coffee but didn't like the taste much. Now the bitter taste stung her tongue and she hoped it would keep her awake.

The news carried video of Nicolae Carpathia's plane landing in New Babylon. An honor guard reverently carried the casket into the airplane hangar. As they watched the round-the-clock coverage, Vicki asked Darrion if she wanted to talk about her bad memories of the summer home.

Darrion nodded and put her coffee on an end table. "I guess I'm ready. Like I told you before, I was mad at my parents, so I wanted to hurt them for not paying attention to me. I got together with a girlfriend of mine. Her brother and another guy drove us. I stole the house key from my dad's key ring."

As Darrion talked, Vicki felt uneasy, but she kept her

composure and didn't overreact. "You've never told anybody?"

Darrion shook her head. "My friend Stacey passed out on the couch. When I told her later, she didn't believe me. I never told anybody else."

"How old were the guys?"

"Her brother was seventeen, the other fifteen. I was about thirteen."

"Do you want to tell me what happened?" Vicki said.

Darrion took a breath. "Stacey passed out from too much beer or too much weed, and the guys started talking to me. They were nice at first."

Darrion's lip quivered, and Vicki put an arm around her. "Something changed and I could tell it. I told them to back off and they laughed. I punched Stacey and tried to wake her up, but she was out cold.

"I ran to the kitchen. I remembered a lady coming to our school saying never be alone with strangers like this, but it was too late. I never thought it could happen to me."

"They ran after you?"

"They were right behind me in the kitchen, so I ran out the back door and into the woods. I'd taken my shoes off, so the rocks and sticks hurt my feet. I heard them behind me, laughing. One of them had a flashlight. I tried to hide, but I was breathing so loud they found me."

Darrion stood and walked to the front window, her back to Vicki. The moon was bright and lit the hillside with an eerie glow.

"I've heard that something like one out of every four women will be hurt like that in their lifetime," Vicki said.

"Yeah, well I'm one of those statistics."

With her back still turned, Darrion told Vicki everything she remembered. "Then, when I got back to the house, they were playing cards in the living room with Stacey. Stacey saw my clothes were dirty and asked what I'd been doing outside. Those guys acted like nothing had happened. They didn't even look up."

Vicki hugged Darrion and whispered, "I'm so sorry. They had no right."

"Stacey didn't believe me!"

"Maybe she thought they'd send her brother to jail."

Darrion clenched her teeth. "That's where he belongs."

"What happened after that?"

"I said I had to go home and they took me. Mom and Dad were waiting. I ran past them to my room. They grounded me, took away my riding privileges at the stable for a week, but we never talked about it."

"And you've carried it with you all this time?"

Darrion nodded, her eyes wet. "That's when I really got into Enigma Babylon One World Faith. I thought I could clear my mind of what happened, focus on the positive, and everything would be all right. But it led me nowhere. I still had all the bad feelings. That's when I met your friend Ryan and he told me about God."

"But you still haven't been able to forget about it, right?"

Darrion shook her head. "I know God loves me and everything, but it still seems like my fault!"

Vicki hugged Darrion again as the girl wept. "You

made some bad choices, but what those guys did was wrong." Vicki took Darrion's face in both hands. "That was not your fault."

Darrion cried on Vicki's shoulder. When she had settled down, Vicki broke away and woke Shelly and Janie, telling them it was their turn to watch television.

"Our time's not up," Darrion said.

"It's okay," Vicki said. She grabbed a flashlight and opened the back door. "Take me to where it happened."

Judd spoke with Mr. Stein about Z-Van's offer. Mr. Stein scratched his head and sat back. "This man is living an ungodly lifestyle. He is not trustworthy. He may say one thing and do another. But perhaps this is a way for you to get back to your friends."

"I've been thinking about Z-Van becoming a believer," Judd said. "He's known everywhere."

Mr. Stein smiled. "That would be wonderful, but be careful. Remember the passage that talks about God using the weak things of the world to confound the wise? We must keep preaching the truth about Jesus Christ. We point people to him, whether Z-Van believes the message or not."

Judd slipped into Z-Van's room and found him sleeping.

When Judd turned, Z-Van called to him and tried to sit up. "Do you know how hard it is to lie on your back all night, your legs covered with this plaster? I need a drink."

"I'll get you some water."

Z-Van cursed. "Don't bother."

Judd hesitated, then took a step toward the bed. "I wanted to talk about your offer. Is it still good?"

"The flight home? Yeah. You want to go, you're in."

"I have a couple of friends who might want to go."

"A package deal, huh? We'll have plenty of room. It'll only be Wes and me. Bring whoever you want."

"When do we leave?"

"As soon as you can get a ride to the airport for us."

Judd looked at his watch. He had a lot to do in a short time.

"Question before you go," Z-Van said. "What kind of place is this?"

"It's a man's house. He used to be a general in the Israeli army."

"Yeah, but I hear people talking, having meetings. What's it about?"

"I'll explain on the plane," Judd said.

Vicki followed Darrion up the hill to a small clearing. The moon was so bright they didn't need the flashlight.

"The brush is thick now, but I think this is where they caught me," Darrion said. She was trembling, her hands clasped tight and her shoulders hunched.

"Okay," Vicki said. She knelt with Darrion, the cold dew quickly seeping through her jeans, making her knees icy. "First I want us to pray."

Vicki began but had to wait for the emotion to pass. "Father, this is the place where something really bad happened to Darrion. You know how much it hurt her. Please, right here, heal Darrion's heart and mind. Help her understand who she is and how much you can help her. In Jesus' name, amen."

Vicki looked at Darrion. "When we get back to the house, I want to show you some verses that talk about how much God loves you. But I brought you out here for another reason.

"Darrion, so many young kids have bad stuff done to them. A lot of them carry that hurt their whole lives and never tell anyone."

"I thought it would go away."

Vicki nodded. "It's scary to tell somebody, and I'm glad you trusted me. I hope it helped."

Darrion bent and pulled some grass, releasing the blades into the breeze. "I still feel like it was my fault."

Vicki took her hand. "You put yourself in a bad place by trying to get back at your parents. You were naïve. But what they did is on them. Nothing justifies that."

Darrion dropped Vicki's hand and stood up, eyeing her. "You seem to know an awful lot about this stuff."

Vicki bit her lip and had to wipe away a tear. "I'm one of those statistics too, Darrion."

6

VICKI sat with Darrion on the hillside until the sun came up, telling her own story. It wasn't easy, dredging up painful memories of a trusted uncle who had taken advantage of her when she was only nine.

"And you never told anyone?"

Vicki nodded. "My mom blew me off. Said her brother would never do that and that she would punish me if I ever said anything like that again. So I never did—at least until I was a lot older. When I'd hear my uncle pull up, I'd run and hide."

"Did you feel like it was your fault?" Darrion said.

"Totally. How could I know better?"

"Until . . ."

"Remember us talking about our pastor, Bruce Barnes?"

Darrion smiled. "Ryan said he was incredible."

"I finally told him. He totally understood. He sent me to a woman counselor he trusted."

"Did it help?"

Vicki looked away. "I'd had nightmares. It's always been hard for me to trust guys. The counselor helped me through that. But then Bruce died and we went on the run. I've had other things to worry about ever since."

"Does anybody else know this?"

Vicki shook her head.

Darrion clenched her fists. "I could kill those guys and that uncle of yours."

"I know the feeling, and I won't say it's easy to get past that."

"I don't suppose you can help me find that counselor."

Vicki smiled and looked into her eyes. "I'm no professional, but I'll talk or listen as much as you need."

———————————————

Judd approached Sam as Lionel packed. When Sam heard about the trip to the States, his eyes widened and then he frowned.

"What's the problem?" Judd said.

"You know how much I would like to go with you, but I don't feel I can leave Mr. Stein and the others. Something is about to happen here, and I don't want to miss it."

"I understand. How would you feel about the two of us going?"

Sam smiled and looked at the floor. "I consider you my brothers. You helped me understand the truth. I will miss you both."

"We need strong, young believers everywhere. You'll

be our main guy in Israel. And if you want to come stay with us, we'll work it out."

Judd phoned Yitzhak's house and reached Kasim's parents. He wanted to speak with them face-to-face, but there wasn't time.

"I keep thinking if I hadn't come here, your daughter and son would still be alive," Judd said, filled with emotion.

"Nonsense," Jamal said. "If it weren't for you, we might never have known Kasim was alive in New Babylon. Go with God. Follow his leading, and we will meet again."

Lina got on the phone to say good-bye. "Don't forget what Nada wrote to you."

Nada's words still haunted Judd. She had sensed there was someone Judd cared about deeply back in the States. Judd could only think of Vicki and was anxious to get home to talk with her.

General Zimmerman said good-bye and offered his limousine to transport them to the secluded airport. Mr. Stein hugged Lionel and Judd, tears in his eyes. "God has used you in miraculous ways, and I pray he will do even more in the future."

Mr. Stein put his hands on their heads and looked toward heaven. "Be gracious to these, your servants, O God. May your face shine upon them and may you give them your peace. Bring others to yourself through their testimony. Amen."

A few of the witnesses carried Z-Van to the limo, and the singer handed them a wad of Nicks, which they all refused. Judd closed the doors and waved good-bye.

His heart was full of emotion as they drove away. So much had happened since they had arrived in Israel. They had lost friends, seen prophecy fulfilled, and witnessed history.

"Who are those people?" Z-Van said as they slowly drove through streets cracked by the earthquake.

Judd turned. Smoke still rose from the rubble of Chaim Rosenzweig's house. Sam Goldberg ran along the street, waving and yelling. Judd and Lionel quickly rolled down their windows and waved.

"They're some of the best friends I've ever had," Judd said to Z-Van.

Vicki awoke with a headache and rushed to see if there was news about Carpathia.

Mark was at the computer, keeping an eye on the coverage and answering e-mails. "I was just going to ask Shelly to get you," he said. "That education guy, Damosa, is supposed to have a special broadcast in a few minutes."

Vicki looked over Mark's shoulder at the new messages. Kids from around the world praised Vicki for her boldness during the GC's satellite transmission. Some wanted more information about how to become a believer.

"There are a few here that look suspicious," Mark said.

He pulled up one from someone who said they lived in Florida. *Hi, Vicki B., I saw you on the satellite feed and think you're really cool. That stuff you said about Jesus is right-on. I'd love to meet with you and your group so I can give you some money to help the cause. Please write back and tell me where we can meet.*

Another from Illinois said: *I heard on television that you live somewhere in Illinois. Or maybe you're not there anymore. Please write me. I have a lot of questions about God, and I have a safe place to stay if you need one.*

"Move over," Vicki said and she started typing an answer. "Both of these sound phony, like they're GC trying to set us up."

"That's what I thought."

Vicki typed: *We know the Global Community is searching for us. Some of you are offering money, a safe place to stay, or have questions about where we are. If you're sincere, thank you. God is taking care of us. If you're a member of the Global Community, nice try.*

"Put that on the Web site," Vicki said.

Mark smiled and typed in the Web site access code. Conrad turned up the sound on the television. "Your pal's on, Vicki."

An announcer introduced Dr. Neal Damosa as the leading educator of the Global Community. He stood in front of a black shroud, dressed in a stunning outfit, as usual. The camera zoomed in on his face.

"I have been asked to speak to the young people of the world and try to make sense out of what happened in Jerusalem last night," Dr. Damosa began. "But I can't make sense of it. Someone, or more likely as we're hearing from our security forces, a group of conspirators decided to take the life of our beloved potentate.

"None of us has words to express the sense of loss we

all feel. In one earth-shattering second, the man who we thought would lead us into a new era of peace and prosperity was taken from us.

"All of the death and destruction we have seen in the last few years could not prepare us for this moment. Most of you have lost fathers and mothers, brothers and sisters, and it may feel at this moment that you have lost another family member."

"Oh, give me a break," Conrad muttered. "Can you imagine having Carpathia as a family member?"

"I'd run away from home," Shelly said.

"In the coming days you will receive instructions about the next round of satellite schools," Damosa continued. "Honor the memory of your fallen potentate. He died in the cause of peace. I urge you to serve the Global Community as he did.

"This is not the end of our dream. It is the beginning. Together we can make the hope of Nicolae Carpathia a reality. It is what he wanted for all of us."

Mark asked Vicki to come to the computer.

"Let me finish—"

"You'll want to see this. It just came in."

Vicki read an e-mail from the pastor in Arizona she had met on her trip west. The message was marked "urgent."

Vicki and the others of the Young Tribulation Force,

A fire was set at the home of Jeff Williams and his father. Sadly, both died in the fire. As you know, they were both believers and growing strong. We can at least be thankful for that.

I have been told that the Global Community knows about our meeting place and that there may be arrests soon. Please pray for us. The Global Community will stop at nothing to ferret out the leaders of any who oppose them.

Be on your guard at all times as you continue to tell the truth boldly.

Vicki sat back and put a hand to her head. Jeff Williams and his father were dead? It seemed like yesterday that she was trying to explain the gospel to Jeff. Now they were gone. She sat the others down and told them Jeff's story. Everyone was saddened by the news of two more deaths, and they prayed for the safety of the other believers in Tucson.

"I wonder if Buck knows," Shelly said after a few moments.

Mark clicked a few keys on the computer. "I don't know if this is related, but Chaim Rosenzweig's home was destroyed by fire last night in Jerusalem."

"How could it be related?" Vicki said. "Unless . . ."

"You think he's become one of us?"

"Let's keep an eye out for other suspicious fires," Vicki said. "This may be the way the GC will try to get rid of believers."

"I've got a bad feeling about Charlie," Darrion said. "What if the GC come back and question that farm couple and Charlie makes a mistake?"

"Have we heard from Charlie or the Shairtons since we left?"

Mark searched through e-mails and came up with nothing. He wrote a quick note to Charlie and asked for an update.

Darrion went out of the room and returned with a cell phone from one of the back rooms. "This is my dad's phone for emergencies. If it works, we could call Charlie and make sure everything's okay."

"Is it GC?" Conrad said.

Darrion nodded.

Vicki turned the phone on and got a dial tone. Mark took it away from her. "Don't risk it. Wait and see if we hear anything from him on e-mail."

Vicki looked worried. She hoped they hadn't left Charlie in a trap.

Judd gasped when he saw the inside of Z-Van's plane. It was almost as elaborate as Nicolae Carpathia's. There were video screens along one wall and a huge seating area. Lionel found a computer and asked if he could e-mail their friends.

"Wait until we get in the air," the pilot said, helping Z-Van get settled. He held out a hand. "Westin Jakes. Nice to meet you."

Judd introduced himself and Lionel, and the two buckled in. "I can't believe we're actually going home."

"About that, we need to take a little detour first," Z-Van said.

"What do you mean?" Judd said.

"I've been thinking about what you said about my fans getting ticked off if I pretend to be dead. Wes and I are working on a welcome back party."

"But you said—"

"Don't sweat, Dorothy. I'll get you back to Kansas."

Judd glanced at Lionel and shrugged. As the plane screamed down the runway, Judd wondered if he had led them into a trap. Had Z-Van heard them talking and figured out who they were?

As they flew over the Israeli countryside, Judd knew there was only one option. He had to confront Z-Van with the truth.

7

VICKI stared at the computer, anxious to hear from Charlie. The others watched news coverage from New Babylon. Already people were spilling into the city to pay their respects to the dead potentate.

Darrion turned to Vicki. "Can you explain one more time what you think's going to happen?"

Vicki ran a hand through her hair. "Dr. Ben-Judah wrote about this, and some people disagreed with him about the wound to the head. They thought the Antichrist wouldn't really die, that he would only appear dead. But Tsion says the best interpretation is that Carpathia will really die and his body will be taken over by Satan himself."

"They're probably embalming the body already," Mark said. "He has to be dead. If they're going to put him in an airtight capsule and let people walk past him like they say on the news, there's no doubt he's dead."

"I can't believe all of this is really in the Bible," Janie said.

Darrion turned up the television as Leon Fortunato appeared at a press conference in New Babylon. He mentioned Rayford Steele's name and said a worldwide search was being conducted.

"Are you sure this man is the shooter?" a reporter asked.

"We have conclusive evidence, including fingerprints, that Rayford Steele is the assassin. I might also add that this man is a Judah-ite, which shows how much they believe in their message of love and peace."

"I can't believe Captain Steele would do something like that," Shelly said.

"Maybe they're framing him for it," Conrad said.

Vicki turned to Mark. "Anything from Charlie yet?"

"No, but a message just came in from . . . hey, it's from Lionel."

The kids gathered around the computer.

Judd and I are on a flight heading home. You won't believe who we're with. I'll tell you all about it when we get close.

You'll probably hear on the news that Rayford Steele is the one who killed Carpathia. Not true. Judd saw the whole thing and it wasn't Rayford.

Write and tell us where you are and how to get there. We're not sure right now when we'll get back or where we'll land, but we can't wait to see you guys.

From the TV Leon Fortunato spoke in the background. "We are committed to doing everything necessary to bring the person or persons guilty to justice . . . and we will have justice."

Another reporter asked about the delivery of the potentate's body. "Can you tell us anything about the mood in the palace?"

"We are all devastated, as you might expect. To lose not only a world leader but also someone you considered closer than a brother, well, it is difficult.

"There was a great outpouring of emotion among the workers, the soldiers. Everyone involved was overcome with tears, and yet, there is a sense that he would have wanted us to carry on in the Global Community tradition."

A reporter started another question, but Fortunato, overcome with inspiration, held up a hand. "As you will see tomorrow at his memorial service, those of us who worked with him behind the scenes believe this was no mere man. Many around the world can testify to the power of his words. He was able to calm our fears and lift us up, even in terrible days."

Reporters paused, then threw up their hands. Fortunato pointed to a female reporter who said, "Can you give us specifics about the ceremony tomorrow?"

"We understand that more than a million people have already come to New Babylon, and we expect more than double that number. There will be a public procession past the body, the time yet to be determined. As far as the service tomorrow, I believe not a person on the planet should miss it. It will be transmitted to every locale that has access to our satellite feed. We will unveil a work of art that I think would please the potentate. Throughout the day we will allow guests to pass by the coffin to pay their final respects. But the main service will begin at noon and the burial at 2 P.M."

"What time will that be here?" Janie said.

Mark had devised a counter that converted times in different parts of the world to Central time in the United States. "Looks like we'll be getting up early again."

For the first time since meeting Z-Van, Judd fully realized who he was with. This man wasn't an ordinary celebrity who could get a table at a busy restaurant. Z-Van was one of the top ten superstars in the world. People paid hundreds of Nicks to see him perform. This skinny guy with tattoos all over his body and wraparound sunglasses oozed power. He was used to people getting him anything he asked for. Judd had seen him listed as one of the wealthiest men in the world.

As he looked at all the rings in the man's ears, nose, and lips, Judd felt a mix of contempt and admiration. There was no doubt Z-Van was a good showman and business operator, but he had no friends. His life was filled with drinking, partying, and concerts, but it was empty.

Lionel logged on to news outlets around the world. The main story, of course, was reaction to the death of Nicolae Carpathia. In entertainment news, Z-Van's death was at the top.

Other members of The Four Horsemen expressed their shock and sadness. The manager of the group, who had been injured by falling debris, said he was the last to see Z-Van alive. "I was outside the music store when the earthquake started. I tried to get back inside, but it was too late. By the time I located a search crew, we couldn't find his body."

"Yeah, right." Z-Van laughed. "That weasel never gave a thought about anybody but himself. And my body-guards ran out faster than anyone."

Z-Van flipped through video channels and found a special program highlighting his career. The program played clips of the satellite school performance in Israel.

"That was a weird gig," Z-Van said. "We were probably seen by more people on the planet than at any other concert, but we were still upstaged by that redheaded chick."

Judd stole a glance at Lionel and smiled. "You still haven't told anyone you're alive?"

"The only ones who know are Wes and your group back in Israel. Now tell me who they are and what you guys are up to."

"Why do you think we're up to something?"

Z-Van lit a cigar and blew a huge plume of smoke toward Judd. "I don't know—holding meetings late at night, a bunch of people with long beards who look like those two crazies at the Wailing Wall. I can guess, but why don't you tell me?"

Judd took a deep breath. "Okay, I'll shoot straight. We're believers in Jesus Christ, followers of Tsion Ben-

Judah, otherwise known as Judah-ites. That group back in Israel is made up mainly of Jewish believers who are telling the world that their only hope for peace is to follow the true God."

Z-Van lowered his head and looked over the top of his sunglasses. "You're not serious."

"Dead serious."

Z-Van shook his head. "How did they trick a couple of smart kids like you into believing that junk?"

"We weren't tricked. This is something we chose to do."

"And I suppose you know that Vicki B. character personally."

Judd nodded. He didn't want to give too much away about the Young Trib Force, but he felt honesty was the best approach.

"Well, that puts an interesting spin on the story."

"What do you mean?"

Z-Van put both hands in front of him, like he was spreading out a banner. " 'World-Famous Singer Kidnapped by Religious Fanatics.' That's probably what the headline will say."

"We didn't kidnap you," Lionel said. "Judd saved your life."

"Yeah, and now you're going to save my soul. Hand me something to write with; this is going to make a good song."

"You've made a career out of bashing believers and making fun of Tsion Ben-Judah," Judd said. "Have you ever thought it might be true?"

Z-Van chuckled, took off his sunglasses, and put the earpiece in his mouth. "All right. Impress me."

Judd asked Lionel to go to the section on prophecies on the kids' Web site. "These things were written about two thousand years ago. Everything from the massive, worldwide earthquake to the one we just had in Jerusalem. The Bible even predicted that seven thousand would be killed in that quake."

Judd showed Z-Van the prophecies about the locusts, the horsemen, and other events of the past three and a half years. "And from what the Bible says, we think Nicolae isn't going to stay dead."

"You guys are crazy. I've seen the video. Carpathia is dead as a stump."

"What if we're right?"

Z-Van waved him off.

"If Eli and Moishe can come back to life, why not—"

"Those two crazies at the Wailing Wall? Carpathia blew them away days ago."

"He doesn't know," Lionel said.

"God raised them from the dead," Judd said. "They went right up into the clouds."

"Wooooo." Z-Van laughed, moving his finger in a circle in the air. "Then why haven't they shown that on the news?"

"I was there," Lionel said. "The GC won't show the replay because they know it'll affect people."

Judd told his story, beginning with where he was at the moment of the disappearances.

When he finished, Z-Van smiled. "So if you and Lionel are such good people, why weren't you taken?"

"Lionel and I knew the truth, but we didn't live it," Judd said. "I was in church as much as anybody, but being in church doesn't make you—"

"I know, doesn't make you a Christian any more than being in a garage makes you a car. Believe me, I've heard it. You probably won't believe this, but I used to go to church when I was a kid too. Stop staring and close your mouths—it's true."

Z-Van pulled himself up in his chair. "Where do you think I got the name The Four Horsemen? They tried to scare me with that stuff when I was a kid."

"Then you know God's trying to get your attention. He's calling you back. Do you know how much influence you could have on people if you—"

"Hold on," Z-Van said. "I'm not trying to influence anybody for good or bad. I'm trying to make a living."

Judd laughed. "You're not influencing anybody? Do you know how many kids dress like you, get tattoos, sing your lyrics, and get wasted because they think it's cool?"

"What people do is their own business. I'm an entertainer. The way I look at it, I have to take advantage of the popularity I have now because it might not be here tomorrow."

"Who took you to church when you were a kid?" Lionel said.

"My mother. She'd be there every Sunday and Wednesday. My dad took off before I was born."

"Where's your mom now?" Lionel said.

Z-Van slammed his sunglasses on and pointed toward Lionel. "Watch yourself. Keep my family out of this."

"It's a fair question," Judd said.

"I say it's not. Drop it."

"What did your mom think of your band and what you're doing now?"

"Things didn't skyrocket until after . . . what happened. I can tell you she didn't like my style." Z-Van smiled and imitated his mother in a falsetto voice. " 'I'm praying for you, Myron. God's going to get hold of you someday.' She'd send me tapes of radio programs she'd heard and books about how to keep your family together."

Judd remembered reading about Z-Van's stormy relationships with women. He had been married at least three times and was frequently pictured with Hollywood actresses in the tabloids.

"She wasn't real happy with the choices I'd made, but how can you argue with success, right?"

"I'll bet you haven't talked with her in three and a half years," Judd said. "Did something happen between you two that night?"

Z-Van shook his head and squirmed in his chair. "You guys don't quit, do you?" He tried to stand, but fell back in the leather seat. Finally, he sighed and said, "She disappeared three years ago or whatever it was. She'd just sent me a fresh box of stuff on the end times. Said with the world as crazy as it was, it wouldn't be long before Jesus came back and I needed to be ready."

"Did you ever answer her or talk to her about it?" Judd said.

"Didn't need to. I knew what she would say."

"One more question and I'll leave you alone," Judd said. "We've been straight with you. You do the same."

"Shoot."

"Is there any part of you that deep down thinks your mom might have been right?"

Z-Van clenched his teeth. "No. And that's the last I want to talk about it." He touched the intercom button. "How much longer, Wes?"

"We've got about another hour until touchdown in New Babylon."

"What?" Judd said.

"Go to the back of the plane. I don't want to stare at you for another hour."

"But you said—"

"Leave me alone!"

8

JUDD and Lionel moved to the back of the plane and talked about their options. Lionel found a rear exit they could use after touchdown, but they both agreed it was a last resort.

"What do you think Z-Van's going to do?" Lionel said.

"He's pretty ticked. He could call the GC and have them pick us up at the plane."

"The pilot seems reasonable. Let's talk with him."

Judd peeked inside the door and saw that Z-Van had fallen asleep. He and Lionel crept to the main cabin and lightly knocked on the cockpit door. The pilot unlocked it and invited them inside.

"Sorry there's no room to sit," Westin said. "Heard a little of your tiff with the big guy. Wasn't smart."

"Do you know what's happening once we touch down?" Judd said.

"I called one of the top GC guys Z-Van knows. I explained what had happened and that we wanted to hold a press conference."

"What about us?" Lionel said.

Westin shrugged. "Z-Van didn't give any instructions about you." He radioed the New Babylon tower and reported their position. Judd and Lionel turned to leave, but the pilot stopped them. "You don't really believe Carpathia is coming back, do you?"

"He could have risen already," Lionel said.

Westin shook his head. "I heard most of what you guys said. Intercom was on. I saw the live video of those two guys come back to life. Incredible."

"Will you help us get back home like Z-Van promised?" Judd said.

"I'll do what I can, but he's the boss."

Judd and Lionel quietly made their way to the back of the plane and buckled in. Judd stared out at the New Babylon skyline. The buildings and elaborate gardens and parks that spread throughout the city were a monument to Carpathia.

As they descended, Judd pointed out a huge scaffold and platform at the front of an open area. Already, thousands of people moved toward the spot. Some would no doubt stay there all night to assure themselves a spot in the funeral service.

Lionel pointed to the vehicles with flashing red lights on the airport runway. "Are those for us or Z-Van?"

Judd shook his head as the plane's wheels touched down.

Vicki and the others watched reports that covered every angle of the potentate's demise. There were replays of Carpathia speeches, reactions from celebrities, and live shots from New Babylon that showed the hurried construction of a viewing area where millions were expected Sunday.

Vicki thought of Charlie and Bo and Ginny Shairton in central Illinois. She prayed for Buck Williams, who would no doubt hear soon about the death of his brother and father. And Vicki thought of Judd. She couldn't believe he and Lionel were finally coming home. When Mark had read the e-mail from Lionel, Vicki hadn't been able to concentrate on anything but the first sentence. She'd felt tears coming and had to turn away. She had thought no one had noticed, but later Shelly asked if she was okay and Vicki whispered that she was excited about seeing Judd again.

There was still no word from Charlie, and Vicki had to resist the urge to pick up Mr. Stahley's phone and dial the number.

The TV coverage switched to an airport in New Babylon, where people of every ethnic background were arriving for the funeral. Incoming flights were sold out, but outgoing flights were empty. No one wanted to leave the city at this historic moment.

A family from Africa stopped to express their feelings. "I have been crying ever since we saw the broadcast," the mother said, holding an infant close. "We were all shocked that this could happen to such a great man."

Her husband grabbed the microphone. "I brought my family here to experience the tragedy firsthand. We want to pass by the body, if that is allowed, and kneel before the greatest world leader in history."

A man from China said, "I brought my wife and my two sons to grieve. It is a time of great sadness, more sadness than we have ever known. But I believe there are great days ahead."

Through an interpreter, a Turkish man said, "The world will never see another like him. It is the worst tragedy we will ever face, and we can only hope that his successor will be able to carry on the ideals he put forth."

"Do you believe Nicolae Carpathia was divine in any sense?" the reporter said.

"In every sense!" the man said. "I believe it's possible that he was the Messiah the Jews longed for all these centuries. And he was murdered in their own nation, just as the Scriptures prophesied."

"Talk about bad theology," Conrad said. "That guy is crazy."

Other people were interviewed on the street. Some speculated about who would succeed Nicolae Carpathia.

"No one has been closer to Potentate Carpathia than Leon Fortunato," a Global Community worker said. "I believe the supreme commander can carry the ideals of Nicolae Carpathia forward so that we can fulfill his dreams."

Mark shook his head. "What a bunch of nonsense."

The report switched to Israel. Vicki thought it would

be an update on the earthquake. Instead, thousands of people gathered in front of a few men in robes.

"This is the scene in Jerusalem, just a day after the murder of Nicolae Carpathia," the correspondent said. People in the crowd ran forward, fell to their knees, and shouted their dedication to Jesus.

"Look," Shelly shouted, "Mr. Stein is one of the speakers!"

The camera zoomed in on the bearded men for a few seconds, then pulled back. Vicki couldn't hear what Mr. Stein and his friends were saying, but the effect was clear. They were using this pivotal moment to tell people the truth about God.

A religious expert was called on to explain the phenomenon. He said that since the leaders of the Global Community and the One World Faith were dead, Carpathia and Mathews, people would try to fill that gap in many ways. The expert said that people turning to Jesus Christ was a fairly recent craze that began shortly after the vanishings.

"Dr. Ben-Judah created an uproar, particularly among Jews, when at the end of the live, globally televised airing of his views he announced that Jesus the Christ was the only person in history to fulfill all the messianic prophecies, and that the vanishings were evidence that he had already come."

"So why doesn't this expert have the mark of the believer?" Janie said.

"This guy knows his facts, but he doesn't know God personally," Vicki said. "And he's right about people looking for something to fill the hole Carpathia left in their lives. Tsion says a lot of people will still believe the truth, but many more will follow false teachers."

"How do you know that?" Janie said.

Vicki pulled up the Bible software on the computer and showed Janie Matthew 24:21-24. "It's talking about what we're about to live through."

"I'm not sure I want to hear it," Janie said.

Vicki read the verses aloud. " 'For that will be a time of greater horror than anything the world has ever seen or will ever see again. In fact, unless that time of calamity is shortened, the entire human race will be destroyed. But it will be shortened for the sake of God's chosen ones.

" 'Then if anyone tells you, "Look, here is the Messiah," or "There he is," don't pay any attention. For false messiahs and false prophets will rise up and perform great miraculous signs and wonders so as to deceive, if possible, even God's chosen ones.' "

"So there are going to be people pretending to do miracles?" Janie said.

"Not pretending," Vicki said. "They're going to perform miracles, and a lot of people are going to think they're from God."

Janie shuddered. "This stuff keeps getting worse and worse."

Vicki checked with Mark. There was still no word from Charlie. Vicki slipped the cell phone in her pocket and walked out of the room.

Judd looked out the window as the plane pulled up to a special hangar at the end of the airport. Several GC vehicles with lights swirling drove close.

"Should we make a run for it?" Lionel said.

Before Judd could answer, the pilot walked into the cabin. "You need to help me get him down the stairs to the wheelchair ramp." When Judd and Lionel hesitated, Westin grabbed Judd's arm. "Now."

Judd looked at Z-Van. "Are you turning us in?"

Z-Van rolled his eyes. "You really think they're interested in a couple of crazy kids when their world has fallen apart?"

"They're ready to crack down on anybody who disagrees with them, and they'll start with followers of Ben-Judah."

Z-Van shook his head. "I'm holding a press conference in the terminal; then I'm meeting with one of Fortunato's aides. I'm telling them you guys saved my life."

"No," Judd said. "Leave us out. Somebody might recognize us."

"Watch the leg!" Z-Van said as they placed him on a ramp. He turned to Judd. "Stay in the plane. I'll know more about our schedule and when we'll leave after this meeting."

"You mean you're still going to give us a ride home?" Lionel said.

"That's what I promised, right? You two just have to promise you won't try to 'save me' again."

Judd and Lionel went back inside the plane and

turned on the bank of televisions. Each channel aired
Global Community news, but from different perspectives.
One channel carried world news while another focused
on finances. Lionel turned to a channel geared toward
younger people. Already several music videos had been
produced with images of Carpathia.

A few minutes later they broke into the regular
programming for a special report. A tall, balding GC official appeared before a blue curtain. Several reporters had
been hastily recruited for the press conference.

"In the midst of some terrible news, we have a ray of
sunshine to report," the man said as his name and title
flashed on the screen. "It was previously believed that the
lead singer for the group The Four Horsemen had been
killed in the earthquake in Jerusalem. However, a few
minutes ago we discovered that not only is Z-Van alive, but
he is also here in New Babylon to pay his respects to the
slain potentate."

The network showed a split screen of the press conference and people inside the terminal. When the pilot
wheeled Z-Van into the picture, hundreds of people clapped
and cheered. Several young people appeared to faint.

Z-Van took the microphone, his eyes shielded by his
patented sunglasses. "First, I want to apologize to everyone
who thought I was dead. I didn't mean to put you through
this, but after I was pulled from the wreckage by a couple
of kids, I didn't have a chance to let anyone know.

"I wanted my first public appearance to be here in
New Babylon, out of respect for the man who means so
much to me and to the whole world."

"Z-Van, how did you first learn of the potentate's death?" a reporter shouted from the back.

"I was in the doctor's office watching the speech on television. When he was shot, I couldn't believe it. I'd give anything to have that man back with us."

"Will you attend the funeral tomorrow?" another reporter said.

"I've just met with one of the supreme commander's aides and they've asked that I participate somehow. I'm honored and if I can help the world express its grief in some way, I'll be glad to do it."

"Who are the young people who helped you escape the earthquake?" a reporter said.

Z-Van smiled. "Just a couple of guys who really don't appreciate my music as much as they should."

Everyone laughed. Another reporter said, "Will they be with you tomorrow?"

Z-Van nodded. "Yes. They'll join us tomorrow."

Judd looked at Lionel. "We have to find a couple of disguises."

Vicki went into an empty room and found the Shairtons' number. She clicked the phone on, dialed, and quickly hung up. She knew she was taking a great risk using Mr. Stahley's phone, but she had to know about Charlie.

She turned the phone on again and dialed. It rang three times, and Vicki nearly hung up before someone picked up and whispered, "Hello?"

"Charlie, is that you?"

"Vicki?"

"Yes. I called to see if you were all right. Why haven't you written us?"

Charlie's voice trembled through the phone line. "Some of those guys came back and asked Bo more questions."

"You mean the GC?" Vicki said.

"Yeah. They matched the tire tracks to the satellite truck."

"Oh no. Get out of there."

"We were packing up to do that when they—"

"What?" Vicki said.

"They're banging on the door."

Vicki heard a noise in the background. Ginny whispered something to Charlie.

"We're in the cellar place, hiding. I'd better not talk."

Vicki heard a clunk, like Charlie put the phone on a shelf. The banging stopped, and then wood and glass crashed. Someone shouted.

"Charlie?" Vicki screamed.

More splintering wood and men yelling. Bo said something that Vicki couldn't understand.

Mark walked into the room and Vicki waved him off. "Something's happening at the farmhouse."

"You used the phone?" Mark said.

Vicki held a finger to her lips.

"It's gonna be okay," Bo said. "They won't find us down here."

Ginny gasped. "What's that? What's dripping?"

"Gasoline!" Bo said.

The phone clunked again. Charlie said, "Vicki, they're going to burn the place down!"

"Get out!" Vicki screamed. "Get out now!!"

The phone crackled and footsteps pounded on the stairs. Vicki heard banging and someone yelled.

Then the phone went dead.

9

VICKI rushed into the living room and told the others what she had heard. The kids tried to assure Vicki that Charlie would be okay, but Vicki wouldn't listen. "I should never have let him stay."

"It was his decision," Mark said.

"Now we know the GC's tactic against believers," Conrad said. "They burned Jeff Williams's house, Chaim Rosenzweig's, and now the Shairtons'."

"We have to go back and see if they're all right," Vicki said.

"If they made it out of the house, the GC caught them," Mark said.

"Then we have to go back and get them released!"

"How about that Morale Monitor you know?" Shelly said. "Maybe she can help."

"We haven't heard from Natalie since the message she sent about Carl," Mark said.

While he wrote Natalie, Vicki gathered the others and prayed for Charlie, Bo, and Ginny. They pleaded with God to keep them safe.

Judd moved awkwardly in the Middle Eastern clothing he and Lionel were wearing. They had turbans wrapped tightly around their heads. Judd didn't want to take any chance that the GC might recognize them.

The air was hot but dry in New Babylon as the two walked behind Z-Van's wheelchair. Westin led them up a ramp and into a courtyard, where hundreds of employees had gathered to see the private unveiling of Carpathia's glass coffin.

Spotlights made it seem like daylight as they passed a barricade. A GC official brought the small group near the stand where the coffin would be displayed. "You can watch the ceremony from here," the man said.

Z-Van thanked him and turned to Judd. "You can leave if you want."

"We'll stay."

"Carpathia could rise any minute," Lionel whispered.

A live orchestra played a somber song as ten pall-bearers carried in the Plexiglas coffin. Two hundred yards away men and women from around the world mourned openly. Some cried and wailed, throwing hands in the air. Others fell to the ground and ripped their clothes. Young children screamed and cried. Judd wondered whether they were devoted to Carpathia or just frightened by all the noise.

Pallbearers carefully laid the coffin on its stand and backed away. Employees walked up stairs and filed past the potentate's body. Two pallbearers removed the shroud that covered Carpathia and people gasped.

"I'm sure it wasn't easy to prepare the body for this," Z-Van said.

"Maybe that's not the real body," Lionel whispered to Judd. "They could have made some kind of wax replica so people wouldn't see how torn up he was."

Employees wept as they passed the coffin. Some leaned over the velvet ropes for a closer look. Several crossed themselves or bowed in a religious gesture. One GC official fell to his knees and spoke in a foreign language.

Only a few employees remained in line when barricades were withdrawn and the massive crowd slowly moved toward the casket. A GC official approached Z-Van. "Would you like us to carry you past the potentate?"

"I'd like my friends to carry me," Z-Van said.

"Fine. Please do not lean on the casket as you pass. No flash photography . . ."

Z-Van held up a hand. "Hey, we don't have a camera and I'm not leaning on anything."

The official bowed. "Of course. Proceed."

Judd and Lionel got on either side of the wheelchair, and Westin lifted from the back. They carried Z-Van up the steps to the platform. Judd nearly tripped over his robe but caught himself in time. Z-Van gave him a stern look. "No funny business, okay?"

Judd nodded and noticed three armed guards next to

the coffin. He had seen dead bodies before. An uncle had died when he was young and Judd had touched his face. Carpathia looked more pale than anyone he had ever seen in a casket. The body was vacuum sealed, like a tube of tennis balls.

Z-Van snapped his fingers. "I need a pen and some paper."

Westin pulled out a small pilot's log from his pocket, and Lionel handed the singer a pen. Z-Van jotted a few notes, and they moved along the platform as the GC official told those behind them what to do and not do.

"Excuse me, Mr. Z-Van, sir," a young man said once they reached the bottom of the steps.

Z-Van looked at Westin. "Tell them I don't do autographs while I'm mourning."

"Supreme Commander Leon Fortunato would like to see you before you leave," the man said.

Z-Van glanced at Judd. "I think we have time for the supreme commander. We'd be delighted."

Vicki watched the endless line of mourners file past the see-through coffin. Newscasters spoke quietly like announcers at a golf tournament, not wanting to spoil the somber mood.

Mark yelled and the kids ran to the computer. He pulled up a message from Natalie at one of the GC posts in Illinois and read it out loud. *"Saw your message. Don't have much information on C and the Ss. I know they were under suspicion because the tire tracks matched the satellite truck. I'll let you know ASAP.*

"I've been assigned in-house work. That means they either don't trust me or think I'm doing some bad stuff. Will keep you posted on any news.

"By the way, the bird is fine. Love, N."

"Okay, so translate," Janie said.

"She doesn't know much about Charlie and the Shairtons," Mark said.

"What's the bird she was talking about?"

"Phoenix. He's okay."

"Think we ought to head back that way?" Vicki said.

Mark shook his head. "Not until there's a good reason."

Judd took a deep breath as Leon Fortunato and a group of followers approached Z-Van's wheelchair. Judd adjusted his robe and pulled his turban as low as it would go.

"I'm so glad to hear that the report of your death was a little—premature!" Fortunato said, laughing at his own joke.

"I was just writing a new song about the potentate," Z-Van said.

"How wonderful. Music can help the grieving process. Would you be willing to perform it for us tomorrow?"

"At the funeral?"

"Of course. You could sing it when we introduce the potentate from the United North American States."

"I have to finish it first, but okay."

"Good. Oh, I want you to meet another artist who is putting the finishing touches on the statue we'll unveil tomorrow."

A man in colorful clothes daintily stretched out a hand and greeted Z-Van. "I'm Guy Blod. I've been a great admirer of yours for years. You have my sympathy about your injury."

"I'd rather be in a wheelchair than in the ground," Z-Van said. He looked at Fortunato. "Any truth to the rumor that you'll be the next potentate?"

Fortunato smiled. "We are moving one step at a time and trying not to get ahead of ourselves."

"Yeah, you're probably on the trail of the assassin."

"Interesting you should say that. After careful review of the video, we have discovered the potentate's last words were an expression of forgiveness to the person who committed this heinous crime. The doctor who performed the autopsy said there was no human explanation for the potentate's ability to speak at all, given the extent of the damage done by the bullet."

Judd flinched, then raised a hand to adjust his turban.

"You mean he shouldn't have been able to talk," Z-Van said.

"Yes. Forgiveness such as this is surely divine." Fortunato looked up at the casket and the people passing by. "This was a good and righteous man. Truly, he was the son of god."

"Which is why we have erected such a statue to proclaim his divinity," Guy Blod said.

"As a matter of fact," Fortunato continued, "many believe there's a place for worshiping and even praying to our fallen leader."

Judd's mouth dropped and he stared at Fortunato. The man squinted at Judd. "This young man looks familiar."

"These are the guys who pulled the boss out of the rubble in Jerusalem," Westin said.

"Worshiping Carpathia," Z-Van said, "not a bad idea. I'll include it in the song."

"Wonderful," Fortunato said, unable to take his eyes off Judd. "If you will excuse us, we need to greet the people. Please call my assistant later about the details of the ceremony."

Fortunato and his lackeys moved to the middle of the line snaking toward the glass coffin. People bowed and knelt and kissed his hands.

"I can't take any more of this," Judd whispered to Lionel.

Westin pointed to the many concession stands and tents scattered about the plaza. "I heard on the news that it's supposed to get above one hundred degrees tomorrow."

Judd saw some emergency medical tents scattered around, but with a crowd expected nearly twice the size of the one at the Jerusalem Gala, he wondered how people would make it in the sweltering heat.

As they rode to the hotel in a special GC vehicle, Judd noticed people with sleeping bags on the sidewalk. Others had built lean-tos with cardboard boxes or slept in parks or hotel lobbies.

"You two will stay with us in the penthouse suite," Z-Van said.

"Have you decided when we'll head to the States?" Lionel said.

"I'll let you know."

Their hotel was jammed with people. Many were sharing rooms with other families. Judd and Lionel helped Z-Van to their room while Westin ran errands. The room was cool compared with the evening heat of New Babylon. Z-Van wheeled to his side of the suite and turned up the stereo to an earsplitting level.

Judd and Lionel retreated to the other side and changed out of their robes. They found two king-size beds and crawled in.

"I feel guilty for sleeping in this kind of luxury while other people are on the street," Lionel said.

Judd nodded. "Do you think it's happened yet?"

"You mean Carpathia? No. And Leon acted like he didn't have a clue about what's going to happen."

"Maybe Tsion's wrong."

Lionel sighed. "That would be a first."

"Do you realize we spent the day with one of the most famous musicians on the planet and stood next to the most famous political figure alive?"

Lionel chuckled. "And I couldn't wait for old Leon to leave. I thought he was going to recognize you."

"I'm just glad he didn't ask me what I thought about praying to Carpathia. Made me want to throw up."

"What's our plan for tomorrow?"

Judd closed his eyes and thought of the rest of the Young Tribulation Force. "We do whatever it takes to get back home."

LIONEL awoke early on Sunday morning and checked e-mail. A message from Sam explained the details of the reports he had seen from Jerusalem.

> *It was incredible to watch. The witnesses were bold, even with the GC there. Mr. Stein was among them, preaching, teaching, and pleading with the people to ask God's forgiveness.*
>
> *Mr. Stein believes we are seeing the fulfillment of prophecies that speak of many coming to Messiah before the end. I had second thoughts about going with you, but this confirms I made a good decision. I will be the Young Tribulation Force contact in Jerusalem.*

Sam wrote that he was praying for Lionel and Judd each day and would also pray for their friends in the States.

Someone knocked at the door. Lionel opened it to find a man with long curly hair, tight jeans, and an open-collared shirt. He carried a guitar case. "Z-Van here?" the man mumbled.

"Yeah, come in."

The man stumbled inside and dropped the guitar. "Where is he?"

Lionel pointed to Z-Van's room, and the man walked in without knocking.

"Boomer!" Z-Van yelled. "Get your stick. Gotta teach you a new song."

Lionel took a walk outside the hotel. The streets were already crowded with people heading toward the plaza. They trudged by, some weeping, others staring off. Lionel knew they were worried about their future without Carpathia. *They should worry about what they're going to do when he comes back,* Lionel thought.

The temperature was already in the high eighties, and Lionel wondered how hot it would be by noon. Street vendors set up stands as people moved closer to the funeral site. Dealers sold umbrellas, bottled water, chairs, sunscreen, and even souvenirs. Every block featured street entertainers—some with guitars, others with different musical instruments. The farther away from the hotel Lionel walked, the rowdier the entertainment became. Jugglers and clowns tried to make people laugh who didn't want to laugh. Fortune-tellers badgered the grieving pilgrims to spend a few Nicks.

A fight broke out between a man playing a saxophone and one of the clowns. Peacekeepers quickly converged and broke it up. Lionel had seen enough. He went back to find Judd.

Vicki relieved Mark at the computer. He had answered questions and posted information on the Web site all day, and Vicki knew he had to be exhausted. "We'll wake you when the funeral begins or if something happens with Carpathia."

The house was quiet except for the droning of the television. She found no new information on Tsion Ben-Judah's Web site, so she clicked on the kids' Web site to retrieve e-mail. Kids from around the world were still writing and a few were angry.

I hope you and that Tsion Ben-Judah die! one person wrote. *You're probably glad Potentate Carpathia was killed. Well, one day it's going to happen to you and I hope I'm there to see it.*

Another person wrote specifically to Vicki. *You cheated us out of a great concert with The Four Horsemen. I hope the Global Community hunts you down like a dog and makes you pay for what you did, you religious freak!*

Most of the e-mails asked specific questions about the future and how to become a true believer in Jesus. The computer blipped and a message from Natalie popped up.

I'm at a safe computer. The farmhouse was destroyed, but the Shairtons and Charlie got out. They're in GC custody and seem to be okay. But the GC is asking questions about the adult Tribulation Force hideout. I don't know why.

With what happened in Jerusalem Friday and the crackdown that's sure to come against believers, I don't think it's a good idea to leave them in the GC's hands. I have an idea on how to get them out, but I need some help. Can you suggest anyone?

Vicki hit the reply button and typed quickly. She gave Natalie information about two of their friends, Zeke Jr. and Lenore Barker.

We'll come back and help, Vicki wrote. *We'll do anything to help get them out. Also, I used a phone that belonged to Maxwell Stahley, one of the GC's higher-ups. Can you check and make sure that phone isn't being traced? If it is, we have to get out of here.*

Vicki sent the message and responded to a few more e-mails. The GC CNN coverage showed live shots of people filing past Nicolae Carpathia's body. Huge screens had been placed throughout the massive plaza and as far as a mile away. Estimates were that as many as four million people would jam the plaza to witness the farewell to Carpathia.

Vicki shook her head. *When is it going to happen?*

Judd and Lionel rode with Z-Van, Boomer, and Westin to the back of the stage. Z-Van invited them to stay while he performed, but Judd said they wanted to join the crowd and meet later at the hotel.

Judd looked out on a sea of people—every national-
ity, color, ethnic background, and religion were represented. People packed together at the front trying to get a
glimpse of the stage and the world leaders. A canopy
sheltered Carpathia's coffin and the dignitaries from the
relentless sun, but people in the crowd fainted and had
to be rushed to medical tents.

Judd and Lionel pushed through the crowd. Without
a cloud in the sky, the heat was suffocating. Judd was glad
he had the turban to cover his head, but any exposed skin
burned quickly. Lionel touched Judd's shoulder and
pointed to a temperature gauge on a huge television
screen. It read 106 degrees.

"Why did you want to come out here?" Lionel said.
"We could have stayed backstage out of the sun."

"In a crowd this size there have to be a few other
believers."

Throughout the vast courtyard were numbered markers,
each staffed by a Global Community Peacekeeper. They
were about a half mile away from the stage when Judd
stopped. Near marker 53 he spotted a female Peacekeeper
talking with a GC official. Both had the mark of the believer.

Judd pointed them out to Lionel, and they pushed
their way through the crowd. By the time they reached
the Peacekeeper, the GC official was gone.

"Can I help you?" the Peacekeeper said as Judd and
Lionel drew closer.

Judd tipped his turban, revealing the mark on his
forehead. The Peacekeeper's mouth dropped open. "If
you need some assistance, come right this way."

The woman took them to her station under a small canopy and gave them both a bottle of cold water from a cooler. Judd introduced himself and Lionel and told the Peacekeeper where they were from.

"I'm Annie Christopher," the woman said. She had short, dark hair and dark eyes.

"Who was that guy that was just here?" Lionel said.

Annie smiled. "My boss. He pulled me into his office one day after I'd prayed and told me I had a mark. We've been working together ever since."

Judd pointed to the draped statue behind Carpathia's body. "Do you know what they're going to do with that thing?"

Annie's radio crackled and she held up a hand. "Sector 53 contained," she said. She put the radio back and sighed. "My boss took a close look at it this morning. They have a fire going inside the statue that was started using Bibles and other holy books. Evidently they got them from the late Pontifex Maximus's collection.

"And that's not all. They want the statue to appear alive so they've somehow made the thing talk."

"You've got to be kidding," Judd said.

Annie shook her head. "On the scaffold this morning, my boss swears he heard the thing say in Carpathia's voice, 'I shall shed the blood of saints and prophets.'"

Judd shuddered and wondered what kind of recording device would work inside a burning statue. "Is that really Carpathia in that glass coffin?"

"As far as we can tell."

A bullhorn from the stage quieted the crowd. Judd

watched the shimmering waves of heat rise from the pavement.

"Maybe we can talk later," Annie said.

"Thanks for your time," Judd said as they moved back into the sun. A glance at one of the huge screens showed that the ten regional potentates and other GC dignitaries were in place. Orchestra members arrived, and an announcer's voice boomed over the public-address system.

"Ladies and gentlemen, Global Community Supreme Commander Leon Fortunato and the administration of the one-world government would like to express sincere thanks and appreciation for your presence at the memorial service for former Supreme Potentate Nicolae J. Carpathia. Please honor the occasion by removing head coverings during the performance by the Global Community International Orchestra of the anthem, 'Hail, Carpathia, Loving, Divine, and Strong.' "

Singers and a troupe of interpretive dancers joined the orchestra. After the performance, a montage of Carpathia's life was shown on the huge screens. Scenes included Nicolae at his fifth birthday party in Romania, his high school graduation, taking office as president of Romania, and speaking at the United Nations three and a half years before.

Fighter jets screamed overhead as video clips showed Carpathia mocking and challenging Eli and Moishe at the Wailing Wall. The ocean of viewers roared as Carpathia shot them dead.

"You notice they didn't show Eli and Moishe rising," Lionel said.

"That's just a silly myth," Judd smirked.

The montage switched to the closing night of the Gala and the slow-motion replay of Nicolae's demise. The body was loaded onto a GC helicopter. As it rose, the chopper was enveloped into a larger image of a man in a dark suit, standing among the stars, looking down on the crowd. It was Nicolae Carpathia.

The jets flew past as the crowd roared its approval. They understood the message: Nicolae may be dead, but because he is divine, he still lives in the hearts of the faithful.

Judd turned to Lionel. "Next up on the program is a group of children singing 'Nicolae loves me, this I know.' "

The music faded and Leon Fortunato gave Carpathia's personal history in a voice filled with emotion. Nicolae had been born thirty-six years earlier in Roman, Romania, and was an only child. He was athletic and interested in academics. Before the age of twelve he was elected president of the Young Humanists and was valedictorian in high school and at the university he attended.

Fortunato recounted the story of Carpathia speaking at the United Nations after the global vanishings and said the world needed "someone to take us by the hand and lead us through the minefields of our own making and into the blessedness of hope.

"How could we have known that our prayers would be answered by one who would prove his own divinity over and over as he humbly, selflessly served, giving of himself even to the point of death to show us the way to healing?"

The crowd applauded. Judd glanced at Annie Christopher and saw her looking through binoculars.

Leon introduced the regional potentates. When they were called, music from the region and loud cheering from his people greeted each potentate. When one potentate mentioned religion in his remarks, Fortunato stood and blasted Jews and followers of Tsion Ben-Judah. He blamed the Judah-ites for Carpathia's assassination and called them closed-minded for believing there was only one way to God.

Suddenly, the statue to Leon's left billowed black smoke. Leon turned and said jokingly, "Even Nicolae the Great has to agree with that."

Fortunato raised a hand as the crowd reacted. "But seriously, before our next potentate comes, let me reiterate. Any cult, sect, religion, or individual who professes a single avenue to God or heaven or bliss in the afterlife is the greatest danger to the global community. Such a view causes division, hatred, bigotry, and pride."

Fortunato then introduced the potentate of the United North American States. "But before he comes, we have a special treat for you. Here with music from the region and a new song written especially for this day is the lead singer for The Four Horsemen, Z-Van!"

The crowd cheered as Z-Van was wheeled onto the stage. Some who had not heard that he was alive covered their mouths and cried. Boomer plugged in an acoustic guitar and sat on a stool a few feet away.

Z-Van started the song a cappella; then Boomer joined him.

> *One man, one heart, one world, one soul*
> *United with a common goal.*
> *To see the flag of peace held high*
> *We honor this man, Nicolae.*
>
> *One spinning bullet can't stop his song*
> *That rang in our hearts for so long.*
> *Beneath the rubble of our lives*
> *No force can silence Nicolae.*

As Boomer strummed, Z-Van moved in his wheel-chair. He seemed to want to get up and run toward the crowd, but he couldn't. He spoke/screamed the words:

> *This man lies in state before you,*
> *Sealed in a man-made coffin.*
> *But no man can seal his ideas or his love.*
> *No force on earth can kill what he stood for,*
> *What he strived for,*
> *The peace he fought for,*
> *And the dream he died for.*
>
> *Worship him now with your heart and soul.*
> *Worship Nicolae!*

The crowd went wild and clapped along as the orchestra joined in the simple tune. When Z-Van had finished, millions stood and cheered. There seemed no end to the hype, but Judd wondered if something worse was ahead. Would Nicolae rise from the dead in front of the cameras beaming the ceremony to every spot on the planet?

11

JUDD felt the effects of the sweltering heat. With the sun beating down from a cloudless sky, he wondered how anyone could stand the soaring temperatures. As the next potentate stood to speak, Judd found a vendor selling lukewarm bottles of water. He bought two and returned to Lionel.

"This guy's speech is falling flat," Lionel said. "There's no emotion."

The potentate, Enoch Litwala, concluded his speech by saying, "The United African States opposes violence and deplores this senseless act by a misguided individual, ignorantly believing what has been spoon-fed him and millions of others who refuse to think for themselves."

Litwala sat and Fortunato seemed caught off guard. He introduced the next two potentates, who also spoke without much emotion.

"I guess there are at least three regions that don't follow Carpathia too closely," Lionel said.

The crowd grew restless and many stood, wanting their chance to pass by the coffin. Fortunato calmed them and asked for attention to his final remarks.

"It should be clear to even the most casual observer that this is more than a funeral for a great leader, that the man who lies before you transcends human existence. Yes, yes, you may applaud. Who could argue such sentiments? I am pleased to report that the image you see to my left, your right, though larger than life, is an exact replica of Nicolae Carpathia, worthy of your reverence, yea, worthy of your worship.

"Should you feel inclined to bow to the image after paying your respects, feel free. Bow, pray, sing, gesture— do whatever you wish to express your heart. And believe. Believe, people, that Nicolae Carpathia is indeed here in spirit and accepts your praise and worship. Many of you know that this so-called man, whom I know to be divine, personally raised me from the dead."

"We've heard it just about every time he opens his mouth," Lionel whispered.

Judd chuckled, then quickly focused on Fortunato. The crowd no longer seemed antsy.

"I am no director, but let me ask the main television camera to move in on my face. Those close enough can look into my eyes. Those remote may look into my eyes on the screen."

"Don't look at him," Judd whispered.

Fortunato lowered his voice and spoke slowly. "Today

I am instituting a new, improved global faith that shall
have as its object of worship this image, which represents
the very spirit of Nicolae Carpathia. Listen carefully, my
people. When I said a moment ago that you may worship
this image and Nicolae himself if you felt so inclined, I
was merely being polite. Silence, please."

Four million people fell deathly silent. Fortunato told
the crowd that they had a responsibility to submit to the
authorities.

"As your new ruler, it is only fair of me to tell you that
there is no option as it pertains to worshiping the image
and spirit of Nicolae Carpathia. He is not only part of our
new religion, but he is also its centerpiece. Indeed, he has
become and forever shall *be* our religion. Now, before
you bow before the image, let me impress upon your
mind the consequences of disobeying such an order."

Rumbling shook the plaza. Fortunato backed slightly
away from the podium and looked toward the statue. A
huge plume of black smoke billowed forth and blotted
out the sun. A voice thundered from the statue, "I am the
lord your god who sits high above the heavens!"

The crowd fell on their faces, terrified. Judd thought
the voice sounded just like Carpathia. Judd and Lionel sat
on the hot ground, not wanting to block anyone's view
but not willing to kneel. Judd had made up his mind long
ago that he would never worship any leader but God.

"I am the god above all other gods. There is none like
me. Worship or beware!"

Fortunato leaned over the microphone and spoke
gently, like a concerned father to little children. "Fear not.

Lift your eyes to the heavens." Leon paused as the smoky cloud disappeared. "Nicolae Carpathia loves you and has only your best in mind. Charged with the responsibility of ensuring compliance with the worship of your god, I have also been imbued with power. Please stand."

As people stood, Lionel turned to Judd. "What kind of power?"

Judd shrugged as Fortunato turned and looked at the ten potentates. Three of them glared at Leon.

"Let us assume that there may be those here who choose, for one reason or another, to refuse to worship Carpathia. Perhaps they are independent spirits. Perhaps they are rebellious Jews. Perhaps they are secret Judah-ites who still believe 'their man' is the only way to God. Regardless of their justification, they shall surely die."

People gasped and stepped back.

"Marvel not that I say unto you that some shall surely die. If Carpathia is not god and I am not his chosen one, then I shall be proved wrong. If Carpathia is not *the* only way and *the* only life, then what I say is not *the* only truth and none should fear."

Vicki and the others gathered as the service in New Babylon started. It was early in the morning in Wisconsin, but no one complained. Some of the kids thought that Tsion might be wrong. Maybe Carpathia wasn't the Antichrist. Perhaps, they said, Leon Fortunato was. When Leon started his hypnotic speech, Vicki leaned close. The camera stayed on Leon's face, and Vicki wondered if people watching around the world would be affected like those in New Babylon.

"It is also only fair that I offer proof of my role," Fortunato said, "in addition to what you have already seen and heard from Nicolae Carpathia's own image. I call on the power of my most high god to prove that he rules from heaven by burning to death with his pure fire those who would oppose me, those who would deny his deity, those who would subvert and plot and scheme to take my rightful place as his spokesman!" Leon paused dramatically. Then, "I pray he does this even as I speak!"

He pointed at three potentates sitting at the end of the platform. Vicki shielded her eyes from the screen as white-hot flames burst from the sky and torched the three. The seven other potentates jumped out of their seats and backed away to avoid the heat and flames.

"I've never seen Carpathia do anything like that," Janie said. "Maybe this Fortunato guy is the real Antichrist."

The kids stared in disbelief as the camera focused on Fortunato. The man smiled as he watched the three potentates burn.

People around Judd screamed and wailed but stayed in their places, paralyzed with fear. As quickly as the fire shot from the sky and burned the three potentates, it disappeared, leaving three tiny piles of ash.

Fortunato assured those who lived in the three potentates' regions that replacement potentates had already been selected.

Judd turned to Lionel. "I wonder what else they've already planned?"

Lionel glanced at Global Community Peacekeepers and guards placed around the plaza. "What'll we do if they make everybody bow to the statue?"

Judd gulped a drink of warm water and pursed his lips. "It's going to be hard to enforce a rule on four million people."

Fortunato encouraged the frightened crowd to express their approval. "You need not fear your lord god. What you have witnessed here shall never befall you if you love Nicolae with the love that brought you here to honor his memory. Now before the interment, once everyone has had a chance to pay last respects, I invite you to come and worship. Come and worship. Worship your god, your dead yet living king."

People nearby fell to their knees and wept. Some lifted hands and seemed to be praying to Carpathia. Officials removed the barricade in front of the viewing line, and slowly people began to walk past Carpathia's coffin. The seven remaining potentates shook hands with Fortunato, leaning close to him to say a few words.

"What do you think they're saying?" Judd said.

"Nice shot?"

In an act Judd couldn't believe was shown on camera, Fortunato stepped to the empty chairs and swept the ashes of the dead potentates away. When the chairs were clean, he clapped and rubbed his hands together and let the dust fall away.

Judd turned to the thermometer fastened to the side of a medical tent. It read 109 degrees. He looked for Annie Christopher, but she wasn't under the GC canopy.

"Look at this," Lionel said.

The statue began to sway and bounce, as if another earthquake was on its way, but no other structures moved. People whispered and pointed as word spread through the crowd. The rocking and swaying continued as the image turned red. Smoke belched and formed black clouds that hovered over the assembly. With the sun blocked, the temperature fell. Many lay with their faces on the ground, terrified.

"Get out of here now," someone whispered to Judd. It was Annie. "This place isn't safe for believers."

"Where should we go?" Judd said.

"Anywhere but here. Just don't make it obvious. Don't run."

At the edges of the crowd people screamed and ran wildly. Annie broke away and headed for a cart. "Stop!" she screamed at the frightened people. "Stay where you are and you won't be hurt!"

The statue roared, "Fear not and flee not! Flee not or you shall surely die!"

A blinding flash knocked Judd and Lionel to the ground. Seconds later thunder shook the earth. Many of those who ran had been struck by lightning from the hovering cloud.

Judd noticed a crowd standing around the nearby cart

and pushed his way through. A uniformed GC officer lay on the ground, her head scorched by a lightning bolt. It was Annie. She had been killed instantly.

"Back away!" a guard said to the group.

Judd and Lionel walked a few paces. The statue continued its angry howling. "You would defy *me*? Be silent! Be still! Fear not! Flee not! And behold!"

Above them, the smoky clouds rolled and churned until the black mixed with red and purple. Like a prelude to some demonic performance, the clouds signaled what was about to come. Judd thought he had seen ultimate evil when he had witnessed the horsemen and the stinging locusts, but this was even more terrifying.

The statue shook and said, "Gaze not upon me." Smoke stopped and the statue was still. It said, "Gaze upon your lord god."

All eyes turned to the coffin where Carpathia lay, and the camera zoomed in on his face. The screen was split—with one side staying on the dead man's face, the other side showing his entire body.

In only a few minutes the temperature had fallen from 109 to the low sixties, and people shivered and rubbed their arms. Lights shone on the coffin.

Judd studied one of the monitors. He thought he saw movement.

"Did you see that?" Lionel said.

"His hand?"

"Yeah. Creepy."

"There it goes again," Judd said. Carpathia lifted a

finger, then let it fall. He uncurled his left index finger
and it looked like it was pointing.

Lightning struck the stage and Carpathia's hands
moved to his sides. Judd looked closely and saw the
man's chest rising and falling. Carpathia was breathing.

Vicki couldn't take her eyes off the coverage. The news
anchor was speechless as Carpathia's hand moved.
Cameras showed anxious faces twisted in terror in the
crowd. As the camera panned the stage, several surviving
potentates fell to their knees.

The screen split into four camera shots. One quadrant
showed Fortunato and the potentates, two others focused
on the crowd, and the upper left corner stayed on
Carpathia's face. Suddenly, Nicolae's eyes popped open.
Several kids in the room screamed.

"Take a look at neon Leon," Conrad said. "He just
turned white as a sheet and can't stop shaking."

"He thought he was going to be the next potentate,"
Vicki said. "Not anymore."

Nicolae's lips separated, and he lifted his head slightly
until it touched the transparent lid. The crowd at the
front of the platform and all the dignitaries collapsed.
Carpathia lifted his knees and kicked something with his
left leg.

"He just broke the vacuum seal," Conrad said. "He's
going to try and get out of there, but the glass alone has
to weigh a hundred pounds."

The once-dead potentate brought his hands and knees

up and pushed at the lid, ripping bolts from the Plexiglas. He kept pushing until the glass popped open and crashed into the podium, knocking it over.

Since everyone else was on the ground, Judd and Lionel sat, as people shrieked and moaned across the plaza.

"What now?" Lionel said.

Judd couldn't take his eyes off Carpathia. "Let's stay here until we figure out what to do."

Carpathia sprang from the coffin like a cat and stood in the narrow end, facing the crowd. Instead of cheering, the stunned crowd was silent.

"Don't they sew your lips together when you're dead?" Lionel said.

"I don't know," Judd said. He remembered the triumph and glee he felt when Eli and Moishe had risen into the sky. Now he felt the exact opposite as he watched Nicolae Carpathia standing in his own coffin.

Nicolae looked like he had just stepped off the pages of a men's fashion magazine. His shoes gleamed, his suit pristine, every hair in place. Judd held his breath as Nicolae raised his hands and began to speak.

12

WHEN Carpathia moved, Vicki backed away from the television. As he stood before millions in New Babylon and countless numbers of viewers, a chill ran up her spine. Tsion had been right. Carpathia was now inhabited by Satan himself.

Behind Nicolae, Fortunato and the seven potentates were on their knees, crying and wailing openly. The microphone had been knocked over by the coffin lid, but Nicolae's voice was crystal clear on the television.

"Peace," Carpathia said. "Be still." The camera kept a close-up on Nicolae's face, and Vicki noticed the scene seemed to get brighter. The dark smoke that had hung over the gathering vanished, and the sun came back.

"Peace be unto you," he said. "My peace I give you. Please stand."

As people throughout the plaza rose, Mark hurried to the computer. "We have to make sure kids know what's going on."

Carpathia continued. "Let not your hearts be troubled. Believe in me."

Conrad shook his head. "This guy is as counterfeit as they come. Those are Jesus' words."

With his hands still raised, Carpathia said, "You marvel that I speak directly to your hearts without amplification, yet you saw me raise myself from the dead. Who but the most high god has power over death? Who but god controls the earth and sky?"

"Vicki, come here!" Mark said.

Carpathia's voice was gentle and soothing. "Do you still tremble? Are you still sore afraid? Fear not, for I bring you good tidings of great joy. It is I who loves you who stands before you today, wounded unto death but now living . . . for you. For you.

"You need never fear me, for you are my friends. Only my enemies need fear. Why are you fearful, O you of little faith? Come to me, and you will find rest for your souls."

Carpathia's speaking more words of Jesus sickened Vicki. She moved to Mark's side and looked at the computer where Mark had pulled up a new message from Natalie: *Cell call traced to Wisconsin. Get out now.*

Judd and Lionel stood with four million others as the sun warmed the plaza again. Within minutes, the temperature had climbed back over one hundred. People were in shock about Carpathia, and only his comforting voice had calmed them enough to obey.

"Only he who is not with me is against me,"

Carpathia continued. "Anyone who speaks a word against me, it will not be forgiven him. But as for you, the faithful, be of good cheer. It is I; do not be afraid."

Judd glanced back and saw two guards loading Annie's body onto one of the carts. Judd wondered if they were setting up a morgue for all who had been struck by lightning.

"I want to greet you," Carpathia said. "Come to me, touch me, talk to me, worship me. All authority has been given to me in heaven and on earth. I will be with you always, even to the end."

People standing in line remained frozen, too frightened to move. Carpathia turned and nodded to someone. "Urge my own to come to me." Slowly, people approached the stairs. "And as you come, let me speak to you about my enemies. . . ."

"Uh-oh," Lionel whispered. "Maybe it's time to get out of here."

Judd shook his head. "Why don't you go back to the hotel. I'll stay."

"What if he makes everyone kneel before him and call him lord?"

"Shh!" a woman next to Judd said.

"I have to stay and see this," Judd whispered. "Go back to the hotel and wait. We'll try to get out of here tonight."

As Lionel slowly slipped into the crowd, Carpathia continued, still standing in his coffin. "You all know me as a forgiving potentate. Ironically, the person or persons responsible for my demise may no longer be pursued for murder. Attempted murder of a government official is still an international felony, of course. The guilty know who they are, but as for me, I hereby pardon any and all. No official action is to be taken by the government of the Global Community. What steps fellow citizens may take to ensure that such an act never takes place again, I do not know and will not interfere with.

"However, individual would-be assassins aside, there are opponents to the Global Community and to my leadership. Hear me, my people: I need not and will not tolerate opposition. You need not fear because you came here to commemorate my life on the occasion of my death, and you remain to worship me as your divine leader. But to those who believe it is possible to rebel against my authority and survive, beware. I shall soon institute a program of loyalty confirmation that will prove once and for all who is with us and who is against us, and woe to the haughty insurrectionist. He will find no place to hide.

"Now, loyal subjects, come and worship."

Loyalty confirmation, Judd thought. *That doesn't sound good.*

Lionel crouched low as he moved through the crowd, trying not to block anyone's view. He noticed a GC guard a few yards ahead and angled away from him. The guard spotted Lionel and yelled, "Halt!"

Lionel stopped and looked around, pretending he didn't know who the guard was talking to.

"Where are you going?"

"Back to my hotel. I don't feel well."

"Your potentate has just risen from the dead. ___ ___
stay and listen." The guard squinted at him. "Unless you
are an enemy of the Global Community."

Lionel swooned, as if he were about to faint. "I
thought I'd watch the televised coverage. . . ." He fell to
one knee, and the guard helped him to his feet.

The guard pointed. "There's a medical assistance tent
there."

"Thank you," Lionel said. He limped toward the tent,
went to the other side, and kept moving through the
crowd.

Vicki and the others hastily gathered their things, listening to the audio from New Babylon. Not long after
Nicolae began speaking, the GC CNN logo featured the
words *Day of Resurrection.*

Vicki knew they couldn't dawdle. If Natalie was right,
the GC could find them any moment.

"You'd think the GC would let their people take a day
off for the funeral," Darrion said.

"It's not a funeral anymore," Mark said, "and I don't
care what Nicolae says about forgiveness, we have to stay
one step ahead of these people."

They all loaded their things into the back of the
Suburban. Shelly took a long look at the Stahley summer
home. "It would have been a great hideout."

"Turn on the radio so we can hear what's going on,"
Janie said.

Mark turned the key and nothing happened. He tried everything but the car wouldn't start.

Judd watched the screen carefully as people passed Carpathia, some shaking hands, others fainting before they even reached him.

Carts with bullhorns zigzagged through the crowd telling everyone that "only those already inside the courtyard will be able to greet His Excellency personally. Thanks for understanding, and do feel free to remain for final remarks in an hour or so."

Lionel found the hotel nearly empty, a few desk workers gathered around a television. He ran to the elevator and went to Z-Van's suite, but his heart dropped when he realized he didn't have a key. The door was locked.

Lionel knocked on the door and waited. Nothing. *If I ask for a key, they'll think I'm a crazy fan.*

Lionel moved to the elevator and stepped inside just as the door to the suite opened. He rushed back into the suite and found Westin, Z-Van's pilot, wide-eyed and jittery.

"I was backstage when Carpathia moved. Z-Van just stared at the guy and didn't move. I said, 'Don't you remember what that kid told you?' But Z-Van wouldn't listen. I came back here alone."

"I came to get our stuff," Lionel said. "We're going to try and get out tonight."

"No! Not before you tell me what I have to do."

"What do you mean?" Lionel said.

"You guys were right. Carpathia came back to life just like you said. And if you're right about that, you must be right about Jesus. Tell me what I have to do to become one of you."

Lionel turned down the sound on the TV and grabbed a Bible. "This is how we know what's true. The prophecies about Carpathia and what's going on in the world are all in here."

"I believe you," Westin said. "Hurry before he calls down lightning on us all."

Lionel showed Westin the passage in the book of John where a man named Nicodemus came to Jesus and asked what he had to do to be saved. "Jesus said you have to be born again."

"I've heard that before," Westin said.

"It means you have to ask God to come into your life. You can't save yourself because you're a sinner and sin separates you from God." Lionel showed him a verse in Romans that said everyone has sinned. "Nobody else but God can help you."

"I believe that, so what do I do?"

Lionel pointed to John 3:16 and Westin read it aloud. " 'For God so loved the world that he gave his only Son, so that everyone who believes in him will not perish but have eternal life.' " Westin closed the Bible and said, "I want that."

"Then pray with me," Lionel said. As Lionel spoke, Westin repeated his words aloud. "Dear God, I need you right now. I believe that you're the only one who can save me from my sin. I believe Jesus paid for the bad things I've done by dying on the cross. He is the true Son of God who was raised from the dead. I ask you to forgive me and save me. I want you to be the leader of my life right now. You are the true king, the real Potentate, and I want to follow you from this day forward. In Jesus' name, amen."

Lionel looked at Westin and saw the mark of the true believer, a cross, on the pilot's forehead. Lionel explained what the sign meant, and Westin said he wanted to hear more.

Lionel smiled. Helping someone come to know God gave him an indescribable feeling. Every time people asked God to forgive them, they went from death to life, from Carpathia's kingdom to the kingdom of God.

Lionel glanced at the television as Nicolae Carpathia moved toward one of the cameras. "Let's watch what the enemy's up to."

Vicki and the others took their things and bolted from the Suburban. Darrion showed them a hiding place in the rocks high above the Stahley home. Mark, Conrad, Shelly, and Janie pushed the car down the driveway and onto the road. Mark tried to start it again, but the battery was dead. They pushed it into some brush, hoping the GC wouldn't find it if they did come, but not wanting to take any chances.

When they were together above the house, Mark

opened the laptop and turned it on. "I want to see what Carpathia says."

Vicki put a hand on his arm and reached to turn the laptop off. Cars rumbled in the distance.

Lionel turned up the volume as an announcer said, "Ladies and gentlemen of the Global Community, your Supreme Potentate, His Excellency Nicolae Carpathia."

Carpathia smiled. "My dear subjects, we have, together, endured quite a week, have we not? I was deeply touched by the millions who made the effort to come to New Babylon for what turned out to be, gratefully, not my funeral. The outpouring of emotion was no less encouraging to me.

"As you know and as I have said, there remain small pockets of resistance to our cause of peace and harmony. There are even those who have made a career of saying the most hurtful, blasphemous, and false statements about me, using terms for me that no person would ever want to be called.

"I believe you will agree that I proved today who I am and who I am not. You will do well to follow your heads and your hearts and continue to follow me. You know what you saw, and your eyes do not lie."

"He's saying he's god," Lionel said. "He's going to convince a lot of people to follow him today."

"God's going to let him get away with it?" Westin said.

"Only for a while," Lionel said.

Carpathia invited anyone who was formerly against him to join the Global Community, then added, "In closing let me speak directly to the opposition. I have always allowed different points of view. There are those among you, however, who have referred overtly to me personally as the Antichrist and this period of history as the Tribulation. You may take the following as my personal pledge:

"If you insist on continuing with your subversive attacks on my character and on the world harmony I have worked so hard to create, the word *tribulation* will not begin to describe what is in store for you. If the last three and a half years are your idea of tribulation, wait until you endure the Great Tribulation."

13

JUDD Thompson Jr. wiped sweat from his forehead, aware that he was watching the beginning of the end of the world. For the past three and a half years he had studied biblical predictions about the Antichrist and the false prophet. There was no doubt in his mind that Nicolae Carpathia and Leon Fortunato, Carpathia's right-hand man, were the evil men described in Revelation 14 through 20.

The sun baked the crowd, still scurrying to greet the potentate. GC personnel in roving carts warned people that the courtyard was filled. "If you want to stay and watch the risen potentate greet others, feel free to do so. Otherwise, please exit the area. Thank you."

The gigantic screens showed Carpathia smiling, energetic, and full of life. Minutes earlier the crowd had wept over the man entombed in his glass coffin. Now, as the Bible had predicted, Carpathia stood in the midafternoon

New Babylon sun and beamed. Like moths to a flame, the crowd worshiped their risen hero.

Judd felt drawn too, but for another reason. Carpathia's final words shocked him. The once-dead potentate had urged his enemies to join the Global Community. Then with menacing eyes the man spoke directly to believers in Christ and warned them not to attack him or the harmony he had worked hard to create. The look on Carpathia's face reminded Judd of the look on his face at the execution of the two prophets, Moishe and Eli. No doubt, Carpathia had the same in mind for other followers of Christ, but how would he try to kill them?

As Judd passed through the crowd, he overheard several people talking about Carpathia. "This is the greatest political comeback in history," a man said.

"There's nothing political about it," another said. "This is a religious experience! He's god!"

Judd shook his head as he headed for the courtyard. A GC guard with a bullhorn asked people to move away from the entrance. Judd pulled out the special pass he had been given when he accompanied Z-Van backstage and held it high above his head. The guard didn't pay attention until Judd came closer. The man inspected the pass, eyed Judd warily, and motioned him through the gate.

"Why does he get to go through?" a woman yelled. "That's not fair."

The gate clanged shut and Judd moved past the line. He looped around the huge speakers and equipment at the front of the stage and found the narrow backstage stairs. He flashed his pass to another guard and the man waved him through.

Invited guests and dignitaries who had planned for a funeral watched in awe of Nicolae. Judd noticed some ashes behind the stage, the remains of the three regional potentates Leon Fortunato had struck with fire. Judd glanced at the statue of Nicolae, a perfect replica. Puffs of smoke lingered, and Judd shuddered as he recalled the voice that had thundered from it.

Judd walked through a series of curtains and almost tripped over Z-Van's wheelchair. A leg cast stuck out from under a velvet curtain. He pulled back the curtain and gasped when he saw Z-Van lying facedown, his hands raised in front of him. His guitarist, a skinny man known as Boomer, sat beside him, equally overcome.

Judd touched Z-Van's shoulder and the man turned, his eyes red. "Don't bother me. This is a holy moment."

"I can't take my eyes off Carpathia," Boomer whispered.

"Don't call him that," Z-Van snapped. "Don't even call him potentate anymore. The term is too low."

Z-Van took a quick breath and covered his face. "He's looking this way. I'm not worthy!"

Judd glanced up in time to catch Nicolae Carpathia staring straight at him.

Vicki's stomach churned as the kids scampered into the shadows of a rocky crag above Darrion's summer house in Wisconsin. The GC had located them through Vicki's phone call, but she could live with that. If she hadn't called her friend Natalie Bishop, they wouldn't have found out about the arrests of Charlie and the Shairtons.

Janie shook her head. "I liked this place. I thought we'd stay here a long time."

Mark cradled the laptop computer and scanned their hideout below. "We have to figure a way out."

Two GC cars stopped near the driveway. Downed trees prevented them from driving all the way to the house. Radios crackled, then went silent as car doors opened and closed. Vicki couldn't see how many officers there were, but by the rustling of the leaves it had to be more than two.

"Be right back," Darrion whispered.

Vicki grabbed her arm. "What are you doing?"

"There's a path behind this rock that leads down to the driveway. I'm going to get a better look. Maybe I'll grab one of their radios."

Mark shook his head. "It's risky."

"I'll go with you," Vicki said.

Darrion squeezed between a tree and a rock, and the two wound around a tiny path. Vicki chose her footsteps carefully. In several places the path was so narrow that Vicki hugged the rock as she inched along.

"Don't look down," Darrion said.

Vicki glanced over the edge and saw tops of huge trees below. *No one could survive a fall that far*, she thought.

Darrion slipped on a loose rock and fell over the edge. She grabbed a small root and hung on as Vicki rushed to her. Rocks landed more than a hundred feet below.

Vicki grabbed Darrion's elbow and pulled with all her might. Darrion struggled to get a foothold and finally pulled herself up to safety. Vicki's heart raced like a frightened animal's as the two sat, their backs to the rock.

"Do you think they heard us?" Darrion panted.

Vicki gasped for air. "Let's go back to the others."

Darrion pointed. "Around this curve the cars will be directly below us. Come on."

Before Vicki could protest, Darrion was on the move. Vicki caught up, being careful not to slip. She leaned over the edge and spotted two GC cruisers near a thicket at the end of the driveway.

"Nobody's there," Darrion said. "Let's go."

"I thought you said the path leads down the hill."

Darrion smiled and pulled a rope from a hole in the rock and threw it over the edge. "My dad and I used to rappel down this rock face."

Darrion showed Vicki how to hold the rope and quickly slid down. When she reached the bottom, she waved.

Vicki took the rope like Darrion had shown her. She wasn't able to go as fast as Darrion, and it felt good when her feet were on solid ground.

They ran to a tree and hid. From there they could see two GC officers outside the open front door of the house. One talked into a radio and gave orders. Darrion tugged at Vicki's shirt, and they crept toward the squad cars.

Darrion peeked inside an open window, grabbed a handheld radio from the passenger seat, and turned it on.

"Negative on the first floor," a man said. "Somebody's definitely been here, though."

One by one guards checked in with reports from inside the house. "This is quite a setup, sir. They've got a huge plasma TV and some pretty sophisticated equipment."

"This was Max Stahley's place," the leader said. "He liked the bells and whistles."

"If it was those kids, how would they have known about this place?" a female officer said.

"Good question."

"Let's go," Vicki whispered.

Darrion shook her head. "We have to think. Maybe we should let all the air out of their tires so they can't follow us."

Vicki glanced at the house again and made sure the officers hadn't moved. Darrion reached inside the car, pulled a lever, and the trunk opened with a thunk.

"What are you doing?"

"There might be stuff in there we can use."

"We don't need anything. Come on."

The leader barked orders to two guards outside. "We've got negative contact. Get the accelerant."

"What's that mean?" Vicki said.

Darrion hopped inside the trunk and pulled Vicki in with her.

Judd locked eyes with Carpathia and trembled. Could this man read Judd's thoughts? If Satan indwelt him, would he be able to see the mark of the believer on Judd's forehead?

Carpathia's face and body looked the same, but there was something different about his gaze. He seemed even more intense than before, as if some unearthly power surged through him. Nicolae turned and glanced at a woman in the receiving line. He smiled and spoke softly, reassuring her that he was alive and well.

Judd studied the back of Carpathia's head. There were no signs of the death wound inflicted by Dr. Chaim Rosenzweig at the closing night of the Jerusalem Gala. Judd relived the scene, remembering how Nicolae fell backward on Rosenzweig's razor-sharp sword. There should have been a huge scar on Nicolae's head, but hair had grown over it. Judd would have loved to inspect the wound closer, but he slipped behind a curtain out of Carpathia's sight. God's archenemy was only a few yards away, and the world worshiped him as if he were the creator of the universe.

Judd looked at Z-Van, still flat on the ground, groveling at the image of Carpathia. Judd heard Z-Van whisper something and he leaned closer.

"Victory to you, our lord and risen king, ruler of the world, head of everything," Z-Van said. "We bow and give you praise; once dead, you're now alive. May peace forever reign with you, our sovereign, Nicolae."

Judd closed his eyes and took a deep breath.

Z-Van turned and said, "If this doesn't make you a believer, nothing will."

Judd winced. He wanted to challenge Z-Van, tell him the truth again, but this wasn't the time or the place.

"Look at him," Z-Van continued. "He's got unbeliev-able power, even over death. When I'm onstage and people scream my name and sing my words, it's an energy rush. But that's nothing compared to this." He looked at Nicolae again, his lower lip trembling. "This man is pure power, and I know he's back to help us."

Judd pulled the curtain back slightly and looked at the long line of people waiting their turn to greet Carpathia. He couldn't wait to get to Lionel and leave New Babylon.

Vicki scrambled inside the trunk, and Darrion pulled the lid down, making sure it didn't latch. A thin strip of light showed around the edge of the trunk lid.

"What if they're coming for this car?" Vicki whispered.

"Accelerant is like gasoline or something flammable. There are no cans in here."

"What will they do?"

"They're probably going to torch the house."

Footsteps hurried by and someone opened the other trunk, closed it, got in, and drove the car a few yards past them, gravel crunching under the tires. As Darrion started to lift the trunk to climb out, the officer in charge barked another order. "Move those fallen trees and bring the other car up here!"

"Told you we should have gone back," Vicki whis-pered.

As the GC guards groaned under the weight of the trees, Darrion fiddled with the trunk latch. "We'll wait until they start the fire and take off while they're not looking. But we've got to figure out a way to—"

Someone ran to the car and opened the driver's door. The car dipped to the left as someone sat. As the engine started, a warning buzzer sounded. The car sped toward the house and slid to a halt. Vicki thought she was going to fly through the backseat.

A man cursed as he slammed the front door. "Wonder who left this open?" The trunk lid slammed shut.

Mark Eisman scooted to the edge of the cliff and looked at the house. A GC officer handed two containers to the others, and the three went inside. Another car raced up, barely skidding to a stop before it smashed the other car. The man got out, slammed the trunk that was slightly open, and went inside.

Shelly crawled beside Mark. "Janie just came back. She said there's no sign of Vicki and Darrion."

Mark gritted his teeth. "We'll have to leave without them."

"No, I won't—"

Mark clamped a hand over Shelly's mouth. "Pretty soon they'll come looking for us and they won't be alone. We have to leave."

"But what if they're hurt? They could have fallen . . ."

"Let's find a safe place and regroup," Mark said. "Tell everybody we'll head along the trail Vicki and Darrion took. Maybe we'll find them back there."

As Shelly crawled away to alert the others, breaking

glass shattered the morning stillness. Someone shouted and GC officers ran from the house.

Then Mark saw it. Smoke poured out of the windows of the Stahley home. Soon, flames licked at the walls. The GC officers were using their weapon of fire again. As the Stahley home went up in flames, Mark wondered what the GC's next weapon would be.

14

VICKI gasped, trying to catch her breath in the closed trunk. The heat and smoke quickly made it difficult to breathe. Darrion fiddled with the latch in the darkness, but it was no use.

"Don't use up all our air," Darrion snapped.

The radio Darrion still held crackled, and the GC leader ordered everyone away from the house. "Search the area thoroughly. I want those kids in custody!"

Someone jumped in the car and raced down the hill. Vicki's head hit the spare tire as she bumped into Darrion, the two rolling like luggage. The car screeched to a halt, and Vicki slammed against the backseat.

"This guy must have gotten his license off the Internet," Darrion said.

"We've found a vehicle," a female officer said moments later. "Illinois plates."

"Run them," the leader said.

"When they find out it's Bo and Ginny's car, the Shairtons will be in even more trouble," Vicki said.

Watching the flames shoot into the air, Mark gathered the others and found Darrion and Vicki's path. When they reached the dangling rope, Mark led them to the other side of the rock. Being careful not to make noise, they climbed behind a pine tree that seemed to grow straight out of the rock.

Squad cars screeched down the driveway, and Mark told everyone to get down. The two cars parked at the main road. "Looks like we're hiking out of here."

"What about Vicki and Darrion?" Shelly said.

"Maybe they've been caught," Janie said.

"We won't be able to help them if the GC catches us," Mark said. "Keep going."

The five headed up a small trail that led into the woods behind the Stahley home. Fire crackled in the distance. Conrad stopped them before they went over a ridge. "Those flames aren't just from the house. The fire's made it to the trees."

"Stupid," Mark said. "They're going to burn the whole forest."

Conrad picked up some brown pine needles and rubbed them between his fingers. The needles crackled and broke apart.

Janie pointed to a dry creek bed. "This place is going to blow like a firecracker."

"Which means firefighters will be here within a few hours," Conrad said. "We have to get out now."

Judd walked away from the stage, sure that he didn't want to be near Z-Van or the worship of Carpathia. He thought of Annie Christopher, the Global Community believer he had met who had been killed by Leon Fortunato's lightning. She had given her life trying to help others. Before she died, she talked about another GC worker who was a believer in Christ, but how would Judd ever find the man in this sea of humanity?

Most of the concession stands were abandoned or had sold out during the ceremony. Judd passed a first-aid station that looked like a mobile hospital. In addition to sunstroke and dehydration victims, doctors and nurses helped those who had been struck by lightning. But from the looks of the charred bodies, there wasn't much the medical staff could do.

Judd had been back in the sun only a few moments when he felt dizzy. He couldn't imagine what others who had been in the sun for hours were feeling. Such was their devotion to their risen leader. He found a strip of shade near another medical tent and sat. Huge monitors showed Nicolae and company still enjoying themselves. Carpathia, Fortunato, and a woman Judd didn't recognize shook hands, touched people's shoulders, smiled, and blessed each passerby.

Judd's shirt was wet with sweat and he was dying for

water. A man peeked out of the tent. "We're tearing down. You have to move."

Judd nodded and walked toward the hotel. He had to get there before he passed out.

In Z-Van's hotel suite, Lionel Washington and Westin Jakes, Z-Van's pilot, watched the continuing coverage of Carpathia's triumphant return. Announcers were still dumbfounded at Nicolae's resurrection. Some commentators called him divine.

"What can you say about a guy who beat the odds like this," a man who had once been a sports commentator said. "With his back against the wall, two outs in the bottom of the ninth, Potentate Carpathia manages to cheat death out of its victory. Amazing!"

Reports from throughout the world showed an outpouring of emotion. People jammed the streets of London, Paris, and Moscow. In America, where the coverage of the funeral services had begun in the wee hours of the morning, people had gathered at sports stadiums to mourn together. When Carpathia came to life, they ran onto fields and courts and knelt before the giant screens.

One man in St. Louis had made a crude replica of Carpathia out of scrap metal. He placed the ten-foot-tall sculpture near the Mississippi River the night before the funeral. Thousands had knelt before the statue and prayed to Carpathia. Now the somber scene was replaced by people elated at the news of the potentate's rising.

Lionel thought of his friends in the States and

wondered if Vicki and the others would come up with a new way to reach out with the truth. He logged on to the kids' Web site and read the latest postings.

Lionel explained to Westin about the Web site and Tsion Ben-Judah's writings.

Westin drank in every word. "I want to learn more. I don't want to waste any time."

"What do you mean?" Lionel said.

"I've spent the last few years flying Z-Van and his friends all over the world. Wild parties, booze, drugs, you name it. I've killed so many brain cells with those guys it's not funny, but now I'm walking away."

Lionel nodded. "I understand. When you know the truth, it's hard to be around people who don't. But you're in an important position."

"I don't follow."

"Z-Van trusts you. He'll listen to you. Even if he doesn't believe what you say about God, you might talk with his band members. Nobody has the access to important people and to travel that you do."

Westin sat on the bed and put his face in his hands. "I thought you'd tell me I needed to get away from these people as fast as I can."

Lionel sat beside him. "We have a couple of friends who had a chance to work directly for Carpathia. They both took the jobs, even though they were believers. They felt God wanted them in that place."

"I don't know," Westin said. "I want to help you and Judd get home, but—"

Westin's phone rang. He spoke softly for a few

moments, then hung up. "That was Z-Van. I need to get him."

"I'll go with you."

When they were sure the GC guards couldn't hear them, Vicki and Darrion tore carpet from the trunk floor to get more air. The heat inside was almost unbearable. By prying the carpet from both taillights they got a little daylight, but they were still short of air.

"Do these backseats fold down?" Vicki said, kicking wildly.

"Don't," Darrion said. "We don't want to get caught."

"We're gonna smother if we don't get out of here!"

"See if we can find anything to help us get out," Darrion said.

Vicki found a crowbar and some roadside flares. Darrion pulled a fire extinguisher and a box from deep in the wheel well. As Darrion tried to open the box, the GC leader barked an order to bring the fire extinguishers from both cars.

"What do we do now?" Vicki whispered.

Darrion opened the box and found only some small tools. She pulled the pin on the fire extinguisher. "When they open the trunk, I'll spray them and we'll both run."

Vicki scooted to the rear so she could spring out. Someone ran past the car, opened the other trunk, and fumbled inside. The trunk closed and keys jangled. A key slid into the keyhole inches from Vicki's head, and she heard the man curse. He tried another key that didn't work. Something clunked on the ground, and Vicki assumed the man had dropped the fire extinguisher.

Before he could try again, the GC leader came back on the radio. "Forget about the extinguishers! The fire's getting away from us. Get out of here before the thing blows the other way."

Vicki sighed and sat back, not knowing whether to be thankful or upset. For the moment, while their air lasted, they were okay.

The GC guards jumped in and three doors slammed. The car turned around and sped toward the main road.

"What do we do with the car we found?" someone said on the radio.

"Leave it," the leader said. "The fire will take care of it and those kids."

As the car sped away, Vicki felt a rush of air. She breathed deeply and gagged. Smoke wafted into the trunk.

Darrion leaned close. "Try not to cough. They'll hear us."

Mark started over the ridge but Conrad stopped him. Flames licked at the top of the rock. Gravel churned in the valley below as the two squad cars raced away.

"You still have the keys to the Suburban?" Conrad said.

"Yeah, why?"

"The GC are leaving. If the fire crosses the road, we could hike for a week and not find our way out of here."

Mark shook his head. "You think you can get it started?"

Conrad nodded. "It's our best chance."

Mark studied the hillside and handed the laptop to Shelly. "You, Melinda, and Janie head down the ridge and get to the road. Stay out of sight in case the GC come back."

"What are you going to do?" Melinda said.

"We're going to meet you at that curve in the road with Vicki and Darrion. Hurry."

Mark and Conrad raced down the embankment and found the trail. Smoke from the fire billowed into the air, and the smell was overpowering. Mark pulled his shirt over his nose and mouth.

The temperature rose as they got closer to the rope. Ashes and burning embers fell around them. Wind seemed to push the fire up the hill behind the house.

Conrad was first to the rope. He scampered down the rock easily, pushing off with his feet and sliding a few feet. A piece of burning ash fell on the rope and Mark stomped it out, but not before it burned a few strands. When he turned, Conrad was at the bottom, waving at him.

Mark pulled on the rope to make sure it would hold. His training with the militia had covered a lot about survival and being prepared, but his rock-climbing experience was limited to a wall back in middle school. He took a breath, tested the rope again, and started down.

"Throw me the keys," Conrad yelled from below.

Mark stopped, found the keys in his pocket, and let them fall. Conrad caught them and ran to the Suburban.

Mark continued his descent one step at a time. He looked at the ground, felt dizzy, and decided it was best to look up. What he saw horrified him. A burning ember had fallen and the rope was on fire.

Mark hurried, trying to imitate Conrad's rapid movements, but he couldn't go as fast. When he was twenty feet from the ground, the rope frayed then snapped, and Mark screamed all the way to the ground. He felt the air whoosh out of him, and for a few moments he couldn't talk, couldn't breathe. Conrad helped him up and Mark pointed to the car.

"Just get it started," Mark gasped.

When Mark arrived, Conrad had the hood up and was spraying something near the engine. "Bo said this might help if the car wouldn't start. I forgot about it until now."

Mark looked at the Stahleys' house, completely engulfed in flames. He yelled for Vicki and Darrion but no one answered. Several explosions rocked the hillside, and Mark wondered what kinds of explosives Mr. Stahley had hidden inside. The flames had spread to the trees behind the house and were working their way around the ridge. A huge plume of white smoke hung over the valley.

Mark climbed a knoll and looked at their way of escape. The wind had swirled the fire toward the road a few hundred yards ahead. He ran back to Conrad. "Get that thing started now!"

"I'm doing the best I can," Conrad said, capping the spray can and climbing into the driver's seat. The engine turned over a few times but wouldn't start.

"We'll have to make a run for it," Mark said.

"What about Vicki and Darrion?"

"Either the GC got them or they're on foot. Let's go."

"Give me one more chance," Conrad said.

As the fire ate more trees, the heat grew unbearable. Mark turned his back to it and covered his face and arms.

Conrad opened something near the engine, sprayed furiously, then slammed the hood and hopped back into the front seat. "God, we need your help." He turned the key and the engine sputtered, then chugged faster and faster until it sparked to life. Conrad floored the gas and the engine revved wildly.

"Woo-hoo, we're in business!" Mark yelled.

Mark pushed the car out of the bushes. He dived into the passenger side as Conrad pulled away. As they rounded the first curve, Conrad slammed on the brakes. The road ahead was a wall of fire.

15

MARK looked behind them and saw the road ended just past the Stahley home. "We'll have to hoof it."

Conrad shook his head. "If we get up enough speed, we can go right through it."

"Won't the gas tank explode in the heat?"

"This thing is built like a tank. Let's give it a shot."

Mark thought of his cousin, John, who had spent his last moments on earth watching a fiery meteor slam into the Atlantic Ocean. "What if the tires start to melt?"

"Trust me. If we get enough momentum, we'll be fine." Conrad slammed the car in reverse and backed around the curve. He threw the Suburban into gear and mashed the accelerator to the floor.

The car was sluggish at first but picked up speed quickly. As they rounded the curve, Mark hung on, afraid they would slide into the trees lining the side of the road. When they hit a straight stretch, the speedometer went crazy.

"How wide do you think the fire line is?" Conrad yelled over the engine noise.

Mark swung his seat belt around his shoulder and clicked it. "Wide enough to cook us if we stop."

"Hang on!" Conrad yelled.

As the GC car sped along the rural road away from the fire, Vicki prayed for her friends. Someone in the other car radioed the leader. Darrion kept the volume down and held it so she and Vicki could hear.

"I want you away from that fire," the leader said, "but set up a lookout just before the main road. If those kids are back there and the fire doesn't get them, that's where they'll probably come out."

Darrion shook her head. "I have to get more air." She wedged the crowbar into the trunk lid.

Vicki saw a little daylight, but some black strips of rubber blocked it. She helped pull at the rubber, and Darrion bent the trunk enough to let in a little more air.

The men in front talked, but the droning of the car's tires made it impossible to hear them. The radio crackled again, and the leader identified himself to the base in Des Plaines. He asked to be patched into GC Wisconsin Emergency Management. Moments later a deep-voiced man asked about the situation.

"Two things," the leader said. "We've got a wildfire in some dense woods north of Lake Geneva. You're going to need a big crew to fight this one."

"We just got a report about that from a civilian," Deep Voice said.

The leader gave them the exact coordinates of the fire. "The other situation is a group of kids who might be on foot. We think they started the fire."

"What?" Vicki said in a hoarse whisper.

Darrion put a finger to her lips.

"You talking rescue?" Deep Voice said.

"Not exactly. We think one is the girl who jammed the GC satellite school uplink."

"I heard about that. Why don't you stay and take care of them?"

"We're leaving one squad near a main road in case they come that way. I need to get back to Des Plaines to interrogate our prisoners. Found some interesting information up here."

"He's going to make the Shairtons pay for giving us the truck," Vicki said.

"We'll keep you informed if we see anything," Deep Voice said. "Chopper's headed that way, and they've scrambled an emergency fire crew."

Judd knew he had been in the sun too long. His lips were chapped and his legs felt numb. Sweat dripped from his face as he moved through the crowd, trying to remember the way back to the hotel. The main stage was a few hundred yards away. He thought the hotel was to his left, but he wasn't sure.

Judd turned and squinted, shimmering vapors rising from the asphalt in the distance. His head felt light and he closed his eyes for a moment. He needed something to lean against.

A speaker stood a few yards away and Judd lurched forward, hoping his momentum would carry him. He needed to collect his thoughts and find some water.

A group of ten passed nearby and a teenager ran up to them, out of breath. "Any luck?" an older man said.

"You won't believe it," the boy said. "I was just at the palace. We were told the potentate cannot see any more visitors than the ones in line."

"Tell us something we don't know," a woman said.

"But a man shouted an idea to one of the guards," the boy continued. "He asked if we could worship the statue! It will be more than an hour before we're allowed in, but they have given the okay."

The group cheered and rushed to get in line, and Judd followed. Suddenly, he heard the high-pitched drone of a small engine and someone behind him shouted, "Look out!" Judd turned to see a man in a golf cart bearing down on him.

He couldn't move. Judd had heard about animals being caught in the headlights of an oncoming car, unable to budge from their spot in the road. Now Judd knew exactly how they felt. The man in the cart slammed on his brakes and slid. At the last second, Judd closed his eyes and prepared for the impact.

Something pushed him and he had the sensation of flying, moving through the air effortlessly.

Then everything went black.

Moments before they hit the wall of flame, Mark had second thoughts. He wanted Conrad to stop, but they were flying now, doing more than eighty miles per hour on a road that didn't even have a posted speed limit. Even with their windows rolled up, Mark felt the fire's heat as they raced toward the orange flames. A burning tree began to fall and Mark pointed at it. Conrad kept going as the tree fell behind them.

The car was inside the inferno only a few seconds, but it felt like an hour. The speed of the Suburban carried them through the firestorm. When they came out on the other side, Conrad and Mark whooped and hollered. Conrad jammed on the brakes and they stopped a few feet short of an embankment.

Mark jumped out to inspect the car. The fire had left black spots on the peeling paint. Conrad sprayed wind-shield-wiper fluid and steam rose from the glass.

A smoky cloud rose above them as the fire devoured everything in its path. It was moving more quickly now, blowing along the road and up both sides of the hill.

Mark jumped back inside and Conrad rushed along the road, keeping an eye out for the others. Mark looked at the mountain engulfed in flames and smoke. *This fire is just like the Global Community*, he thought. *It ruins everything it touches.*

"We're coming to the curve you showed the girls,"
Conrad said.

Mark asked him to slow down and the two kept
watch for any movement. A rock banged off the roof and
Conrad stopped. Shelly, Melinda, and Janie climbed over
the road's edge and got in the car.

"What took you so long?" Janie said.

"Had a little problem getting it started," Conrad said.

Shelly looked around inside. "Where are Vicki and
Darrion?"

Mark explained what they had found.

"You think they could have been in one of the GC
cars?" Melinda said.

Mark shook his head and took the laptop from Shelly.
He had no idea where Vicki and Darrion were or if they
were still alive.

Lionel was amazed at the number of people in the street,
singing, dancing, and chanting about Carpathia, their
new god. Several people banged on the side of their vehicle, asking for a ride to get closer to Carpathia. Westin
told Lionel not to roll down the windows, and the people
finally backed away, clearly upset.

They made it through the crowd and the gauntlet of
GC security poised near the courtyard. Lionel walked
behind Westin as they approached the stage where
Carpathia, smiling, still greeted people. It seemed like
every third person fainted as they prepared to shake
Carpathia's hand.

As Westin went for Z-Van, Lionel studied the monitor behind the stage and listened closely as Carpathia soothed each person with his voice. He must have said "Bless you" a hundred times while Lionel watched.

What shocked Lionel most was hearing Leon Fortunato speak to all the people as they passed. "Worship your king," he said. "Bow before his majesty. Worship the Lord Nicolae, your god."

Guards in the background tried to move people along, but Carpathia and Fortunato didn't seem concerned about the thousands still waiting in line. They drank in the praise together.

Lionel looked over the audience, hoping to spot Judd. The sector Lionel had left him in was deserted. Candy wrappers and drink cups littered the ground, but there was no breeze, just the hot sun beating down on the asphalt. *He's probably back at the hotel watching this on TV,* Lionel thought.

Westin wheeled Z-Van to the stairs. The singer beamed and mumbled something as they carried him to the van. Lionel leaned close and heard Z-Van say, "The face of god. I've seen the face of god."

Throughout the ride to the hotel, Z-Van rambled on about Carpathia and his powers, Leon Fortunato's lightning show, and the crowds. Lionel listened but didn't talk. Finally Z-Van looked at him and said, "I saw your friend earlier. Where is he?"

"I'm hoping Judd's at the hotel. We got separated after Carpathia—I mean, Potentate Carpathia came alive."

Z-Van stared out the tinted window. "Nobody's ever experienced what we did today. I know you guys believe Jesus came alive, but that was in some cave in Israel, and nobody saw it happen. This was live, in front of cameras and millions of people. His Excellency doesn't do anything in secret."

Lionel sighed. He wanted to ask Z-Van about Judd but he held his tongue.

Westin spoke up. "What's up next on the schedule?"

Z-Van stared straight ahead. "He looked at me—he spoke with his eyes. He said he had heard the song, even though he was dead."

"You mean Carpathia?" Westin said.

"He spoke to my heart." Z-Van suddenly sat up. "That's it! I'll make a monument to him, just like the one they had in the courtyard, only this one will be music dedicated to Lord Carpathia."

Lord Carpathia? Lionel thought.

"Cancel everything and get the band together," Z-Van continued. "I want no interruptions."

"What about Judd and Lionel?" Westin said.

"Who?"

"The kids who saved your life," Westin said, pointing to Lionel. "You told them you'd give them a ride back to the States."

Z-Van shook his head. "They'll have to wait."

———————————

As Conrad drove toward the main road, Mark turned on the computer and checked the Web site for any e-mail.

He found a message from Natalie, who had been reassigned to GC headquarters in Des Plaines.

Good news, Natalie wrote. *The adult Tribulation Force
made it out alive. No one was taken into custody. I don't know
how they did it, but the GC around here are pretty upset.*

*Also heard a report that you guys set a fire up there. Please
let me know your situation as soon as possible.*

"She didn't say anything about Vicki and Darrion
being taken into custody," Mark said.

"They can't be in the woods," Conrad said. "We yelled
at the top of our lungs."

The road wound around a hill and angled down. Dust
rose behind them. Shelly pointed ahead. "There's the
main road."

Conrad picked up speed and skidded sideways onto
the pavement. Mark looked back to see a perfect view of
the mountain, dense smoke rising above it.

Something moved from behind a row of bushes near
the road, and Janie screamed. "It's a GC squad car!"

16

MARK watched the GC car speed up. It was newer, faster, and would overtake them quickly.

"Floor it!" Mark said.

"I am," Conrad said, watching the speedometer slowly climb.

"They're gaining on us!" Shelly said.

"Is there anything in the back we can throw out to slow them down?" Mark yelled.

Shelly and Janie climbed over the backseat. "There's a spare tire and a tire iron," Shelly said.

"I found a bunch of nails and screws in a little box," Janie yelled.

Mark turned to Conrad. "Go as fast as you can. We'll slow them up a little."

Conrad nodded and kept his eyes on the road as Mark climbed over the seats. He grabbed the tire iron, smashed the back window, and muttered, "Sorry, Bo."

Vicki tried to get comfortable in the trunk. Darrion held the crowbar in place so they would continue to get air.

"Where do you think they're going?" Darrion whispered.

"Probably back to Des Plaines where they're holding the Shairtons and Charlie."

A frantic voice came on the radio, calling the leader. Vicki's heart sank as she heard a young officer say, "We've got those kids, sir. They're in that old car we spotted in the bushes. They're about a quarter of a mile ahead of us."

"How many?"

"Can't tell, sir. They passed us going pretty fast. Probably at least four or five."

"Where are they headed?"

"Toward Lake Geneva, sir."

"Good," the leader said. "The roads are torn up that way. You should be able to catch them."

"We'll need some backup to transport that many, sir."

"Right. I'll arrange it. Just catch them!"

"Sir, they're—whoa!" the young officer said. His radio went dead.

"What's wrong?"

"Sir, they're throwing things from the back of the car. We had to swerve around some debris of some sort—watch out!"

The radio went dead again, and then the young officer came back on, breathless. "They just threw a tire out. We're trying to get back on the road."

"Stay a safe distance behind," the leader shouted. "Just keep them in sight until we can get the chopper headed your way."

Judd's first thought was of heaven. Have I died? He moved his head back on the pillow and struggled to open his eyes. When pain shot through his body, he knew he wasn't in heaven. He yelped and settled back on the pillow.

He felt a bandage on his left arm and noticed his legs were wrapped tightly with gauze. Red spots showed at his elbow, and his shirt was torn and bloody. A bag of fluid hung beside his bed, and there was a needle in his left hand. Every breath was like swallowing shards of glass through this crack down his parched throat.

Cots filled the room as emergency medical personnel hurried about. The tent flap opened, and two GC officers with huge sweat stains showing through their uniforms carried a body inside.

"Not in here," a woman said. "Next tent."

"Sorry, ma'am," the officer said.

Judd lifted his head slightly and studied the patient next to him. The man's face was as red as a cooked lobster. On the other side of Judd was a woman lying on her side, her back to him. She had long, brown hair and her knees were drawn to her chest.

When a nurse approached, Judd tried to talk. The woman shook her head and put a finger to her lips. "I'll be with you in a moment."

The nurse knelt by the cot of the brown-haired

woman. When the patient didn't respond to her questions, the nurse felt for a pulse, then turned the woman on her back. To Judd's horror, a black mark ran down the side of the woman's neck. The nurse quietly covered the woman's body and moved to Judd.

"Water," Judd managed.

The woman asked someone to bring a bottle. She knelt by Judd, felt his forehead, and checked his bandages. "You gave us a scare."

"What happened?" Judd said.

"The man who brought you in said you stepped in front of his cart. He slammed on his brakes, but the impact knocked you down and you fell on the pavement." She pulled the bandage back from his arm and winced. "Fortunately, you didn't land on your head. They said the asphalt is one hundred and twenty degrees in the sun."

Judd tried to sit up, but his head became light and he felt sick to his stomach.

"You've lost a lot of fluid," the nurse said, checking the IV. "We need you strong so you can join in the worship of the risen potentate."

"I need to get to my—"

"Lie still," the nurse said, pushing Judd back on the cot.

Judd glanced at the dead woman. "What happened to her?"

"Lightning," the nurse said. "There were many who ran when the supreme commander told them not to. It's a shame. Maybe this is a way to weed out those weak in faith."

Judd closed his eyes and wanted to scream. Some of those who had been struck were believers in the true

God. Others had apparently been scared of a dead man coming back to life.

The nurse gave Judd a bottle of water with a straw. He grabbed her hand as she turned to leave. "I need to get a message to my friend."

She pulled a pencil and a scrap of paper from her pocket. "Write it down and I'll be back later to check on you."

"But—"

"People are dying. I have to go."

Judd turned on his side and tried to write but his eyes stung. Whatever the doctor had given him for the pain was wearing off. The scrapes on his arms and legs burned like fire. The smell of the dead turned his stomach and he thought he would be sick. Finally, he turned over on his cot, buried his head in the pillow, and fell asleep.

Lionel wondered about Judd as he stared at the locked door to Z-Van's room and listened to the clanging of the man's guitar. Glass smashed and Z-Van cursed.

Boomer, Z-Van's lead guitarist, lit a cigarette and slid down the wall to the floor. "He always gets like this when he's in one of his creative moods. You can bet this is going to be a good album if he's working this hard."

Lionel pulled Westin into another room. "I'm worried about Judd. I need to know what he said to Z-Van backstage."

"You don't know what you're asking," Westin said.

"That guy could have turned Judd in for all we know. He could be in GC custody. I want to find him and get out of here before Z-Van goes berserk."

"You're this scared of him and you want me to stay and work for him?"

Lionel sighed. "I don't know what you should do, but I can't wait any longer. It'll be dark soon. Please."

Westin knocked on Z-Van's door, and the man flew into a rage. A mirror shattered and something hit the wall and broke. Finally, Z-Van opened the door and Westin slipped inside. Z-Van screamed, a lightbulb shattered with a pop against the door, and Westin yelled back.

As the noise increased, Boomer stood, stretched, and said he was going to rest in another bedroom. A few minutes later Westin returned, holding a cold soda can on a red welt above his eye. "That went well." Westin smirked.

"Did he tell you about Judd?"

"Just about the song he was composing when Judd interrupted his worship of Carpathia. He said Judd looked a little sunburned, but he didn't remember him saying much."

"You don't think Z-Van turned him in?"

"I don't think Z-Van has thought two seconds about anything but Carpathia. He's bought the lie big time."

Lionel grabbed a bottle of water and opened the front door. "I'll call in an hour. If Judd comes back, tell him to stay put."

Mark threw everything he could get his hands on out the back, hoping to slow down the GC car. They had swerved at each load he threw, but the car kept coming.

"I see the lake," Conrad shouted from the front.

Mark turned and saw water to their right. The road wound around the lake and into town, a couple of miles away.

"Where should we go?" Conrad said.

"Head for town," Mark said. "We've got a better chance of losing them there."

Conrad sped up. Janie handed Mark an ashtray and the rest of the food. "Only thing left is the laptop."

"What about the seats?" Shelly said.

"Good idea," Mark said. "Help me unhook them. Janie, see if you can get the back door open."

Mark, Shelly, and Melinda worked furiously to unlatch the two bench seats. They pushed and pulled the seats to the open door in back.

"Don't fall out!" Conrad called out, looking in the rearview mirror.

The GC car had gained ground and followed only a few car lengths behind. Janie held the door open as Mark and Shelly prepared to launch the smaller bench.

"The guy has a gun!" Janie said.

Mark heard the first ping of a bullet glance off the fender. "They're trying to shoot out our tires!"

"The town's coming up," Conrad yelled. "There's a bridge ahead."

"I don't remember a bridge around here," Mark said.

"Maybe they built it after the earthquake," Conrad said.

Another bullet pinged, and the kids threw themselves behind the seats, the back door swinging wildly.

"When I say, we push both of these out at the same time," Mark shouted.

An explosion rocked the car and the Suburban careened out of control, almost hitting the guardrails on the bridge. Mark smelled rubber burning as one of the back tires shredded. The Suburban slowed as the GC car swerved onto the bridge. "Get ready!"

The GC car wasn't far behind when the kids shoved the seats out. They landed on top of each other, skittering on the pavement in opposite directions. The car turned and avoided the smaller seat, but it hit the larger one full force, pinning it under the front tires. The car skidded to a stop.

It was dark as Lionel walked toward the palace, thousands of people filling the streets, celebrating, drinking, and dancing. Loud music blared from speakers hastily set up outside restaurants and hotels. Anyone who passed by was drawn into the celebration.

A young woman grabbed Lionel and pulled him into a crowd screaming Carpathia's praises. She took his arms, danced in a circle, and shouted, "He is risen!"

Lionel smiled, but the woman jerked on his arms. "Come on, say it!"

"He is risen," Lionel muttered.

"No, you're supposed to say, 'He is risen indeed.' "

"Yeah, right. He is risen indeed."

The woman danced again, hopping and skipping, running into others in the crowd as she circled with Lionel. "He is risen," she shouted again.

"He is risen indeed!" a man said, pushing Lionel away and moving toward the woman.

Lionel slipped out of the crowd, glad to be away from the revelers. He shuddered as he walked toward the palace. Early Christians had used those same words about Jesus. *Is there anything followers of Carpathia won't do?*

Mark led the cheers as the kids screamed. He fell to the floor and kicked his feet high in the air as the GC officers got out and tried to dislodge the seat.

"There's no time to celebrate," Conrad yelled. "We can't go any farther on this bad wheel."

Mark tried to close the back door, but it was stuck. The shredded tire was almost gone, and the wheel made a *ka-thunk* sound each time it went around. The metal rim was surely bent.

A louder thumping beat the air outside the car. Mark glanced out the back and saw a helicopter swoop low behind them.

"We've got more company!" Mark shouted. "Go faster!"

"I've got it to the floor," Conrad said. "We have to ditch this thing."

Smoke rose from the shattered tire. Mark knew it could catch on fire, and if the sparks reached the gas tank, they'd be blown sky-high.

Shelly put a hand on Mark's arm. "What now?"

17

MARK crawled to the front of the car as Conrad turned down a tree-lined street. A brick building stood to the right and the lake lay beyond it. The helicopter hovered overhead.

"Can you get us to the main street?" Mark yelled.

"No way!" Conrad said. "Get in the back. I'll tell you when to jump."

Mark wanted to argue, but he knew Conrad was right. They had to get out now. Mark gathered the others at the rear.

"What about Conrad?" Shelly said.

"He'll get out. Just be ready."

"I don't like this," Janie said.

Mark cradled the laptop in his arms. He hoped to time his jump and protect the computer.

Conrad drove off the pavement and onto a small knoll under an oak tree. "Now!"

Janie, Melinda, and Shelly jumped out and rolled on the grass, the car still moving. Mark jumped, landed on his feet, and rolled backward, narrowly missing a fire hydrant. He patted the laptop and turned to watch the Suburban.

The car accelerated over the knoll, and Mark lost sight of it for a moment. It raced up an embankment that led to a short pier, careened off the edge, and landed in the water.

"Come on!" Mark shouted. He and the others raced to the brick building and watched the Suburban sink into the muddy lake.

Shelly put a hand over her mouth. "We have to help Conrad!"

The GC helicopter passed overhead and hovered over the choppy water. The car lay on its side, sinking quickly. Mark noticed several people on the sidewalk near the main pier, watching the scene.

Shelly started toward the lake and Mark grabbed her arm. "He wouldn't want you to put yourself in danger!"

Shelly pulled away, put her head on Melinda's shoulder, and cried.

"Look!" Janie said.

Conrad scampered up the hill in the cover of some shrubs. "What's all the blubbering about?"

Mark socked him in the shoulder and Shelly hugged him. Conrad caught his breath and said, "I wedged my shoe onto the accelerator and jumped out just over the hill. I don't think the GC saw me."

Mark looked toward the road leading to town. It was their only hope. The kids ran away from the brick building and crossed the street, making sure they kept trees between them and the helicopter. They passed a long building with a screened-in area, and Mark remembered it had once been a seafood restaurant.

People from the town crowded near the pier, pointing and asking questions. A teenage boy in cutoff jeans said he had seen the whole thing. "That truck passed the library and headed straight for the water. I don't think anybody could have survived a crash like that."

An older woman shielded her eyes. "How many were in it?"

"I don't know. The driver was probably drunk."

The kids turned left and ran up another street. Before the disappearances the town had been a vacation spot for Chicago area families. Now shops that once sold ice cream and T-shirts were boarded up.

The helicopter moved from its position over the water, apparently convinced that the kids weren't in it or hadn't survived. Mark pulled the others into a doorway until the chopper passed. A siren wailed in the distance.

"Come on," Mark said.

The kids ran farther up the street, passing more boarded-up businesses. Mark darted into an alley and the others followed.

Conrad grabbed Mark's arm. "I think we can get in this building."

Conrad pried two boards from a rickety door that led to one of the abandoned shops. The doorknob fell off, Conrad kicked, and the door flew open. Once inside, Conrad replaced the boards.

Mark and the others moved through a narrow hallway to the front of the store and were surprised to find it had once been a bookstore. Shelves lined the walls, and there were still a few books in piles on the floor. A large window in the front gave them a view of the street and part of the lake.

Mark pulled out his wallet, checked his cash, and made a face.

"What is it?" Melinda said.

"The cash box. Did anybody remember it?"

Conrad groaned. "It must still be in the glove compartment."

The kids went through their pockets but came up with only a few Nicks. Because no one had eaten since the day before, they pooled their money, and Shelly volunteered to find some food.

"I don't think we should go out before dark," Conrad said.

"I'm starving," Janie said.

"I won't go far," Shelly said. "If I see any GC, I'll come right back."

Mark paced the floor as Shelly climbed out the back. A few minutes later a GC car passed and the kids hit the floor. The car's engine sounded funny, and Mark peeked through a hole in the boarded-up window. "It's the GC car that followed us."

"How can you tell?" Janie said.

"Front end's out of whack," Mark said. "Must have taken a while to get that seat out."

The GC turned on the car's loudspeaker. "Citizens of

Lake Geneva, we need your help locating some enemies of the Global Community and the risen potentate. We believe they are between the ages of fifteen and twenty. If you see anyone you do not know, please report them immediately to this squad car or the GC post set up at the pier."

Shelly returned and Conrad helped her inside. She placed a paper bag on the floor and pulled out a loaf of bread, some bologna and cheese, and a few bottles of water. "I would have bought more, but I ran out of money."

Shelly explained that she had found a gas station a few blocks away that had a few high-priced supplies. She hadn't heard the GC loudspeaker.

"We'll lay low until dark and try to make a break," Mark said.

Lionel moved in the darkness toward the courtyard. Pilgrims had formed a new line in front of the giant statue of Nicolae. As they passed it, some reached out and touched the legs of the image. Others knelt, bowed, or lay prostrate before it, praying and worshiping the idol.

Lionel's mind raced thinking about all the things that might have happened to Judd. He could have been arrested by the GC, or worse, he could have been struck by Leon Fortunato's lightning.

Many of the medical tents were empty. Others bustled with activity as medical personnel tried to care for the injured and those suffering from the heat. He stumbled into one tent that was eerily quiet and smelled like smoke. A guard approached.

"I'm looking for a friend of mine."

The guard said something in a different language. When Lionel shook his head, the man said, "Dead here. You look for lightning dead?"

"No. I mean, I don't know."

The man pointed to a tent a few hundred yards away, and Lionel thanked him. A nurse approached Lionel in the next tent, and he explained what Judd looked like. The woman shook her head. "I haven't seen anyone who fits that description, but I've only been here an hour."

"Can't you look up his name?"

"We've been treating people as they come in. We don't have a database yet. Look around, but don't bother anyone and don't get in our way."

Lionel tiptoed through the rows of cots, looking into faces of strangers. Most were asleep, trying to overcome the effects of the hot day. Others moaned.

One man reached out to Lionel as he passed. "Something for the pain!"

"I can't help you."

The man grabbed Lionel's shirt, but Lionel pulled away.

Other patients stirred and a nurse ushered Lionel outside. He tried to explain, but the woman wouldn't listen. "Don't let him back inside," the woman said to a guard.

Judd saw his friends running away and he shouted, but they kept running. One of them fell and turned toward him. It was Nada. Judd called out as someone helped her up, and he realized it was his old friend Ryan Daley. A dog barked. Judd turned and saw a hideous dragon, eyes red and tongue full of fire.

Someone grabbed Judd and pulled him toward the others. It was Annie Christopher, the GC employee he had met at Carpathia's funeral.

Judd's legs were heavy. He tried to run, but he felt the hot breath of the dragon behind him. He glanced back and screamed as the dragon came close, its breath horrible, fangs bared, ready to strike.

Judd sat up in bed, out of breath. The dream had been so real he was shaking. He looked for a nurse and saw one at the front of the tent, ushering someone outside. He blinked and tried to focus. Could it be?

"Lionel!" Judd said weakly.

Judd ripped the needle from the back of his hand and jumped to the floor. His legs gave way and he fell, catching himself on the side of the next cot. He wasn't going to let his friend leave without him.

Vicki tried to stay awake as the car drove on. She didn't want to be overcome by any fumes, so she stayed close to the opening Darrion had made, breathing in the clean air.

Throughout the trip, Vicki heard radio reports about the kids in Wisconsin and the wildfire that was completely out of control. One guard contacted the other car and asked if they had seen his radio. Darrion stifled a laugh.

When someone reported that the Suburban had plunged into Lake Geneva, Vicki's heart sank. A few minutes later the chopper pilot said no one had come to the surface.

"If they're not dead, they're on foot," the leader said.

"Search the town. I want those kids brought in for questioning, especially the one that interrupted the satellite feed."

Darrion smiled at Vicki. "What's it feel like to be a wanted teenager?"

Vicki rolled her eyes. "Really special."

The GC stopped and Darrion took the crowbar from the trunk. One officer got out and returned with drinks for the others. Vicki realized how thirsty and hungry she was.

An hour later a report from the emergency management team informed the officers that the wildfire was gaining on the town of Lake Geneva. "We're digging a fire line to see if we can contain it. It's already destroyed a number of homes. It'll be a miracle if we can stop it before it gets to town."

"I can't believe they're blaming us for the fire," Darrion said.

"Typical."

The next time they stopped, all the officers got out and Vicki heard other car doors slam nearby. Darrion put the crowbar under the trunk lid and lifted an inch or two. They were at a police station.

"You think this is where they're holding Charlie and the Shairtons?" Darrion said.

Vicki smiled. "Wasn't it nice of them to give us a ride?"

Darrion tried to use the crowbar to break the latch. When she couldn't, she started to bang and Vicki touched her shoulder. "Somebody might hear us."

Vicki concentrated on the backseat. She pulled the covering material away and kicked as hard as she could. The seat gave a little.

"There must be some kind of latch up front that pops the thing forward," Darrion said.

Vicki felt along the top of the seat but couldn't find a button or a latch. "Let me try," Darrion said.

Darrion ran the crowbar along the top edge of the seat until it pushed through. A sliver of light shone and Vicki squealed. Darrion and Vicki pushed until the seat leaned forward an inch.

"Hold it with your feet and I'll see if I can unlatch it," Darrion said.

Vicki pushed with all her might as Darrion reached through the opening. "I found the latch, but it won't budge."

"Try the other side," Vicki gasped, trying to keep pressure on the seat.

Darrion put her arm through but couldn't reach the other side. "Let me try," Vicki said.

Footsteps approached, and the girls sat back and listened. Someone opened the front door and fumbled through the glove compartment. Another door opened and someone climbed in the backseat. "If I don't find that radio, they'll make me buy a new one."

"Maybe you put it in the trunk when you went for the gas," the other officer said.

"I don't think I even opened this trunk, but it's worth a shot. The thing's not under the seats or in the glove compartment."

The two climbed out of the car and Vicki's heart raced. Darrion grabbed the crowbar as the officer jangled his keys.

18

VICKI found the fire extinguisher and angled it toward the back of the trunk. The officer inserted the key, then cursed and fumbled with the others. Darrion quickly put the crowbar against the mechanism and snapped a wire.

The man inserted the key, turned it, but nothing happened. He did it again and again, but the trunk didn't open. "This is weird. I know this is the right key."

"Curt has a set of masters to all these cars," the other man said. "Find him and you'll get your radio."

The two walked away. Darrion pushed the seat open with her feet while Vicki stuck her arm through. She strained to reach for the latch but was a few inches short.

"Push it harder!"

"It's as far as it will go."

Vicki lunged against the backseat, cracking one of the panels. She tucked her head, pushed her shoulder against the seat, and reached through. She felt the latch with the tips of her fingers and used her feet to push farther. "Another inch and I've got it," she grunted.

Darrion gave one more furious push and Vicki grabbed the latch. The seat flew forward and Darrion crawled through. Vicki followed, leaving the radio behind, and the two crept onto the floor. They pushed the seat back to its normal position.

Vicki peeked out the back window toward the building and opened the door. "Come on." They crawled out, keeping their heads down and crab walking around the door. Vicki closed it quietly and moved away from the building. When the front door to the station opened, Vicki and Darrion rolled under another squad car and lay still.

"If you used the right key, the master's not going to do you any good," a new man said. "Did you try to get in through the backseat?"

"Didn't think of that."

A door opened. "How did the seat get torn up? It wasn't that way when we drove here."

A latch clunked and the first officer shouted, "Here it is!"

"Hold it," the other man said. "Somebody's been back here. Get the chief, quick!"

Lionel thought he heard something as he was led outside the tent, but when he turned, the guard grabbed him by the shoulder and shoved him away from the opening. Lionel was surprised by the move and lost his balance, tumbling onto the asphalt. The sun had been down for hours, but the asphalt was still warm from the soaring temperatures of the day. Lionel rolled onto his side.

Someone inside shouted and Judd burst through, carrying his shirt, the IV tape still on the back of his hand.

The guard reached for Judd's arm. "You can't leave!"

"This isn't a hospital," Judd snapped, wrenching away from the guard's grip and nearly falling. "I can go when I'm ready."

Lionel stood and put one of Judd's arms around his own neck. They walked toward the palace, Judd gasping for air and putting more weight on Lionel's shoulder.

"I'm not sure if I'm really ready," Judd whispered, "but when I saw you, I knew I had to get out of there. What time is it?"

"After midnight," Lionel said. He asked Judd what had happened, and Judd told him what he could remember. Judd shuddered as they passed the statue of Carpathia, thousands of people still standing in line for the chance to worship their idol.

Lionel was excited to tell Judd about Westin, Z-Van's pilot, and that he had prayed with Lionel after seeing Nicolae come back to life. "He remembered what we had told Z-Van on the plane and said we were dead-on with our prediction."

Judd asked to rest as they moved toward the hotel. The celebration continued in the streets. Lionel and Judd exchanged information about Z-Van and considered their next move.

"Something tells me we don't want to be here when Carpathia puts his next plan into action," Judd said.

"What's that?"

"Tsion says Carpathia's going to make everyone swear loyalty to him by forcing every living soul to take some kind of mark."

"They're probably planning how they're going to do it right now."

"Which means they're also planning what they're going to do to everyone who won't take it."

Lionel shook his head. Three and a half years had passed since the disappearances of his family and the treaty Carpathia had made with Israel. Now that Carpathia was indwelt by Satan, the gloves were off. He didn't need to hide his evil deeds. With people blindly worshiping his image, he had the world right where he wanted it. They would follow him like sheep to the slaughter, not knowing their beloved leader was evil in the flesh.

When they saw their chance, Vicki and Darrion ran from the parking lot. When they were a safe distance away they slowed to a walk.

Vicki's hair was matted with sweat. She ran her hands through it as they walked. She hadn't been in this town for so long she hardly recognized it. The earthquake had changed streets and buildings. Damaged homes had been demolished, and the town was littered with empty lots.

They stopped for a drink of water at a fueling station, and Vicki remembered Zeke's place. The girls were hungry and tired, but Vicki said once they found Zeke, they would have all the food they could eat.

They cut across lawns and through alleys. When they heard a siren, they hid. Finally, Vicki turned down an alley, sure that Zeke's was not far away. A suspicious-looking car sat at the end of the alley near Zeke's gas station.

"Why don't we call him?" Darrion said.

"Do you have your dad's cell phone?"

Darrion shook her head. "I got rid of it when they traced your call."

The girls backtracked into a neighborhood. Neither had much money and finding a working pay phone was almost impossible.

"Let's try one of these houses," Darrion said.

Before Vicki could protest, Darrion walked up to the first house and knocked on the door. A man wearing a dirty T-shirt opened the door a few inches. "What?"

"We're with a youth project trying to find people who are skeptical about the resurrection of Potentate Carpathia," Darrion said.

"Skeptical?" the man said. "It's been all over the television the whole day. You'd have to be a fool not to believe it."

"Right, but are there any in the neighborhood here who have acted strangely? You know, still buying into Christianity?"

The man opened the screen door and looked up and down the street. When he saw no one, he scratched at his stubbly beard and said, "I don't want to get Margaret in trouble."

"She won't be," Darrion said. "We just want to talk to her."

"Well, she's been trying to get me to read this guy's Web site . . ."

"Tsion Ben-Judah?"

"Yeah, that's him."

"Lots of silly predictions, right?"

The man leaned close. "Margaret says it's not silly. She's been trying to get me to read the Bible too."

Darrion sighed. "It's one of the telltale signs. Which house does she live in?"

"Other side, three doors down. The light blue one."

"Don't tell anyone you gave us this information," Darrion said. "It's strictly between you and us."

The man went back inside as Vicki and Darrion hurried down the street. Before they reached the house, Vicki took Darrion aside. "I don't like it that we lied to that guy back there."

"I'm just trying to find someplace safe to hide."

"I know, but I feel like we used him. He needs to know the truth too."

Darrion shoved her hands into her pockets. "So if the GC ask if we're Judah-ites, we're supposed to say yes?"

Vicki looked away. "I don't have all the answers about everything we should and shouldn't do. I'm just saying I feel bad about that guy. What if we just pushed him further away from God?"

"What do you want me to do?"

"Let's talk through what we're going to do and decide together next time."

Darrion nodded and the two climbed the steps to the house. Vicki knocked loudly, and an older woman with graying hair opened the door. When she saw the marks on Darrion's and Vicki's foreheads, she hugged them both. "Come in, come in. How did you find me?"

Darrion explained about the neighbor and Vicki's concern that they had deceived the man. The woman led them to the kitchen. "I've been working on just about everybody on the block. Don't worry about him. I'll talk to him after you've gone. I'm Maggie. What are your names and what brings you here?"

Vicki and Darrion introduced themselves and quickly told Maggie their story. "We wanted to visit a friend in the area, but I saw a suspicious car in front of his place and want to make sure everything's okay."

"Would you like something to eat while you're making your call?"

"That would be great," Vicki said.

Darrion helped Maggie while Vicki looked up Zeke's number. When she found it, she remembered there were two phone lines into the gas station. One was the regular line anyone could use and the other was a secret line that was different by only one number. Vicki dialed and let it ring until an answering machine picked up.

Hearing Zeke's voice again made Vicki smile. "It's me, just leave a message," he said on the recording.

After the beep, she said, "This is Vicki Byrne. You might not remember me—"

"Vicki?" Zeke said as the machine beeped again. He spoke quickly and didn't seem himself. "You shouldn't have called me here."

"We were headed to your place and saw—"

"Don't come near," Zeke said. "It's crawling with GC."

"They found you?"

"They arrested Dad this morning. Charged him with subversion and took him away. Ever since then there's been at least one GC car watching our place like a hawk. Anybody who comes for gas gets arrested. I've been watching them through the cameras I rigged up around the place. I didn't see it in time to warn Dad."

"Why didn't they take you?"

"I don't go outside much, and they must not know about our underground hideout. I'm hoping to get out after dark. I'm packing right now."

"Okay," Vicki said, "we won't bother you."

"Hey, good job on that satellite deal. I heard about how you guys stirred things up with the GC."

"Hopefully we'll do more in the future."

"I'll be praying for you," Zeke said.

Judd nearly passed out as he got into the hotel elevator. He had walked what felt like miles and didn't think he could go another step. Lionel helped him to the room, propped him against the wall, and lightly knocked on the door. Westin opened it and helped Judd inside.

With part emotion and part exhaustion, Judd hugged Westin. "Welcome to the family."

Westin carried Judd to the couch and found him a pillow. "I think Z-Van just went to sleep. He's been banging away at his new songs all night."

"We have to get out of here," Judd said when he caught his breath.

"I know that," Westin said, "and I plan on helping you. But I'd love it if you'd stick with me for a week or two and teach me everything you know."

Judd glanced at Lionel. Since Carpathia's rising he could think of nothing but getting out of New Babylon and away from all the trouble. He knew, of course, that there would soon be trouble everywhere and finding a hiding place would be nearly impossible. Still, his heart ached to see the others, especially Vicki.

"Let's talk about it after we get some rest."

Mark and the others at the abandoned bookstore rested throughout the day and waited for nightfall. Several GC cars passed, but the kids stayed hidden. When evening came and the sun began its slow descent over the hillside, Mark smelled smoke and wondered how close the fire would come to the lake.

As soon as it was dark, Mark pulled Conrad aside and asked him to come with him. He told the others they would be back soon and to be ready.

Mark and Conrad slipped through the quiet streets until they came to the old library. A tow truck was parked along the bank, a few yards from where the car had plunged into the water.

"Doesn't look like they've pulled the Suburban out yet," Conrad said.

"That's what I was hoping," Mark said as he took off his shirt and shoes.

"What are you doing?"

"We need cash. We don't have much of a chance without it."

"You heard Vicki's last count," Conrad said. "There's maybe a hundred Nicks left down there in the cash box."

"That's a hundred more than we have right now, and I'm going to get it."

"What about the tow-truck operator?"

"Distract him," Mark said. "I'll swing around and get in the water up the beach. You keep him busy."

Conrad shook his head. "I'm not very good at that stuff. Let me do the dive. I'm a stronger swimmer."

Mark agreed and put his clothes back on. Conrad ran up the beach a few hundred yards, and Mark walked toward the tow truck. A man sat inside smoking a cigarette. Yellow tape wound around the site where the Suburban had gone into the water.

"How's it goin'?" Mark said as he stepped up to the truck.

"It'll go a lot better for you if you get out of here. GC doesn't want anybody bothering this place until they can get a bigger rig to pull that car out."

"So one really did go in, huh? I didn't know whether to believe it or not."

"Believe it and get out of here. Besides, I just heard on the radio that the fire's only about three miles away. You should have been evacuated a long time ago."

Mark noticed Conrad slipping up to the pier and

heading out in the water. "I didn't know it was that close. Why are they making you stay?"

"I told you, to keep everybody away from this site."

"Who was in the car?"

"A bunch of kids. Now leave me alone before I call the GC."

Mark held up his hands. "Just curious. Didn't mean to bother you."

Mark stepped away and looked at the water. Conrad surfaced and Mark coughed to cover the noise. "Smoke's getting close. I'll be seeing you."

"Yeah," the man said.

A few minutes later Conrad returned to the library holding a box and the shoe he had wedged onto the accelerator. "Couldn't see a thing down there. It took me a couple of dives to find the car, but once I got inside, it was easy." He opened the box and picked up the soaked cash.

"We'll count it back at the bookstore," Mark said. "Come on."

———————————

Vicki and Darrion explained what they had been through since the disappearances. Maggie listened with interest, covering her mouth when Darrion told of the deaths of her father and mother.

Vicki described Charlie and the couple he had stayed with. "They're in GC custody now, but we have someone on the inside who said she'd help get them out."

Maggie bit her lip. "First thing you need is a good night's rest."

"What about your story?" Darrion said.

The woman smiled. "In the morning. Let me get you some nightclothes."

Vicki awoke from a dead sleep a few hours later. A thunderous explosion rocked the neighborhood and a plume of fire and smoke shot hundreds of feet into the air. Vicki and Darrion changed into their clothes and ran outside. They wound their way through the neighborhood until they reached the fire. Vicki's heart sank. Zeke's gas station was completely engulfed in flames.

19

MARK led the way back to the bookstore in the soft glow of the moon. The smoke was getting thicker and his eyes stung. They were only a block away from the hideout when a GC vehicle passed slowly, its lights flashing. Mark and Conrad ducked out of sight.

"Attention: all residents are to leave immediately. This is a forced evacuation. For your own safety, exit the city and go east. The wildfire has jumped the fire line over the main road. Again, exit quickly and orderly."

When the car passed, Mark and Conrad raced to the bookstore and found the others. Shelly was angry that they took the risk but grateful they had money.

Conrad pulled a wad of cash from his pocket and counted the Nicks. They had more than two hundred, which wouldn't buy them a car, but it would be enough for food.

"You don't think this is a trick to lure us out?" Melinda said.

"The smoke's enough to convince me," Mark said.

Cars jammed the main road out of town. The five stayed out of sight as much as possible, slowly finding their way through woods and farmland that ran parallel to the road. Shelly suggested they follow the lake and look for a campsite.

"This whole place is going up," Conrad said, pointing behind them. In the distance flames licked at the tops of trees and moved toward the town.

Janie shook her head as they walked through a field of tall grass. "I don't understand any of this."

"What do you mean?" Shelly said.

"Vicki and Darrion are lost or were taken by the GC, and we're running from a wildfire with no place to stay and not much money. Charlie and the Shairtons are locked up in some holding tank in Des Plaines. Why would God let us go through all this if we believe in him?"

"Just because you believe in God and accept his forgiveness doesn't mean you don't have trouble," Shelly said.

"Yeah, think about Jesus' friends," Conrad said. "They just wanted to follow God and tell people the Good News. Most of them were killed because of what they believed."

Janie rolled her eyes. "That's comforting."

"Believers have gone through tough things all along," Shelly said. "Sometimes becoming a Christian gets them in trouble with their family. Friends turn their backs. The government cracks down on them or they have a hard time at their jobs. Trouble doesn't mean God's abandoned you or that he isn't in control. He promises to go through the hard times with you."

"But what's the point?" Janie said. "Wouldn't it be a lot easier if we just went along with the GC until Jesus comes back?"

"God never promised easy," Conrad said. "From the time I first believed until now, it's been a struggle. My brother's dead, all the family and friends I've known are gone, but it's still worth it."

"Why?"

"Because the Bible is coming true every day. God is real. He keeps his promises. We could hide in some cave, but I don't think that's what God wants us to do."

Janie stopped and turned away from the others. "Even though I can see things coming true, like Carpathia rising from the dead, I still don't understand."

Shelly put an arm around Janie. "I learned from Vicki a long time ago that we'll always have questions and doubts. That you struggle with them is proof that your faith is working on you. God is making your faith more real every day. He's preparing you for something."

Janie looked up with tears in her eyes. "You really think so?"

Shelly nodded. "There's a verse in Jeremiah that says God knows the plans he has for you. 'They are plans for good and not for disaster, to give you a future and a hope.' "

Janie smiled and the two walked together. Mark led the kids into the night. They all prayed for Vicki and Darrion as they went.

———————————

Vicki awoke the next morning to the smell of a home-cooked breakfast. She let Darrion sleep and stumbled to the kitchen table. Eggs and bacon sizzled in a skillet.

"I took a walk this morning and looked at that gas station," Maggie said. "There's nothing left but a big hole in the ground."

Vicki noticed an old computer in the corner of the room and asked if it still worked.

Maggie nodded. "I mostly used it to write my grandkids before the disappearances. Now I read what Tsion Ben-Judah says and keep up with the news. You can use it if you'd like."

Vicki logged on to the kids' Web site and gasped at the hundreds of e-mails that had piled up without being answered. She quickly typed a message to Mark and the others saying she and Darrion were okay. She gave them the bad news about Zeke's father and the gas station. *I don't know about Zeke, but it doesn't look good,* she wrote. *I hope you get this and that you're all right.*

She sent the e-mail and scanned the incoming messages. She recognized Natalie's address and quickly pulled up her e-mail.

> *Vicki, where are you? There was a big commotion last night about someone breaking into a GC car that had been up to Wisconsin. Do you know anything about it?*
>
> *I found out more about Charlie and the Shairtons. They're still here being questioned. The GC had watched the farmhouse after they found the satellite truck a few*

*miles away. When you didn't show up, they moved in
and arrested Charlie and the Shairtons.*

*They've brought in another man on charges of subver-
sion, and I think that's what they'll charge the Shairtons
with. They've moved Charlie to a separate holding area, so I
think if we're going to get him out, we'd better do it soon.*

*I hope you get this message and that you're okay.
If I don't hear from you soon, I'll try something myself.*

*Love,
Natalie*

Vicki quickly typed back: *Darrion and I are in Des
Plaines. We hitched a ride in the GC's trunk without them
knowing it. We're ready to help. Have you heard anything
about Mark and the others? Give a safe phone number where I
can call you. And be careful, Natalie. These guys mean business. Love, Vicki.*

"Your breakfast is ready anytime," Maggie said.

Darrion walked in rubbing her eyes, and the three sat
at the table. Maggie offered to pray. "Lord, you know our
needs better than we do, and we thank you for giving us
this food. We're going to enjoy it and the days we have left
before your return. Protect Vicki, Darrion, and their friends
and give them what they need. In Jesus' name, amen."

Vicki and Darrion ate hungrily. Vicki could tell from
the meal the night before that Maggie was a good cook,
but breakfast was even better.

"What's your story?" Darrion said.

Maggie spread jam on a piece of toast and sat back.
"I've been a widow for almost ten years. Before that, my

187

husband and I were agnostics. You know what that means?"

"That you don't know whether God exists or not," Vicki said.

"Right. We didn't think there was really enough evidence. My husband taught science at a community college so we were big on proving things. We didn't vote for anyone who couldn't prove they'd do a good job. We didn't buy products that didn't live up to their promises, that kind of thing.

"Our children were raised that way too. Twins—a boy and a girl. But something went wrong when they got to college. They got mixed up with this campus group of Christians, and the next thing you know, the kids are home trying to convert us."

"What did you and your husband do?" Darrion said.

"We listened, of course, but we believed they'd been brainwashed. Finally, we told them it was all right with us if they wanted to throw away their minds, but they should stop trying to change ours."

"What did they do?"

"They stopped. They didn't mention God or Jesus or the Bible one more time, so I thought it was something they'd snap out of. But when they both got married to Christians, I realized they were committed."

"They never talked about it again?" Vicki said.

"They didn't have to," Maggie said. "They lived it. They showed a love to their kids I'd never seen. They were there for me when Don died—that's my husband. Sometimes I'd wonder if I could have what they had, but I'd push the thought away. It was too painful to think that Don and I had missed out on the greatest truth of the universe."

"What happened?" Darrion said.

"The Rapture. I had e-mailed my granddaughter something the night before. She always got up early and wrote back. It was exciting to read her notes every morning.

"Well, there was no message that day. I didn't think much about it until I turned on the news and saw what was going on. I was devastated to learn that my whole family was gone. My kids had never talked about the Rapture, but I knew this had something to do with God."

"That's when you saw Tsion Ben-Judah?" Vicki said.

"No, that's when I picked up a Bible off the shelf and started reading." Maggie closed her eyes. "I read the New Testament straight through in a couple of days. When I got to Romans, I finally understood that the proof I had been looking for was right under my nose. Jesus had made such a difference in the lives of my kids. If he did rise from the dead and do all those miracles, what more did I need?

"I asked God to forgive my hard heart and change me. And he did. It was sometime later that I came across Tsion Ben-Judah and his writings."

Maggie asked what Vicki had found on the computer, and Vicki told her everything about the Young Tribulation Force. Vicki logged on again and found a message from Natalie that included a phone number.

Hurry, Natalie wrote.

Lionel let Judd sleep most of the next day. He called a few airlines about commercial flights to the States. Several companies reported that flights into New Babylon had been full before the funeral, but flights out had been nearly empty.

"Everybody wanted to get here for the memorial service," one attendant said, "and now nobody wants to leave."

Lionel found a flight that would get them close to Chicago. It was more money than he and Judd had, but a good option, especially considering Z-Van's deepening loyalty to Carpathia.

Lionel decided to wait and talk with Judd before going ahead with the plan.

Mark awoke in a school that had been converted into an emergency shelter. Earlier that morning he and the others had split up before going inside, not wanting to attract attention. He had been given some bedding, a number, and was pointed down a long hallway to the gymnasium. The gym floor was littered with sleeping bags, mattresses, and old cots. Those who couldn't afford hotel rooms farther away had moved frantically east to this spot.

Mark noticed Conrad on the other side of the gym and gave him a nod. Conrad returned the greeting and lay down on his cot.

Women slept in classrooms while men stayed in the gym. There were a few teenage boys present, but most were married men whose families were sleeping in a classroom.

Mark looked for any other believers as he walked to the bathroom. He overheard two men talking about the fire. The GC had reported that the wind had switched directions just before it reached Lake Geneva and that the town might be saved.

"I'll bet if Carpathia were here, he'd be able to stop the fire in no time," one man said. "You saw what happened. This man is god!"

When he returned to his cot, Mark took the laptop from under his covers and looked for a power outlet. He found one near Conrad's cot.

Mark made small talk with Conrad, as if they had just met, and pulled up the kids' Web site. He let Conrad read Vicki's message, and they were both relieved to know the girls were safe.

"That makes our job easier," Conrad whispered.

"How's that?"

"We don't have to look for Charlie and the Shairtons. We simply find a place they can bring them."

Mark agreed and wrote Vicki about it. He also sent a quick message to Judd and Lionel in case they returned to the country and didn't know where to find the Young Trib Force.

"I'll go tell the others the good news," Conrad said.

"Get ready to leave," Mark said. "The GC could inspect this place anytime."

Mark looked at the hundreds of e-mails that had come in during the last two days. So many kids had questions. The unbelievers were mostly anxious and afraid. A few scolded the kids and praised Nicolae Carpathia as god. But the believers simply wanted to know Carpathia's next move and how they should prepare.

As Mark thought about what he could say, he noticed an e-mail from Tsion Ben-Judah. He opened it quickly and read:

> Dear Mark,
> I am sending the following letter so you can relay it to kids around the world. I trust you to make my words easy to understand for your readers. There is no longer any question about Nicolae Carpathia. I am persuaded that Leon is his false prophet. Those who have ears will not be deceived, but they must hear this message.
>
> I pray for you and the rest of the Young Tribulation Force every day. You do not know what an incredible impact you are having. Keep up the good work, and may God give you the courage you need to stand for him in this difficult time. Remember, even though Satan now indwells Carpathia, greater is he who is in you, than he who is in the world!
>
> Your friend,
> Tsion Ben-Judah

Mark smiled. Tsion didn't know it, but he had just given Mark the very thing he needed to answer the hundreds of e-mails in front of him.

20

JUDD awoke with a pounding headache. Lionel stood over him and placed a few sheets of paper on his bed. "Feeling well enough for some good news?"

Judd sat up and winced. "Tell me."

Lionel explained what Mark had written about Vicki and the others. Though the kids were separated, they were all accounted for. The only ones in immediate danger, it seemed, were Charlie and the farm couple who had befriended the kids in Illinois, the Shairtons. "Oh, Zeke's dad was arrested too."

"What's this?" Judd said, picking up the papers.

"Mark's translation of Tsion Ben-Judah's latest letter. It's long, but he answers a lot in here."

Lionel brought some food and water, and Judd propped himself up with a few pillows. He drank in every word from Dr. Ben-Judah.

To: The beloved tribulation saints scattered throughout the earth, believers in the one true Jehovah God and his matchless Son, Jesus the Christ, our Savior and Lord

From: Your servant, Tsion Ben-Judah, blessed by the Lord with the privilege of teaching you, under the authority of his Holy Spirit, from the Bible, the very Word of God

Re: The dawn of the Great Tribulation

My dear brothers and sisters in Christ,
As is so often true when I write you, I come in both joy and sorrow, delighted yet sober in spirit. Forgive the delay since I last wrote, and thank you all for your concern for me. My comrades and I are safe and praising the Lord for a new base of operations. And I always want to thank God for the miracle of technology that allows me to write to you all over the world.

Though I have met few of you personally and look forward to that one day, either in the kingdom Christ sets up after his return or in heaven, I feel we are drawn together like a family as we share the riches of Scripture in these letters. Thank you for your prayers that I will remain faithful to my calling and healthy enough to continue for as long as the Father himself gives me breath.

Tsion wrote that readership of his Web site had passed the one-billion mark. Though the Global Community denied the figures, Judd knew it was true. Dr. Ben-

Judah revealed the process he went through for interpreting prophecy. Judd knew if this letter reached those who were undecided about God, many could be persuaded about the truth.

> *While the prophecies that foretold Messiah were fairly straightforward and led me to believe in Jesus as their unique fulfillment, I prayed that God would reveal the key to the rest of the prophecies. He did this by impressing upon me to take the words as literally as I took any others from the Bible, unless the context and the wording itself indicated otherwise.*
>
> *In other words, I had always taken at its word a passage such as "Love your neighbor as yourself," or "Do for others what you would like them to do for you." Why then, could I not take literally a verse which said that John, the writer of Revelation, saw a pale horse? Yes, I understood that the horse stood for something. And yet the Bible said that John saw it. I took that literally, along with all the other prophetic statements (unless they used phrases such as "like unto" or others that made it clear they were symbolic).*

Judd had to go back over Tsion's words a second time, but he finally understood. Tsion's straightforward reading of the Bible helped the teacher discover the order of the Seal and Trumpet Judgments and that the Bowl Judgments yet to come would be even worse than those they had witnessed.

> *Believers, we have turned a corner. Skeptics—and I know many of you drop in to see what we are up to—we have*

*passed the point of politeness. Until now, I have been
direct about the Bible but somewhat cautious about the
current rulers of this world.*

*No more. As every prophecy in the Bible has so far
come true, as the leader of this world has preached peace
while swinging a sword, as he died by the sword and was
resurrected as the Scriptures foretold, and as his right-
hand man has been given similar evil power, there can be
no more doubt:*

*Nicolae Carpathia, the so-called Excellency and
Supreme Potentate of the Global Community, is both
anti-Christian and Antichrist himself. And the Bible says
the resurrected Antichrist is literally indwelt by Satan
himself. Leon Fortunato, who had an image of Antichrist
erected and now forces all to worship it or face death, is
Antichrist's false prophet. As the Bible predicted, he has
power to make the statue speak and to call down fire
from heaven to destroy those who refuse to worship it.*

*What's next? Consider this clear prophetic passage in
Revelation 13:11-18: "Then I saw another beast come up
out of the earth. He had two horns like those of a lamb,
and he spoke with the voice of a dragon. He exercised all
the authority of the first beast. And he required all the
earth and those who belong to this world to worship the
first beast, whose death-wound had been healed.*

*"He did astounding miracles, such as making fire
flash down to earth from heaven while everyone was
watching. And with all the miracles he was allowed to
perform on behalf of the first beast, he deceived all the
people who belong to this world. He ordered the people of*

the world to make a great statue of the first beast, who was fatally wounded and then came back to life.

"He was permitted to give life to this statue so that it could speak. Then the statue commanded that anyone refusing to worship it must die. He required everyone— great and small, rich and poor, slave and free—to be given a mark on the right hand or on the forehead. And no one could buy or sell anything without that mark, which was either the name of the beast or the number representing his name.

"Wisdom is needed to understand this. Let the one who has understanding solve the number of the beast, for it is the number of a man. His number is 666."

It won't be long before everyone will be forced to bow the knee to Carpathia or his image, to bear his name or number on their forehead or right hand, or face the consequences.

Those consequences? The Bible calls this the mark of the beast. Those without it will not be allowed to legally buy or sell. If we publicly refuse to accept the mark of the beast, we will be beheaded. While it is the greatest desire of my life to live to see the Glorious Appearing of Jesus Christ at the end of the Great Tribulation (a few days short of three and a half years from now), what greater cause could there ever be for which to give one's life?

Many, millions of us, will be required to do just that.

Judd put the page down and closed his eyes. To think of millions of believers losing their lives because they wouldn't obey Carpathia was almost unbelievable. How would the Global Community carry out so many executions? Would Judd be asked to give his life?

Judd read the next few sentences, which included Tsion's belief that every believer called on to give his or her life would be given strength by God to endure the beheading. Tsion also wrote that taking the mark would forever condemn a person to eternity without God.

> While many will live in secret, supporting one another through private markets, some will find themselves caught and dragged into a public beheading. To live, the only alternative is to reject Christ and take the mark of the beast.
>
> If you are already a believer, you will not be able to turn your back on Christ, praise God. If you are undecided and don't want to follow the crowd, what will you do when faced with the mark or the loss of your head? I plead with you today to believe, to receive Christ, and cover yourself with protection from God.
>
> We are entering the bloodiest season in the history of the world. Those who take the mark of the beast will suffer at the hand of God. Those who refuse it will be killed for his blessed cause. Never has the choice been so stark, so clear.
>
> God himself named this three-and-a-half-year period. Matthew 24:21-22 records Jesus saying, "For that will be a time of greater horror than anything the world has ever seen or will ever see again. In fact, unless that time of calamity is shortened, the entire human race will be

destroyed. But it will be shortened for the sake of God's chosen ones."

In all God's dealings with humans, this is the shortest period on record, and yet more Scripture is devoted to it than any other period except the life of Christ. The Hebrew prophets spoke of this as a time of God's revenge for the slaughter of the prophets and saints over the centuries. But it is also a time of mercy. God compresses the decision-making time for men and women before the coming of Christ to set up his earthly kingdom.

This is clearly the most awful time in history, but I still say it is also a merciful act of God to give as many as possible an opportunity to put their faith in Christ. Oh, people, we are the army of God with a massive job to do in a short time. May we be willing and eager to show the courage that comes only from him. There are countless lost souls in need of saving, and we have the truth.

It may be hard to recognize God's mercy when his wrath is also increasing. Woe to those who believe the lie that God is only "love." Yes, he is love. And his gift of Jesus as the sacrifice for our sin is the greatest evidence of this. But the Bible also says God is "holy, holy, holy." He is righteous and a God of justice, and it is not in his nature to allow sin to go unpunished or unpaid for.

We are engaged in a great worldwide battle with Satan himself for the souls of men and women. I do not say this lightly, for I do understand the power of the evil one. But I have placed my faith and trust in the God who sits high above the heavens, in the God who is above all other gods, and among whom there is none like him.

Scripture is clear that you can test both prophet and prophecy. I make no claim of being a prophet, but I believe the prophecies. If they are not true and don't come to pass, then I am a liar and the Bible is bogus, and we are all utterly without hope. But if the Bible is true, next on the agenda is the ceremonial desecration (or defiling) of the temple in Jerusalem by Antichrist himself. This is a prediction made by Daniel, Jesus, Paul, and John.

Tsion wrote specifically to Jewish readers and prepared them for what was to come in Jerusalem. Nicolae would go into the holy temple and sacrifice a pig on the sacred altar.

If you are Jewish and have not yet been persuaded that Jesus the Christ of Nazareth is Messiah and you have been deceived by the lies of Nicolae Carpathia, perhaps your mind will be changed when he breaks his covenant with Israel and withdraws his guarantee of her safety.

But he shows no favoritism. Besides reviling the Jews, he will slaughter believers in Jesus.

If this does not happen, label me a heretic or mad and look elsewhere than the Holy Scriptures for hope.

Thank you for your patience and for the blessed privilege of communicating with you again. Let me leave you on a note of hope. My next message will concern the difference between the Book of Life and the Lamb's Book of Life, and what those mean to you and me. Until then, you may rest assured that if you are a believer and have

*placed your hope and trust in the work of Jesus Christ
alone for the forgiveness of sins and for life everlasting,
your name is in the Lamb's Book of Life.*

And it can never be erased.

*Until we meet again, I bless you in the name of Jesus.
May he bless you and keep you and make his face to
shine upon you, and give you peace.*

Judd stared at the wall. So this was it. Everything was
out in the open. Tsion Ben-Judah hadn't held back
anything about Carpathia.

"What do you think?" Lionel said.

Judd sighed. "I think what we've already been through
will seem easy compared—"

The door opened and Westin walked in. "Z-Van just
got off the phone with someone from Carpathia's office.
They've asked him to go to Jerusalem for another celebration."

Judd gripped the pages. "What's the celebration for?"

"They told Z-Van they were going to give true worship
to Carpathia and deal with his enemies."

Judd nodded and looked at Lionel. Tsion's words
were already coming true.

21

VICKI dialed Natalie's number but got a GC answering machine. She hung up and tried a few minutes later, again getting the machine. More than an hour later, a man answered.

"I'm looking for Natalie Bishop," Vicki said.

"Sorry, not in this department."

"She gave me this number."

The man sighed and clicked a few keys on a computer. "She's been reassigned. What do you want with her?"

"She's a friend of mine and—"

"She's not here. If you want to leave a message—"

"What's her new assignment?"

"Corrections. I know there's been a lot of activity down there. Now, if you don't mind—"

"Can you transfer me?"

"Miss, this is not a chat room. If it's not official GC business, I suggest you contact her on her personal time."

"Okay, can you tell me when—"

THE YOUNG TRIB FORCE

Click.

Vicki told Darrion what she had learned, and the two agreed to wait for Natalie to get in touch. Darrion handed Vicki a sheet of paper she had printed from the kids' Web site. It was a new message from Tsion Ben-Judah.

Mark wanted to show the others Tsion's letter, but they didn't dare stay at the school with the GC so close. Mark kicked himself for not getting out earlier and asked Conrad to round up the rest of the group and meet behind the school near a tree. He walked past new arrivals in the gymnasium, trying to find anyone with the mark of loyalty to Christ. There was no one.

The others emerged from the school one at a time, just as Mark had suggested. Shelly and the others said they hadn't noticed any believers in the women's area.

"Before we leave, I think you ought to know what we're up against," Mark said. He opened the computer and read every word Tsion Ben-Judah had written. The kids were quiet as Mark read, and the further he went, the more concerned they looked.

"Well, if Tsion wasn't on Carpathia's most-wanted list before, he's there now," Conrad said.

"Can you believe Fortunato is the false prophet?" Shelly said.

"What's that mean?" Janie said.

"Basically the Antichrist's vice president," Conrad said.

Melinda scratched her head. "What's the thing about the image?"

"You know, the statue at the funeral," Mark said. "My guess is they're going to cart it around and make people worship it."

Conrad shook his head. "They'll probably mass produce them and have one in every town."

"What's that stuff about the right hand and 666?" Janie said.

"Remember how we talked about Satan counterfeiting everything God does? Well, he's doing it again. Satan's plan is to destroy as many people as he can, so he's making everyone take his mark on the hand or forehead. If you want to buy or sell something, you have to have the mark."

"Then believers are going to starve to death!" Janie said.

"That's why Chloe Williams and the others put together the commodity co-op. They've been storing food and supplies so believers won't starve. People like Zeke and Pete have helped get it where it's needed most. Hopefully, it will be enough to last."

"I used to know a guy who thought his social security number was the mark of the beast," Conrad said. "Guess he was wrong."

"So if we don't take the mark, they cut off our heads?" Janie said.

Shelly shuddered. "What an awful way to die. And there will be millions."

"I don't know if I could do it," Melinda said. "I mean, I know Dr. Ben-Judah says God will help us, but what if we crack?"

"They'll give you a choice between worshiping Carpathia or worshiping God," Conrad said. "Unless that seal on your forehead is fake, God won't let you make the wrong choice."

"Plus, they have to catch us," Mark said.

"I guess there's good news in all of this," Shelly said. "People still have time to choose God. After they take the mark, they won't have a choice."

"Which means we have to tell readers on the Web site to be bold," Mark said.

Janie stood and turned her back on the group. She walked a few steps toward the school.

"What's wrong?" Shelly said.

Janie put a hand to her face and shook her head. "If Dr. Ben-Judah is right, and I believe he is, the people in that school are going to take Carpathia's mark and they'll suffer." Janie turned and wiped away a tear. "I don't want to be caught by the GC, and I sure don't want them to chop my head off. But we ought to tell these people the truth rather than run away from them."

"Let's take a vote," Mark said. "Who wants to get out of here right now and find a place to hide?"

No one moved.

"Who wants to tell these people the truth about God?"

Everyone raised a hand and Mark smiled. "Then we'd better pray and get to it."

In the afternoon, Vicki and Darrion watched news of people's reaction to Nicolae Carpathia's resurrection. Thousands still waited in line in New Babylon for their

chance to worship the statue. There was talk of construct-
ing other statues in different parts of the world.

Religious experts said the world had never seen such a
widely exposed miracle. "This godlike display of power
can only be compared to the mythical accounts of the
Bible," one expert said. "In those stories, the miracles
were only viewed by a few people. This one was seen all
over the world at the same time."

"That's not true," Darrion said. "Lots of people saw
the miracles in the Bible, didn't they?"

Vicki nodded.

Maggie yelled when an e-mail came in from Natalie
that included a new phone number.

Natalie answered on the first ring and took the phone
into another room. "I have a roommate who's true-blue
Carpathia."

"What happened?"

"My transfer to corrections came through after I sent
the first message."

"Have you seen Charlie and the Shairtons?"

"I saw Charlie today but didn't talk with him. I don't
want him to know about any of this until it's time. The
Shairtons are in the adult groups, but they're okay."

"Have they brought in more people?"

"An older guy yesterday who ran a rebel gas station."

"That's Zeke!" Vicki said.

"How did you know he was named Zeke?"

Vicki told Natalie the story of the gas station and how
Zeke and his father had helped them.

"They think the guy is part of a conspiracy against the

GC. They arrested anybody who stopped at his station to buy gas."

"How many?" Vicki said.

"About ten are still in custody. But most of them just saw that his station was open and stopped for gas."

"What's the plan?" Vicki said.

Natalie had several ideas and told Vicki all of them. Vicki thought they were all too dangerous.

After a few minutes, Natalie said she needed to go because her roommate wanted to use the phone. "One more thing. Our division received a message from GC headquarters in New Babylon. They said they're producing loyalty enforcement facilitators."

"What's that?" Vicki said.

"Guillotines, as in chop your head off."

"That's awful."

"The message said each sector of the United Carpathian States should have them up and cutting within thirty days."

"Hopefully we won't be anywhere near when that happens."

"I'll call or e-mail you from work tomorrow."

Vicki hung up and told Darrion the ideas. When Vicki finished, Maggie scooted her chair closer. "If you get those people out of jail, they'll be in more trouble than they're in now. If they don't charge them, the GC might let them go."

"With those guillotines on their way, we can't take that chance," Darrion said.

"You need to be willing to get thrown in jail yourself before you do this."

"We are," Vicki said.

Maggie smiled, a twinkle in her eyes. "So am I. Let me help."

Mark and the others went back inside the school. A GC sponsored relief organization provided sandwiches and drinks for lunch. The kids decided to split up and talk with people individually. Mark sat by a man and his teen-age son and asked where they lived.

"A couple of miles on the other side of the lake," the man said. "I thought we'd be okay once the fiery hail burned a bunch of trees a while back. Now this."

"I'd like to get my hands on the people who started the fire," the boy said.

The man said he had lost everything he had in life, except the clothes on his back, the truck parked outside, and his son.

"Were you married?" Mark said.

"Divorced," the man said. "My ex fought it the whole way, but I had to be free. She got custody of the kids. Then all of them disappeared, except for Quin here."

The boy looked at his father. "I like living with my dad. Don't have to go to church every week and do all that stupid religious stuff."

Mark nodded, frustrated that the conversation wasn't going better. He wanted to show them Tsion's letter or stand on tables and shout the truth to everyone. These two needed God, but Mark couldn't force them to believe. "You ever think about all the stuff that's happened and wonder why?"

"All the time," the father said. "And I think we got our answer."

"Really?"

"Yeah, all of this has been for a purpose, to show that Nicolae Carpathia really is a god."

"If we ever get enough money," Quin said, "I want to go to New Babylon and see where he came back to life."

Mark excused himself and threw away his trash. Conrad joined him, also discouraged with the people he had talked with.

Janie ran to them with a thin young woman holding a baby. "Terry, these are the guys I was telling you about. They helped me understand."

Mark and Conrad shook hands with the woman and sat at a table in the back of the room. "How can we help you?" Mark said.

"I'm scared for my child. I used to think there was a God, but now I'm not sure."

Mark leaned over the table. "There is a God and even in the middle of all this ugliness, he loves you."

"Really?"

Janie moved across the room and talked with an older man. Mark turned back to Terry and asked if he could tell her some things about the Bible.

"The Bible talks about this? I thought it just listed the things you shouldn't do."

Mark opened his computer and showed Terry verses that predicted what they had experienced the past three years. Terry read each word and seemed eager to hear more.

"Jesus said that he came so that people could have life, and have it to the full. Most people are either living just to stay alive or they're following Nicolae Carpathia."

"I just want a safe place for me and my baby."

"I understand," Mark said, "but what if I told you that you can know real safety and have a lasting peace in your heart?"

"What do you mean?"

Mark explained sin and that a holy God can't accept anything that's not perfect. "That's why Jesus was born. He was God in the flesh. He lived a perfect life and was sacrificed so that you and I could be forgiven and live forever with God."

The baby cried and Terry held it close. "I know I've done bad things, but I want to be forgiven. I want peace."

Mark thought of Tsion Ben-Judah's words. "You need to know that if you choose God, those who hate God are going to be against you."

"What does that mean? I thought you said I would be safe."

"You'll be safe from the judgments God is pouring out, but God's enemies might try to hurt you."

The baby screamed and Terry stood. "Let me think about it."

22

MARK talked with people until a GC official arrived and called everyone together in the gymnasium. A janitor plugged a microphone into a wall jack, and the man's voice was amplified through small speakers.

"There's good news for a lot of you," the official said. "It looks like the fire missed Lake Geneva."

People whooped and yelled, giving each other high fives. Quin and his father didn't celebrate.

"The wind changed direction and it's blowing the opposite way. We've counted about two dozen homes in the forest that didn't make it. Those people will be eligible for assistance through the Global Community."

The officer said those who lived near town might be able to return home in the morning. "But we'd like your help locating those we think started the fire." The man held up a picture of Vicki. "We think this girl and some others were involved. They are religious zealots and if you

213

have any information, please see me. People rushed up to the man when he was finished, asking questions about their homes and the GC assistance.

Mark and everyone but Shelly slipped away together. Each of the kids reported they had talked with a few people but that no one had prayed.

Shelly rushed up to the group. "A couple just drove up in a big van. They have the mark of the believer and said we could stay with them."

"Where do they live?" Conrad said.

"On a farm east of here. They heard about the emergency shelter and brought some food."

Mark quickly met the man and his wife and explained what they were doing. "We'll wait here until you're ready to go," the man said.

"Are there any more GC people around?" Mark said to the others.

"They just left," Shelly said.

"Then everybody get your stuff together. Conrad, grab the laptop."

"But what about these people?" Janie said. "We haven't talked to all of them."

Mark put a hand on Janie's shoulder. "We'll take care of that right now."

Mark approached the janitor, who was unplugging the microphone. "I want to say something. Could you wait?"

The janitor nodded and stood to the side, his arms folded.

"If I could have your attention," Mark said into the

microphone. The room hushed and Mark began to sweat. He cleared his throat as people looked at him. "My friends and I have been talking with some of you about what's happened the past three years. We've found something that's made sense, and we'd like to share it with any of you who want to listen."

"What are you talking about?" a woman in the back yelled.

"By listening to people who know the Bible, we believe that what happened in New Babylon was predicted a long time ago. And things are going to get worse."

"Hey, pal," Quin's father said, "Carpathia just rose from the dead. I'd say that's a good thing."

"That depends on what you believe about Carpathia. If we're right, he'll make everybody worship him and take some kind of identifier on their forehead or their right hand."

"Why shouldn't we worship him?" Quin's father said. "If he can come back from the dead he has to be god."

"Let the kid talk," someone said.

"Fine, but I get my say too! For all we know, this guy set the fire."

Mark looked nervously around the room. He hadn't planned on starting a debate; he simply wanted to tell people the truth. Now all eyes were on him. "If you want to follow Carpathia, that's your decision. But if you feel like there's something wrong with the whole Global Community, please come up front."

Mark moved away from the microphone and thanked the janitor. The room buzzed with conversation, some asking who these kids were, others getting their cots ready for bed. A few came forward.

The first person who reached Mark was Terry, the woman with the baby. "I've thought a lot about what you said earlier," she said. "I don't care what the GC do to me. I need God to forgive me."

Mark smiled. Conrad, Shelly, and Janie came to the front. Quickly, Mark went through the information he had shared with Terry. "Anyone who wants to pray right now, come with me."

Terry and three others joined Mark in the corner. The janitor still stood with his arms crossed, one foot on the side of the wall.

"Pray with me. God, I'm sorry for my sin, and I want to turn from it right now and accept the gift you're offering me. I believe that Jesus died on the cross and paid the penalty for my sin. I accept your offer of mercy and grace, and I ask you to come into my heart and make me a new person. Change me from the inside out."

The people next to Mark prayed the prayer out loud with him. Mark concluded: "I thank you for saving me from my sin, and I ask you to be the Lord of my life from this day on until you come again. Give me the strength to live for you. In Jesus' name, amen."

Mark looked at Terry and smiled. On her forehead was the mark of the believer. The others around her had the mark as well and they asked what it was for. As Mark explained, he noticed the smiling janitor had a mark too.

Melinda rushed forward and grabbed Mark's arm.

"They're onto us. I just heard a man calling the GC on his cell phone."

Mark went to the group of new believers and held up a hand. "I'm sorry to cut this short, but we're in danger. We have to leave. If you prayed and you want to go with us, come now."

The kids gathered their things and headed outside.

A man in the back yelled, "Stop! I've got some questions!"

"That's the one," Shelly whispered.

"Sorry," Mark yelled at the man, "maybe another time."

Mark pushed the others out a side door. The janitor followed with a broom and stuck it through the handle. Someone on the inside pounded on the door and shouted.

"Go!" the janitor said. "I'll take care of the GC."

Mark shook hands with the man and ran to the waiting van. As it pulled away, Mark and the rest of the passengers saw flashing lights coming from town. The driver of the van turned off his headlights and drove the other way. A few miles later they crested a hill, and the man turned onto a dirt road that led into the countryside.

"Don't worry, kids," the driver said. "The GC won't find you now."

Vicki awoke early the next morning and helped Maggie make breakfast. She pulled up the kids' Web site, but there was no word from Natalie. She found a message from Mark sent late the night before. He explained about their time at the emergency shelter and talking with people about God.

Last night we met some believers who have an awesome hideout, Mark wrote. *We brought some people we had met at the shelter, and every one of them has decided to follow God!*

The people here are willing to help us in any way. They said they'd even come to Des Plaines and help spring Charlie and the Shairtons. I'll tell you more about them later.

Stay safe and let us know how we can help.

Darrion and Maggie read the e-mail, and the three thanked God for keeping their friends safe.

"I'll bet the GC up there are really ticked about them getting away," Darrion said.

The phone rang. "Bad news," Natalie said to Vicki. "They lifted your fingerprint from the radio in the car and matched it to the ones they found at the schoolhouse."

"So? They know I had their radio, but they don't know where we are."

"They're going door to door with a picture they got from the satellite broadcast. Lay low."

"What about Charlie and Bo and Ginny?"

"There's not much I can do for the Shairtons. I haven't had any contact and I'm not sure they'll let me into the adult area."

"And Charlie?"

"I'm going to pitch an idea to a deputy commander today. Tell me about the woman you're staying with."

Vicki told her about Maggie, and Natalie gave Vicki a phone number. "This is Deputy Commander Henderson's cell number. Keep it. We might need it if my plan works. My meeting is at ten. Pray for me."

Vicki hung up and told Maggie and Darrion what she knew. Someone knocked at the door, and Maggie shooed the girls downstairs. The basement was dark except for a little light coming from the front. Vicki and Darrion quietly crept to a small window and listened as Maggie opened the door.

"May I help you?"

"Ma'am, we're looking for this girl and another one she might be traveling with," a man said.

Paper rattled and Maggie said, "Is she in some kind of trouble?"

"Just tell us if you've seen her, ma'am."

"She's awfully pretty. Kind of looks like my grand-daughter in a way, but I can't help you."

"Ma'am, the gentleman down the street said two girls came to his house a couple of days ago, saying they were with some youth project and looking for people who were skeptical of the potentate's resurrection. He said he sent them over here."

"Why would he do that?" Maggie said. "You've seen the replay. There's no denying Potenate Carpathia is really alive."

"Ma'am, he said they walked over here. Did you see them or not?"

"Let me look at the picture again." Maggie didn't speak for a few moments. "I've been having trouble remembering things lately."

"It's okay, ma'am. Take your time."

"You know, now that you mention it, this girl does look like someone who stopped by here. Her hair is different in the picture, but yes, I'm sure of it."

"Could you tell us where the two might have gone?"

"No, they didn't say anything about going anywhere. Wanted to talk to me about Carpathia and, well, that's not my favorite subject. You see, the Global Community denied my insurance claim back after the—"

"I'm sorry about that, but do you know which way they went?"

"N-no, I don't . . . ," Maggie stammered and began to cry. "I don't know what's wrong with me. One minute I can think straight and the next I'm all mixed up."

"All right. If anything comes to you, would you please call me? I'd be grateful for any information."

Maggie sobbed and closed the door. Vicki watched the two officers walk away, glancing back as they reached the next house.

23

JUDD and Lionel spent the next few days with Westin, talking about the prophecies of the Bible and what would happen before the return of Christ at the end of the Great Tribulation. Westin asked about the adult Tribulation Force and how they were operating inside the Global Community.

After resting a day, Judd started to regain his strength. Z-Van had Westin run errands, order room service, and keep the place quiet while he was working. Westin drove Z-Van to a meeting at the palace one afternoon.

When they returned, Z-Van lingered outside Judd and Lionel's room. "You guys still believe that Bible stuff?"

"Don't you?" Lionel said. "It's all coming true."

Z-Van smiled. "You're in good company. So does Leon Fortunato."

"What?" Judd said.

"The Most High Reverend says the potentate is going to use your holy book against you."

"The most high what?" Lionel said. "I thought he was supreme commander."

"He was until His Excellency gave him the responsibility to head the new religion that will replace all others. Leon Fortunato is now the Most High Reverend Father of Carpathianism."

Judd looked away.

"The world will now have a personal deity, someone people can look to for guidance, someone they can trust, someone they know has power since he raised himself from the dead."

Westin carried papers and drawings through the hallway. Z-Van pointed to his bed. "Put them there." He turned to Judd and Lionel. "The potentate has asked that I sing at the dedication of his image in Jerusalem."

"What are you talking about?" Judd said.

"You haven't heard? Statues of the potentate are being built in major cities throughout the world. The Most High Reverend Father gave me a copy of the plans for inspiration. Each city will construct a life-size image of the potentate and display it for worship."

Judd glanced at Westin. They had talked about that very prophecy only hours before.

"The potentate hopes his resurrection will help change the minds of those who are against him. The mark he's devised is pure genius. Each one has a set of numbers that identifies where you're from. A biochip is injected under the skin so they'll know every person on the planet."

"And if we don't take the mark?" Judd said.

Z-Van smiled. "Trust me, you'll take it. I'm hoping to get mine while we're here in New Babylon. I want to do it in the city of my god, Nicolae Carpathia."

Natalie Bishop waited in the office of Deputy Commander Darryl Henderson. When he finally returned, Natalie stood, shot out her hand, and shook firmly.

Henderson was a tall man with dark, bushy eyebrows and a weird smile. He took off his glasses and rubbed at the red marks on his nose. "I see you just moved to corrections. Something wrong?"

"Sir, I'd like to help catch these kids. They're a disease to the Global Community, and I can't stand the thought of them getting away with what they've done."

Henderson sat down and leaned back in his chair. "We could use more people like you . . ." He squinted, trying to read Natalie's badge.

"Bishop, sir."

"Right. What do you want to do?"

"I've read the statements this kid Charlie has made. I think he knows more than he's letting on."

"He's not the brightest bulb, if you know what I mean." Henderson scrolled through his computer screen. "We're shipping him out to a juvenile facility Saturday."

Natalie flinched. "Let me talk with him, sir."

"You think you can do what our trained interrogators couldn't?"

"I know how these religious wackos think. I had a good look at what was in that schoolhouse. If I can convince him I'm one of them, he might lead us to them."

Henderson shook his head. "I don't know . . ."

"I'd like to talk to the man and woman from the farm too."

"Out of the question. But I will give you ten minutes with the kid."

Mark walked around the compound with the driver of the van, Colin Dial. The house had two bedrooms and was built near a mound of earth. A compact car sat in the garage and a few tools and bicycles hung on the wall.

"If I were the GC, I'd never suspect you," Mark said.

"That's the point," Colin said. "Those people at the shelter saw a big van drive away. There's no van here."

"Where's it hidden? I was too tired to notice last night."

Colin took him to the other side of the mound. Looking closely, Mark saw tracks on the grass that led to the side of the hill. At the base of the mound was a huge pile of firewood. Colin pointed a handheld device at the wood, and suddenly the pile split in two, revealing an underground bunker.

"I poured the concrete and rigged the opening myself," Colin said.

"Must have taken years."

They walked inside and Colin closed the door. "I used to be into the militia. Way before the disappearances I started digging this, storing food and supplies, and getting ready for a nuclear holocaust. I didn't want to die."

"Did you know about God?"

"I'd been to church a lot and listened to sermons, but it didn't sink in. To me the Bible was a codebook with lots of secrets. When my wife finally showed me Tsion Ben-Judah's Web site, I knew I had missed what the Bible is all about."

Mark put the laptop next to a bank of computers that kept track of everything from the latest Global Community news to the local wildfire. "So you've turned this place into a hideout for believers?"

"Didn't plan it that way, but that's what it's become. We're real happy to have you kids and the others. Stay as long as you like."

Natalie stood outside Charlie's cell as the guard unlocked the door and left. When Charlie saw her mark, his mouth dropped open.

"My name is Natalie," she said quickly, pulling a chair to his bunk. Natalie lowered her voice. "We're just going to talk, and you're not going to say anything about seeing me before, all right?"

Charlie nodded. "I got it."

"Have they been treating you okay?"

"Yeah, the food is pretty good, and I've met a bunch of kids who need to know the truth."

"You've talked to them about God?"

"Sure. Was I not supposed to?"

Natalie smiled and leaned forward. "I'm going to get you out of here. They're sending you to a detention center this Saturday, so it has to be before then."

"What about the Shairtons?"

Natalie frowned. "They won't let me in to see them."

"Is the GC going to hurt them?"

"They're going to make everyone decide between God and Nicolae Carpathia."

"That's easy."

"Listen carefully. In order to get you out, you have to lead us to Vicki and Darrion."

Vicki and Darrion stayed out of sight in Maggie's house, watching televised coverage of the excitement over Nicolae Carpathia's return.

Dr. Neal Damosa, the head of the Global Community Department of Education, announced that the satellite schools would again hold meetings. Damosa encouraged young people to use their creativity to come up with songs, artwork, poems, and stories that celebrated the resurrection of Nicolae Carpathia. Damosa gave the address of a Web site that would soon display young people's work.

Vicki shook her head. "Next thing you know they'll have a contest for a trip to meet Carpathia in person."

Vicki asked Darrion to turn the TV off. They sat alone in Maggie's basement and talked about the other kids in the Young Trib Force and how they had been brought together.

"You really couldn't find people who are more different," Vicki said. "You and Judd come from wealthy families. I grew up in a trailer park."

"It's funny how even though we're different, our problems are pretty much the same."

Vicki nodded and ran a hand through her hair. "I keep thinking about Lionel and Judd, wondering if they'll ever get back."

Darrion smiled. "You're especially thinking of Judd, right?"

"What do you mean?"

"I could tell the first day I met you that you two had chemistry. You're going to get together. It has to happen."

Vicki blushed. She told Darrion about Judd and Nada. "I guess they were pretty serious before Nada died. I don't know how a person can rebound after something like that."

"It takes time. I'll bet when Judd gets back you'll be fighting like old times."

"I miss him so much, it's scary," Vicki said. "I keep wondering if he'd have done something different with the schoolhouse, gotten out earlier."

Darrion put a hand on Vicki's shoulder. "It's going to be all right."

"Not for the Shairtons. If we had left the schoolhouse earlier and if I hadn't done that last satellite broadcast, the Shairtons wouldn't be behind bars."

"And if we hadn't met them, maybe Mr. Shairton wouldn't have prayed to accept Christ. Have you thought of that?"

Vicki nodded. "I just don't want anything bad to happen to them because of us."

"You've helped me see that God is in control. At first I was scared at just about everything that happened and thought it was up to us to stay alive. Now, even if the GC gets hold of us, I know that God can work something good out of anything. I'll bet the Shairtons feel the same."

Natalie tried to meet with Deputy Commander Henderson before lunch but couldn't. At two in the afternoon she finally sat in his office and told him her news.

"I had a breakthrough with that Charlie kid. He totally believes I'm one of the Judah-ites."

Henderson sat forward. "Good work. Did he tell you anything about where this Vicki girl is?"

"I guess the kids used to live near Mt. Prospect. I asked if he could take us there and he agreed if we get his dog."

"What dog?"

"From the abandoned schoolhouse. I found the thing and tried to get it to follow the kids' trail but it didn't work."

Henderson looked at his watch. "I suppose there's no harm. Let's get the dog and go."

"He doesn't want to go until tonight. He's freaked about the GC following us."

"I have an appointment tonight. Either we go now or forget it."

"He won't go in the day. Sorry. I told Charlie you were one of the Judah-ites, and he was looking forward to meeting you. I thought you wanted those girls, but maybe they're not that important."

Henderson buzzed his secretary. "Cancel my meeting tonight."

The sun was going down as Vicki took the phone from Maggie. Natalie gave exact instructions about what they were to do.

Vicki put a hand to her forehead. "Okay, we'll be across the street. I've got the phone number and how we'll get Charlie and Phoenix, but you haven't said anything about yourself. Are you coming with us?"

"Let me play this out with the GC. I don't think they'll suspect I'm working from the inside."

"That's crazy!" Vicki said. "You know you have to get out of there before they start giving people the mark of the beast."

"Calm down. I'm a lot more valuable to you guys in here. If I can't pull it off, I'll run."

"But it might be too late."

"All my life I've wanted to do something that counted. You guys have reached so many and now I have a part in it. I want to take as many people to heaven with me as possible, so let me do this. I might even have a chance to get the Shairtons and that Zeke man out of trouble."

"I understand, but if things get hairy, promise you'll come with us."

"I promise," Natalie said.

Vicki looked at her watch and told Maggie and Darrion what to do. She sent an e-mail to the others in the Young Trib Force and asked them to pray.

24

VICKI sat in the driver's seat of Maggie's car across from the woman's house. Maggie and Darrion sat in the back, watching the street. For the fiftieth time, Vicki made sure Maggie's cell phone was turned on.

Darrion scooted down in her seat. "What other plan did Natalie have?"

"She was going to bring Charlie out of his cell and spray something in the guards' eyes if they got in her way," Vicki said.

"This is better," Maggie said.

Vicki and Darrion had tried to convince Maggie that she should come with the kids to Wisconsin, but the woman wouldn't listen. "I've lived here a long time, and there are a lot of people around who still need to hear the message."

"If they see your license plate, they'll find you," Vicki said.

"Took it off," Maggie said, smiling. "The rear plate is in the trunk. Put it on when you're safe."

"What are you going to do when this Henderson guy comes?" Darrion said.

"I'm going to keep him busy while you get away," Maggie said.

"You know they'll suspect you," Vicki said.

Maggie shook her head. "You really underestimate me. You think I'm just some old woman who doesn't know how to take care of herself. I've thought about it a lot.

"After you get away, they'll ask me what happened. I'll tell them how you two forced your way in and how scared I was. Then I'll make them coffee and offer some sweet rolls. They'll probably give me some kind of medal for bravery."

Vicki smiled. She hoped the GC would treat Maggie well. She looked at the cell phone again and made sure it was still on.

———

It was drizzling as Natalie escorted Charlie from the building in handcuffs. Deputy Commander Henderson signed Charlie out at the front desk. The clerk at the front questioned Henderson. Natalie thought about jumping in the GC vehicle and taking off, but the man cleared up the problem and followed as she got Charlie in the backseat. Natalie climbed in next to Charlie and fought off Phoenix as he licked his friend's face. Charlie laughed, awkwardly trying to pet Phoenix.

Natalie leaned toward the man and whispered, "It

might be good if we took his cuffs off. You know, a show of faith."

Henderson winked and handed her the keys. "Charlie, we're going to get you out of those so you can pet your dog."

"I sure appreciate it, sir," Charlie said. "I had no idea I'd meet two followers of Dr. Ben-Judah here. How did you find out about him?"

Henderson smiled as he drove toward Mt. Prospect. "Oh, you know, I saw his Web site, read his message, and pretty soon I was just praying away."

"Has it changed your life like it has mine?" Charlie said.

"Oh yes, definitely. I'm a much better person now that I believe . . . uh, what you believe. God is so much more real to me now."

Henderson turned right on Mt. Prospect Road. It was fine in places, torn up in others, so the man slowed. A few of the streetlights worked. Others were broken or had burned out long ago.

"Did the kids meet in a house or some other kind of building?" Henderson asked Charlie.

"It was sort of a house, but they used it like an apartment building. I think I'll know it when I see it."

"Natalie says you don't remember the street?"

"Didn't you say it started with a *C?*" Natalie said.

Henderson glared at her. "Let him talk, Bishop."

"Yeah, I think it started with a *C,*" Charlie said.

"Central?"

"Yeah, that's it."

Henderson found Central and drove a few blocks. Natalie placed her hand inside her coat, found her cell phone, and secretly punched the number Vicki had given her. She gave it time to ring and hung up.

"Anything look familiar?" Henderson said, slowing at an abandoned business and two burned-out cars.

"Nothing yet, sir."

Henderson pulled to the side and stopped. Charlie's eyes darted and Phoenix whimpered.

"Tell me the truth," Henderson finally said.

Natalie sat forward. "Sir, I told you—"

"I'm not talking to you. I'm talking to him." Henderson grabbed Charlie's arm and pulled him forward. "You don't know where those two are any more than I do."

Charlie looked wildly at Natalie and back at the man.

"You told me you knew where their hideout was," Natalie said.

"You're supposed to be my friends," Charlie said. "I don't understand."

Henderson threw the car in gear and turned around. He tossed the handcuffs into the backseat. "Cuff him. We're taking him home."

Natalie couldn't believe Vicki hadn't phoned. Was it possible Natalie's signal hadn't gone through? She pulled Charlie's arms behind his back and clicked the cuffs but didn't put them on. "Just keep your arms behind you," she whispered.

Natalie pulled out her cell phone. "I don't believe this. I'm calling headquarters and telling them we're coming back in."

She dialed Vicki's number and made sure it rang. She ended the call and threw the phone onto the floor. "I hate this thing. I can never get through."

"Don't bother," Henderson said. "They don't need to know we're coming back."

"Sir, I'm sorry. I thought for sure he was legit."

Henderson shook his head. "I should have known better than to trust—"

Before he could finish his sentence, Henderson's phone rang. He wrestled with his coat and pulled it from his pocket. "Yeah."

Henderson held the phone away from his ear. Natalie leaned forward and listened.

"Is this Mr. Henderson?" an older woman said.

"Who is this?"

"I just called your office and they gave me this number."

"Well, they shouldn't have. If you have business with the Morale Monitors, call me there in the morning."

"But—"

Natalie's heart sank as Henderson hung up. "Who was that?"

"Some old bat."

The phone rang again. Natalie was afraid he was going to turn his phone off. Instead, he answered it and cursed.

"You watch your language, young man," the woman said. "I called to give you information on those two girls you're looking for, but if you're going to treat me like that, I'll just hang up."

"No, no! I'm sorry. I've had trouble with people in the office giving out this number." He pulled to the side of the road and stopped. "Please, what two girls are you talking about?"

"The two they were looking for the other day. Teenagers. Young, pretty little things. I had a hard time believing they were the ones you wanted until I tried to get them to leave."

Henderson pulled out a pen. "Okay. Give me your exact location."

The woman rattled off a street address near the GC station. "I'm using my cell phone so they won't hear me. I'm telling them I'm ordering a pizza, so ring the bell—"

"No!" Henderson shouted. "Don't tell them anything. Just leave the front door open and I'll come in."

"I'll try, but they notice everything."

"I'll find a way inside. Just keep them there. I'm about fifteen minutes away."

"I'll do my best."

Henderson hung up and raced down the road. Charlie tried to keep his hands behind him as they bounced.

"What's happening?" Natalie said.

Henderson scowled. "Your friend back there wasn't even close. We're going to nab those two girls tonight."

Vicki took the cell phone from Maggie, and the woman got out of the car. Vicki and Darrion got out and hugged Maggie. "We don't know how we'll ever be able to thank you," Vicki said.

236

Maggie smiled. "You just keep telling people the truth about God. That's payment enough for me."

The three stood in the drizzling rain until Maggie told Vicki and Darrion to get into the car. "You two are going to catch your death of cold before we get that boy back."

"What about the car?" Vicki said.

"It's yours. You and your friends use it however you see fit."

Maggie went back into her house. Rain poured, pelting the windshield. Vicki watched the drops trail down the glass.

Finally, a car turned onto the street and turned off its lights. As it slowly approached, Vicki and Darrion scooted toward the floor and waited.

Natalie took a deep breath as they approached Maggie's house. She knew the next few moments might mean the difference between freedom and a GC prison for the kids.

She had hoped Henderson wouldn't call for backup. She knew he had an ego and wanted to make the arrest himself. As he slipped the car into park, he dialed his cell phone and asked to speak to an officer on duty.

"I thought you were one of us," Charlie said. "You don't believe in God?"

Henderson turned with a smirk. "I got news for you, pal. The only god I believe in rose from the dead last weekend. You'd better get used to following his orders."

The rain came harder, drops banging onto the roof.

Natalie glanced to her left and noticed an older car parked opposite Maggie's house. She nudged Charlie.

Henderson gave the address and asked for a squad car to back him up. The officer said it would take another five minutes for someone to get there, and Henderson hung up. "I'm not going to wait any longer."

Natalie opened her door. "I'm going with you."

"No way. You stay with him and watch the front."

"I didn't sign up to do baby-sitting," Natalie spat.

Henderson paused. "I gave you a direct order. Stay here and make sure they don't come out the front."

"What if they do?"

"Get out and use your Mace to subdue them."

Henderson closed the door quietly and crept up the sidewalk. Charlie started to speak, but Natalie put a finger to her lips. She glanced at the car across the street and saw some movement on the driver's side.

Henderson looked in a window at the front of the house, then rounded some bushes and tried to see in another.

"Come on, Henderson," Natalie whispered to herself, "go to the back before those other GC goons get here."

Phoenix jumped into the front seat and Charlie grabbed him. "Hold on to him," Natalie said.

Henderson tried to get in the backyard but couldn't. He circled the front yard again, glancing at the car as he passed. The front door opened and an old woman waved Henderson inside. "That must be Maggie," Natalie said. "But what's she doing?"

Henderson ran into the house and Maggie waved

excitedly. Natalie threw open the squad-car door and yelled at Charlie. He came bounding out with Phoenix in his arms.

Vicki started Maggie's car and Darrion opened the back door. When Phoenix saw Vicki he yelped. Charlie jumped in after him.

"Get in!" Vicki yelled at Natalie.

"No," Natalie said, her hair soaked from the rain. "I can handle this. Just get out of here before . . ."

Vicki glanced in the rearview mirror and saw two headlights and flashing lights approaching. Maggie's front door opened with a crash, and Henderson shouted from the top of the stairs.

"Hurry!" Natalie said as she slammed the back door.

Judd awoke with a start early in the morning in New Babylon. He walked through the massive hotel rooms, but no one stirred. Z-Van had worked late into the night and still snored. Lionel, Westin, and the others slept soundly.

Judd went back to bed and lay there. He thought of Z-Van's trip to Jerusalem and what would happen there. Judd felt like he was being drawn back to Israel . . . but why? He pushed the thought from his mind and suddenly had the impression that someone was in trouble.

Judd knelt by his bed and asked God to protect his friends. He prayed first for Vicki.

25

VICKI mashed the accelerator to the floor and glanced in the rearview mirror. Flashing lights from an oncoming Global Community squad car cast an eerie glow in the rain. A shadowy figure darted across the wet street. *Natalie should have come with us*, Vicki thought.

Charlie craned his neck to see, and Vicki told him to stay down.

"You think they're going to shoot at us?" Darrion said.

Vicki shrugged. "Just stay down."

Phoenix squirmed in the backseat. Charlie grabbed his collar and pulled him to the floor. "He's excited to see you!"

"I'll be excited to see him once we get away," Vicki said, gripping the steering wheel. She kept the lights off, hoping the GC car wouldn't spot them in the rain. Vicki's heart raced so fast she found it hard to breathe.

She remembered the driving instructions Conrad had given during their trip west. "Make sure you stay calm behind the wheel," Conrad had said. "If you're angry or scared, don't drive."

"Great," Vicki had said. "I'll never learn because I'm always angry or scared."

Conrad had helped Vicki get comfortable with driving in all kinds of weather. During a severe rainstorm in California, she drove in an empty parking lot, sliding when she made sharp turns. Now, as she rushed down the wet road, the practice was paying off.

"Where are we going?" Charlie said.

Vicki quickly explained about the kids in Wisconsin. "We may not make it tonight, but we'll try." She turned a corner without touching her brakes and grazed a parked car.

"They're stopping at Maggie's house," Darrion yelled.

Vicki drove on, wondering what Natalie would say to her boss.

Natalie Bishop leaned against the car, rain dripping from her hair, as Deputy Commander Darryl Henderson stumbled down Maggie Carlson's front steps. He fell in the wet grass with a thump.

Natalie screamed in mock pain. She quickly reached into Henderson's car, stuffed his keys in her pocket, and kept screaming. She fumbled with her key chain—a combination pocketknife, flashlight, and Mace dispenser.

Natalie had seen a few prisoners who had been

maced. Their eyes turned red and filled with tears. She could only imagine the pain.

"Bishop!" Deputy Commander Henderson shouted. The man was on his feet again. "Bishop, what happened?"

Natalie pulled the Mace dispenser close as lights swirled from the oncoming GC squad car. She glanced at the car Vicki was driving and saw it move around a corner.

This is my only hope, Natalie thought. She had planned it this way, and so far everything was working. Vicki and the others were gone, and if Henderson believed her, she might be able to keep working for the GC.

"Where are they?" Henderson screamed as he opened the car door.

Natalie closed her eyes tightly, pressed the nozzle, then opened them as the spray filled her eyes. For several moments she could hear nothing but her own screams. Unbelievable, searing pain! Her eyes felt on fire. She covered her face with her hands and rolled on the pavement, unable to focus on anything but the pain.

"Where are my keys!?" Henderson said.

Another GC squad car pulled up, and an officer tried to help Natalie. Henderson screamed for the man to follow the car that had just pulled away.

"I didn't see any—"

The officer sped off and Henderson barked orders into his radio. An older woman arrived, and Henderson questioned her about her car. She gave him the information, and he called for all available units to respond.

The woman knelt by Natalie and asked what was wrong. Natalie said she had been sprayed with Mace, and the woman helped her into the house. "We need to flush your eyes with water."

As Henderson combed the yard for his keys, the woman took Natalie to the kitchen. "That was a brave thing you did for those kids," she whispered.

Natalie tried to open her eyes but couldn't.

"It's okay," the woman said. "I can see by the mark on your forehead that you're a believer. I'm Maggie Carlson."

Natalie sobbed, forced to her knees by the pain. "I took Henderson's car keys so he couldn't follow," she whispered. "If he finds them—"

"Where are they?"

Natalie patted her right pants pocket and Maggie took them out. "I'll care for them. Keep your eyes under the running water."

Judd Thompson Jr. sat alone on a leather couch in Z-Van's hotel suite and prayed for his friends. He had sensed danger several times before, but never so strong as now.

As the New Babylon sun peeked over the palace a few blocks away, Judd took a bottle of water from the small refrigerator and walked into the main living area. Z-Van's sheet music lay stacked on the grand piano, but Judd couldn't look at the words. The man had seemed possessed since the day Carpathia had risen from the dead, spending every waking moment writing his tribute to the risen potentate. Judd knew Nicolae could take power over people's minds. Was Carpathia controlling the singer?

Judd used a laptop to log on to the kids' Web site. He read Tsion Ben-Judah's latest message again and shuddered at the prophecies about the Antichrist. Soon the Global Community would require every living being to receive a mark on the hand or forehead and swear allegiance to Carpathia. Anyone who willingly took that evil mark would never be able to come to God.

That's why we have to tell as many people as quickly as we can, Judd thought.

Around the world, loyal citizens were prepared to kneel before Carpathia's image. The GC had been working on biochip technology that would accompany the mark, but Judd didn't know how long it would take to distribute the machines used for the injection.

Judd thought of the trip Z-Van had planned to Jerusalem. It would be safer to hide or get out of New Babylon altogether. But something in Israel tugged at him. Was it Sam? Mr. Stein? Nada's family? Lionel felt it too, so they had stayed.

Judd typed a short note to his friends in the Young Tribulation Force and asked about everyone. He knew Charlie had been taken by the GC and wondered if this was the reason he felt the need to pray.

Judd was astounded at the number of e-mails to the Web site. He had known when they started it that many would read its contents, but he had no idea hundreds of kids would e-mail every day from around the globe. They asked everything from how to become a true believer to what was coming next on the prophecy timeline. Mark and the others had done a good job of listing the most frequently asked questions, or FAQs, but some wanted a personal response.

One girl from the former country of France gave a first name of Eleta and wrote:

> *I grew up knowing nothing about God. My parents and teachers never talked about spiritual things, believing religion was unimportant or just superstitious. Now that Nicolae Carpathia and Leon Fortunato have performed miracles, many are saying Carpathia is truly a god. They want to worship him, but I'm not sure. The things you have posted make me wonder if Carpathia is really evil. Please help me understand the truth so that I can tell my family.*

Judd's heart leapt. This was exactly the kind of person the kids had hoped to reach. Judd sent a message, quickly explaining more about what the Bible revealed about God and how important it was to not follow the Global Community's twisted religion.

Sadly, others wrote in support of Carpathia. One man said he was monitoring the Web site and had notified local GC authorities. *It's only a matter of time until they find you and shut you down!*

Judd heard someone stir in the next room. He started to leave the Web site, but a new message sparked his interest. The subject line read *New Babylon believer—help.*

Lionel walked into the room with Westin Jakes,

Z-Van's pilot who had become a believer. Judd waved
them over and put the e-mail onto the full screen.

> *Dear Young Trib Force,*
> *I am seventeen and a believer in Jesus. I have been visiting*
> *New Babylon with my parents. My father is a huge sup-*
> *porter of N. C. and came to pay his respects at the funeral.*
> *He and my mother do not know of my faith in Christ.*
>
> *My father wants me to work for the GC. Though I'm*
> *still in high school, I have a number of skills with*
> *computers. The GC have given us a free apartment until I*
> *can be processed for employment.*
>
> *The last thing I want to do is work for the Global*
> *Community, but my father insists. We have had argu-*
> *ments and he will not listen. Me working for Carpathia is*
> *an honor greater than anything my father can imagine.*
> *Can you help me? I have only two believers I can talk to*
> *right now. Please write as soon as possible.*
> *C. W.*

Lionel studied the message. "You think it's a trick?"

"Looks genuine to me," Westin said.

Judd nodded and typed a reply. "I think this is someone in a real jam."

"We have no idea who this C. W. is," Lionel said.

"Doesn't matter. If he's a fellow believer, he deserves
our help."

"What advice are you going to give him—or her?"

Judd smiled. "No advice. I'm going to set up a meeting."

Vicki made her way through backstreets and alleys, trying to stay out of sight. A few minutes after they had escaped, she took a wrong turn down a dead end. As they turned the car around, a GC squad car passed on the street in front of them, its lights flashing.

"Maybe we ought to find a place to hide," Darrion said.

Vicki shook her head. "The GC will be crawling all over here by morning. It's dark and raining. We should try to get as far away as we can."

Lightning struck nearby and the sky thundered. Phoenix whimpered in the backseat and Charlie tried to comfort him.

With their lights still off, Vicki found what was left of Rand Road and headed north. Anytime she saw the lights of GC squad cars, she turned at the nearest street and stayed out of sight.

Charlie leaned forward. "When are we going back for Bo and Ginny?"

Vicki stole a glance at Darrion. "Natalie couldn't get to the Shairtons."

"You mean we're just going to leave them?"

Darrion turned in the seat. "We need to get you to safety, and then we'll see about them."

"I don't want to get to safety. I want to help them. They were like a mom and dad to me. Can we turn around?"

Vicki shook her head. "I don't expect you to understand, Charlie. We need to keep going."

Charlie slumped in his seat and put his face in his hands. Lightning flashed and Vicki spotted a sign that said "Wauconda." Several headlights approached from behind. A few miles later, Darrion spotted a street sign and asked Vicki to turn. They followed a muddy road into the countryside.

When they reached what looked like an old general store, Vicki parked in the back. With each flash of lightning they spotted abandoned barns, cornfields, and old farm equipment.

Vicki fished Maggie's cell phone from her pocket and called Mark in Wisconsin. He was glad to hear they were safe and asked about Natalie. Mark offered to meet them, but Vicki said they would keep driving and call again before daybreak.

The three sat in the car, staring out at the darkness. The only sounds were the patter of raindrops on the roof and Phoenix panting. Finally, Darrion broke the silence. "My mom and dad used to bring me up here every fall to pick apples. I wish I could get a mug of hot apple cider right now."

Vicki smiled. "Or a caramel apple." She turned and put a hand on Charlie's shoulder. "It's good to have you back."

"Didn't think I was going to get out."

Vicki scooted down in her seat. "Tell me more about picking apples."

"My dad would hold me on his shoulders so I could get the high ones. Then I'd find the biggest pumpkin, and he'd carry it back to the car."

"Petting zoo?" Vicki said.

"How'd you know?"

"One of our neighbors knew a farm family. I always liked the hayrides."

"The place we went to had a corn maze. They'd cut rows out of a cornfield and you'd have to try and find your way to the middle."

Vicki thought of her little sister, Jeanni. Just the sight of cows by the side of the road made the girl squeal with delight. Vicki closed her eyes and began to cry. Darrion put a hand on her shoulder.

"I'm okay," Vicki said. "I was just thinking about my sister petting those farm animals. She always laughed when she fed the goats. For some reason I can't remember her face anymore. I try hard, but . . ."

A light flashed inside a house behind them. Tears ran down Vicki's cheeks as she started the car and headed for the main road.

26

NATALIE Bishop let the water cascade over her eyes for almost a half hour. She looked at her red, puffy face in a kitchen mirror and rubbed her eyes with a fresh towel.

Deputy Commander Henderson was picked up by another squad car to direct the search. Maggie slipped outside and put his keys under his car as another Peacekeeper came to take Natalie's statement.

"So the kid with the dog maced you and got out of the car?"

Natalie nodded.

"Wasn't he handcuffed?"

"He was, but Deputy Commander Henderson said we could take them off, just to show him we were his friends."

"And you didn't put the cuffs on after you got the call from the woman?"

Natalie rubbed her eyes. "I thought I did, but I guess he tricked me. Maybe he got the key. I can't remember."

The Peacekeeper went in the other room and talked with Maggie. Deputy Commander Henderson returned a half hour later.

"Did you catch them?" Natalie said.

Henderson shook his head and ignored her, looking around the house. He spotted the computer and asked Maggie if the girls had used it.

"They sure did. They were on it almost the whole time they were here."

Henderson turned the computer on and looked at Natalie. "You okay?"

"I'll feel better when this stuff wears off."

"I read your statement. Something's not right."

"What do you mean?" Natalie said.

Maggie brought Henderson some coffee and a sweet roll and sat at the kitchen table. "This girl has been through a lot. I don't think she's the one to blame."

"I didn't even want to stay with that guy," Natalie said. "I wanted to come with you."

Henderson scratched his chin. "Doesn't make sense. These two girls leave your house before we get here and wait? How would they know this Charlie kid is with us?" He turned to Maggie. "Tell me the truth."

"I already told you. They forced their way into the house and took over. I was so scared I hardly knew what to do. They used the computer and ate like they were starving. It was a miracle I was able to break away and call you when I did."

"And they found out you were talking to me?"

Maggie nodded. "I tried to get them to think it was a

friend, but they knew I had called the GC. They grabbed
my car keys and ran. What could I do?"

Henderson went back to the computer and started
typing, but the machine beeped. "They must have erased
the hard drive."

Maggie shook her head. "These kids are smart. Maybe
they were going to steal your car. Then they saw this
Charlie kid and took off."

"Maybe . . ."

"I'm sure you'll catch them eventually."

"Eventually's not good enough," Henderson said,
taking a bite of the sweet roll and sipping his coffee. "I
have to say you were brave, ma'am. And you're right. We
will catch them. We have roadblocks set up from here to
the northern border. Plus, I've asked for assistance with
satellite imaging."

"What's that?" Natalie said.

"GC Security and Intelligence can snap pictures from
miles above the earth. If we give them the coordinates
and the weather cooperates, they can detect movement
and give us reports."

Maggie gave Natalie a worried look, then turned back
to Henderson. "So you will catch them."

"You bet." He took another sweet roll. "And believe
me, when we have them in custody, your contribution to
the search will be recognized."

Maggie smiled and brought more food and coffee for
the other Peacekeeper. She turned to Natalie. "Why don't
you go upstairs and lie down in my room. I'm sure resting your eyes will help."

253

"Go ahead," Henderson said. "We'll wait on the satel-lite report."

Maggie patted Natalie on the back and pressed a piece of paper into her hand. When Natalie got to the top of the stairs, she opened it and found a phone number along with a note. *Call them now.*

A noise at the bottom of the stairs startled Natalie. She turned to see the other Peacekeeper looking up at her.

Mark Eisman studied the hastily drawn map Colin Dial had made of the upper Illinois/lower Wisconsin area. Vicki would need to work her way around several lakes to get to the new hideout.

"The earthquake cut off a lot of roads," Colin said, pointing to an old map. "These two lakes are dry craters, and it's impossible to get through except on foot. The GC made a main road toward Lake Geneva, but I don't think she should go that way." Colin traced a route and told Mark to call Vicki.

"She's driving blind," Mark said. "How's she going to find roads in the dark that don't even exist on a map?"

Vicki drove back to the main road and continued north. The rain had slowed, and she flashed her lights every minute to make sure she was on course.

"You think those people back there in the house will phone the GC?" Charlie said.

"I hope they'll go back to bed and forget about us."

The cell phone rang and Vicki pulled over.

"Vicki, it's Mark. We have directions to get you here, but it's complicated. Where are you?"

Vicki told him and Mark talked with his friend, Colin Dial. "Okay, head north on Route 12. When you get to Fox Lake, which isn't there anymore, pull off and call me."

Vicki followed Mark's directions. The clouds were clearing and she could finally see moonlight.

"As long as we keep our lights off, they won't be able to see us, right?" Charlie said.

Vicki nodded.

Natalie smiled at the Peacekeeper, and the man returned to the kitchen. She slipped into Maggie's bedroom, closed the door quietly, and picked up the phone by the bed. No dial tone. It was either the storm or the GC had cut the lines. *Do they suspect Maggie?*

Natalie fell onto the bed and buried her face in a pillow. Her eyes still stung, but she couldn't think of that now. She had to figure out a way to warn Vicki. "Please, God, help me get in touch with her."

Natalie heard a commotion and went to the top of the stairs.

Deputy Commander Henderson paced as he talked on his cell phone. "That would fit," he said, covering the phone with a hand. "We just got a report from Wauconda. A suspicious car was seen outside a home. They left a few minutes ago."

Henderson put the phone back to his ear. "I don't know how they got that far, but we won't miss them this time. Give me the satellite coordinates."

Natalie went back downstairs and stood in the kitchen doorway. She gave Maggie a worried look.

"All right, I want three cars at the northern roadblock at Richmond to move south toward Wauconda," Henderson said. "We should run right into them."

Lionel Washington sensed an old feeling creeping up on him. Judd was at it again, doing what he thought was right and not caring about anyone else. Though they had fought during their time together in Israel and in New Babylon, Lionel liked Judd. It was impossible not to like him. But when Judd made up his mind, nothing and no one could stop him.

Like other mornings, Lionel went to the lobby for some food. He knew Z-Van had spent thousands of dollars on room service and Lionel could order anything he wanted, but he felt guilty eating what he considered "Carpathia food."

Lionel grabbed a tray and went through the complimentary buffet of muffins, doughnuts, fruit, cereal, and juice. People gathered around small breakfast tables and talked about the events of the past week. Nicolae's rise from the dead was replayed on wall-mounted televisions. When Leon Fortunato called down lightning on the crowd, many in the dining room clapped. All of the clips were in preparation for a live news conference at the GC Palace.

When Leon Fortunato appeared on the screen, many applauded, then called for quiet. "Hail Carpathia," Leon began.

"Hail Carpathia," people said to the television.

"I am here to outline plans our beloved potentate has put into effect in the last few days and to keep everyone abreast of the schedule we have laid out to celebrate the resurrection of our lord and risen king.

"I want you to know that I will no longer be supreme commander of the Global Community."

Many around Lionel gasped and the room fell silent.

Leon smiled. "At the potentate's request, I have accepted, with great enthusiasm I might add, the new position of Most High Reverend Father of Carpathianism. The former Enigma Babylon One World faith will be replaced with a more perfect religion, one that worships a worthy object. That is, the one who raised himself from the dead, Nicolae Carpathia."

This was not news to Lionel. He had heard it from Z-Van, but clearly those in the room were surprised and joyful at the report.

"As has been relayed to you through news channels," Fortunato continued, "the image of His Excellency is being reproduced around the world in every major city. Each image will be a life-size replica of His Excellency.

"Let me say another word about our worthy lord. While our beloved potentate lay dead, he gave me power to call fire from the sky and kill those who oppose him. He also allowed me to give speech to the statue so we could hear his own heart. This confirmed my desire to

serve him as my god for the rest of my days, and I shall
do that for as long as Nicolae Carpathia gives me breath."

Leon said he would take questions from the press
after one final announcement. "To further the cause of
world peace and unity, the Global Community is beginning a massive identification plan that will encompass
every man, woman, and child on the planet. This loyalty
mark will be on a biochip embedded just beneath the
skin. It will contain a series of numbers matching the
world region where each person lives. There will also be a
physical representation of this mark on the body."

Leon paused for what seemed like dramatic effect. The
breakfast room fell silent. Even people walking through
the lobby stopped to listen as Leon continued, his voice
peaceful and soothing.

"Every man, woman, and child, regardless of their
station in life, shall receive this mark on their right hand
or on their forehead. Those who neglect to get the mark
when it is made available will not be allowed to buy or
sell until such time as they receive it. Those who overtly
refuse shall be put to death, and every marked loyal citizen shall be deputized with the right and the responsibility to report such a one. The mark shall consist of the
name of His Excellency or the prescribed number."

Lionel felt goose bumps. Fortunato had just
announced the death penalty for anyone refusing the
mark, but people around him seemed eager to identify
with Carpathia.

A reporter raised a hand. "Sir, what is the potentate's
position on those who oppose him, specifically the

Jewish contingent in Jerusalem and the Judah-ites who are spread around the globe?"

Fortunato smiled. "We believe these misguided groups will see the errors they have made when the potentate returns to Jerusalem in the beloved Holy Land. The Jews are looking for their Messiah, and Nicolae Carpathia will return there, triumphant. Each person will have an opportunity to repent and see the light.

"The Judah-ites believe Messiah already came and went. They think Jesus is their Savior." Leon seemed to look around the room. "But I see him nowhere. If the Judah-ites want to see the true and living God, let them come to Jerusalem, for that is where he shall soon be. In the city where they slew him, they shall see him, high and lifted up."

Another reporter said, "The controls that you're putting on citizens—such as the mark and the biochip—are we to conclude that citizens aren't to be trusted?"

"On the contrary. Most people believe in and follow the tenets of the Global Community. It is only that small percentage I have just mentioned who are not loyal. We seek peace and unity for all, and in order to accomplish that, all must comply."

"Ask him when we'll be able to take the mark!" someone shouted in the breakfast room. Everyone laughed.

"If someone should choose against the loyalty mark," another reporter said, "how will they be . . . handled?"

Fortunato smiled again. "I'm sure you will agree that no thinking person would choose against allegiance to a man who has proved his divine nature by raising himself from the dead. Let us hope there will be no need to even address that question."

"How will the mark be applied?" another reporter said.

"The miniature biochip will go under the skin as painlessly as a vaccination. It takes only a matter of seconds. Citizens may choose either their hand or their forehead. The procedure will leave a thin, half-inch scar, and to its immediate left will be the home region number in black ink. Some may also choose the initials *NJC* or even the name *Nicolae,* which would cover the left side of the forehead.

"The embedded chip will not only give evidence of loyalty to the potentate, but also will serve as a method of payment and receipt for buying and selling."

"When will this start?"

"We intend to implement the mark as soon as possible. First, those who are behind bars will have the opportunity to show their loyalty and then members of the Global Community workforce."

Lionel grabbed the tray of food and walked to the elevator. Fortunato could fool members of the press and other viewers, but followers of God knew what was about to happen. Those who took the mark would lose their souls for eternity. Those who didn't would lose their heads. Simple as that.

27

NATALIE followed Deputy Commander Henderson to the street. She pointed at something shiny under the car, and Henderson retrieved his keys.

"You're not going. Your eyes—"

"I'm fine. I need to be there when you get these jerks."

Henderson sighed and tossed his bag in the backseat. "No complaining. We're staying out as long as it takes to find them. I'm not having it on my record that I let a prisoner escape and meet up with other suspects."

"I understand, sir."

The other Peacekeeper turned on the dome light and studied a map. He pointed out the roadblock location and the Wauconda sighting.

Natalie glanced at Henderson's bag beside her, which held an extra gun, ammunition, important papers, and his cell phone. She unsnapped the phone compartment and felt inside. Empty.

Henderson started the car and handed his phone to

the Peacekeeper. "Call the satellite office and see if there's anything new."

The Peacekeeper dialed the number and cursed. "We must be out of range."

"Let me try," Natalie said. "I'll keep dialing until we get through."

The Peacekeeper handed the phone to Natalie.

Vicki flashed her lights and saw the sign for Fox Lake. She pulled to the side of the road and turned off the car. Charlie had fallen asleep in the backseat beside Phoenix.

"What did Mark mean about Fox Lake not being here anymore?" Darrion said.

"I'm guessing the earthquake drained it," Vicki said. She looked at the fuel gauge and saw they still had a quarter of a tank. "We should be able to get to Wisconsin on this."

Vicki dialed Mark and told him where they were.

"Good. I'm going to let Colin give you directions. Do you have a pen and some paper?"

Vicki fumbled in the glove box and found a pen. Darrion pulled a manual from under her seat, and Vicki wrote on the inside cover.

"Listen carefully," Colin said.

The phone beeped and the screen said "Low battery."

"Do you have a recharger?" Colin said.

"Not unless it's in the glove compartment," Vicki said.

"Look for it and call me in five minutes. I'll try to make the directions as simple as I can."

Vicki turned off the phone and crawled through the car looking for the phone cord that plugged into the cigarette lighter. Charlie slept through the futile search.

"How much time is left on the battery?" Darrion said.

"I think the warning light comes on a few minutes before it actually runs out. We should have enough power to get the directions."

Vicki turned on the phone and dialed, but before she could hit the Send button, the phone rang. She picked up and heard static.

Then someone said, "I'm not getting anything. We're still out of range."

"Who is it?" Darrion said.

"It sounds like Natalie, but—"

"How did you come up with the idea for the satellite, Mr. Henderson?"

Vicki covered the phone's mouthpiece. "It is Natalie. I think she's trying to warn us."

Henderson said something in the background. Then Natalie said, "So as soon as we get in touch with the satellite guys, we'll know their exact location?"

Vicki told Darrion what she had heard, and the phone beeped a low battery signal again.

"If they're heading north on Route 12," Natalie said, "and those three cars from the Richmond roadblock are heading south, we're sure to catch them."

Vicki whispered, "Thanks, Natalie." She punched in the number for Mark.

Colin answered and Vicki explained what she had learned. "That changes things," Colin said. "If they know your location, it won't matter how many back roads you take. Plus, you'll lead them right here."

"My battery's almost gone. What do I do?"

Colin spoke with Mark quickly and said, "Okay, see if you can find a good place to pull off the road ahead and hide. When the southbound GC cars pass you, keep going north until you get to the Richmond roadblock. Park and head out on foot. Mark and I will—"

Click.

The phone went blank. Vicki tried turning it on but it was dead. She told Darrion what Colin had said.

"About a mile back, there was a turnoff," Darrion said.

Headlights shone in the distance and Vicki gunned the engine, spinning the car around and heading south. "Just tell me when we get close."

Natalie had heard Vicki's whisper and turned the phone off. She scrolled through the directory and erased the call so Henderson wouldn't know what she had done.

When she dialed the number for the satellite station, it rang. She handed the phone to Henderson, and the man beamed.

"Give me an update. . . . Cloud cover? What's that got to do—? . . . Okay, so it's lifting now. That means you should be able to see something."

Henderson gave the satellite operator the proper coordinates and asked him to look for three cars heading south and one probably going north. Natalie sat helpless, praying for clouds and rain.

Judd told Lionel that their mysterious contact inside the palace, known as C. W., had written back almost immediately and agreed to meet in a park not far from the hotel.

Lionel shook his head. "You're walking into this blind. We should be getting out of here, not meeting people who could be GC."

"I don't know who this guy is," Judd said, "but I think he's a believer. If he's really in trouble, I want to help."

Lionel stared at the television as Leon Fortunato continued his press conference. Judd changed and headed for the door of the suite. Westin offered to drive, but Judd said he would walk. He looked back once more before he left, but Lionel simply stared at the television.

Judd left the hotel lobby and headed toward the palace. It had been almost a week since Nicolae's body had been returned to New Babylon. The city looked much different now. Gone were the people mourning in the streets and the windows draped with black curtains. Now people from around the world searched for mementos of their visit.

One booth Judd passed sold necklaces with Nicolae's name embedded in a jewel. Another offered a prayer cloth with the face of Nicolae pictured on the front. The busiest kiosk sold miniature replicas of the Carpathia statue. Judd picked one up and pushed a button on the back. A deep voice said, "Hail Carpathia, risen from the dead." Judd nearly dropped it.

As Judd made his way to the park, he noticed freshly planted trees and a new water fountain. He sat on a bench and looked at the beautiful garden. The last time he had been in the area, Nada had been waiting.

Nada.

He whispered her name and a wave of emotion swept over him. He had recently e-mailed Sam and asked him to pass along some questions to Nada's mother.

"Why did you choose the name *Nada*?" Judd had asked.

"In some countries the name means 'hope,' " Nada's mother answered. "That certainly fits her personality. She was full of hope and promise for the future. But in our part of the world the name means 'giving.' "

Judd closed his eyes. *Giving.* That definition fit as well. Nada had given her life for him, jumping in front of a jailer just as the man's gun fired. One moment she was full of life, the next she was on the floor, her breath and blood escaping like some wounded animal's.

Judd leaned forward, elbows on knees. Just thinking about the scene in the Global Community jail took his breath away. He closed his eyes and tried to think of something else. Anything. Z-Van. Westin.

He took another breath and thought of Lionel. *Am I walking into a trap?*

Footsteps crunched on the walking path nearby. "Are you all right?" someone said.

Judd looked up. A Global Community Peacekeeper stood over him.

Vicki sped south on Route 12 with the GC cars gaining on them. She drove without lights and several times found herself careening around curves and running off the road.

"Don't use your brakes or they'll see the lights," Darrion said.

Charlie woke up as they lurched off and back on the road. "What's going on?"

"Just stay down and buckle up," Vicki said.

Charlie held Phoenix and lay across the backseat.

Vicki rounded a corner and Darrion pointed. "There it is, on the left!"

Vicki glanced in her rearview mirror. She couldn't see the lights of the oncoming GC cars, so she slammed on her brakes and turned the steering wheel to the left. The rear of the car slid around on the wet pavement. She pushed the accelerator and the car screamed down an embankment, metal scraping against dirt and rocks, then concrete. Something banged underneath as they stopped and the car rumbled loudly. Vicki pulled forward a few more feet into a clump of willows.

"That doesn't sound good," Darrion said.

Vicki turned off the car and rolled down her window. Crickets chirped in the night and she drank in the fresh, earthy smell. The three sat in silence as the hum of car tires approached from the north. Vicki turned and looked at Charlie and Phoenix. She put a finger to her lips as headlights flashed high above. Phoenix whimpered, as if he knew something was happening.

The first car passed and the second followed. Vicki listened for the squeal of brakes, but the cars continued until the whine of the tires drifted off on the wet breeze.

"They passed us!" Darrion said.

"Wait. Natalie said there were three cars coming from the north. That was only two."

"Maybe she was wrong," Charlie said.

Vicki held up a hand. In the distance, the third car approached slowly, shining a bright light on either side of the road. "This guy is going to see us if he's going that slow."

"Quick," Darrion said, "everybody out and cover the top!"

The kids got out, making sure Phoenix stayed in the backseat. The girls grabbed leaves, sticks, and even chunks of earth and threw it all on top of the car. Charlie grabbed armloads of dead willow branches and scattered them on the roof. Near a huge drain Vicki found piles of tin cans and trash. She scooped it all up and frantically threw it on the hood and trunk.

"He's getting close!" Darrion whispered.

Charlie put one more armload of branches on the side of the car and followed the girls into the drain that ran under the road. Water from the recent rain was knee-deep and difficult to walk through. They sloshed their way to the middle of the long tunnel. Vicki couldn't see a thing until the car passed above them. The light shone on the right side of the drain, and Vicki saw the silhouette of her two friends beside her.

"Please, God," Vicki whispered, "let him pass."

The light switched to the left side of the road where Maggie's car sat under a mound of debris. Vicki's heart sank as she heard a squeal of brakes above them.

28

VICKI held her breath as the light focused on the culvert where they had left the car. She wondered if they had hidden the car well enough.

"What if Phoenix barks?" Charlie whispered.

Vicki shrugged. "Nothing we can do now."

Darrion pointed to the other end of the drain. "We should go out that side and run."

A radio crackled above, and Vicki moved to the other end of the pipe. She guessed it was Deputy Commander Henderson calling for an update. "Have you found anything?"

"Still looking, sir," the Peacekeeper above them said. "Thought I saw something just now, but it was just a broken tailpipe."

"So that's what happened when we went down the embankment," Darrion whispered.

"Keep looking, and let us know if you find anything," Henderson said.

"Yes, sir."

The car slowly pulled forward. Darrion climbed out of the tunnel and checked their car. She waved Vicki and Charlie up, and they pushed the limbs and debris away.

"Guess we did a pretty good job of hiding it," Charlie said.

Phoenix barked wildly, and Darrion opened the back door and petted him. "Good boy. Way to be quiet."

When the GC car was out of sight, Vicki hopped in and turned the key. The engine roared so loud that Vicki turned off the ignition.

"Can't worry about that now," Darrion said. "Let's go."

Natalie watched the countryside roll by, pretending to dial satellite operations.

Finally, Henderson asked for the phone and dialed himself. It rang through and he pulled to the side and asked for an update. "No, there are three cars, all heading south," he said. "Where? . . . Okay, how far would you say the third car is from them?"

When Henderson hung up he got on the radio. "You've passed them," he said. "Satellite ops said there's a car traveling north between you and the roadblock."

"I couldn't have passed them, sir. I've gone over every inch of road."

"Somebody pulled out a moment ago and is driving north at a high rate of speed. It has to be them. They must have hidden in some cornfield and are trying to get by the roadblock. Catch them!"

"I'm on it, sir."

The other two cars radioed and said they were turning around as well. Henderson spun gravel as he drove from the roadside. "We've got them now."

Judd was startled by the Peacekeeper and looked for a place to run. He noticed the young man's nameplate read "Donaldson."

"I said, are you okay?"

"Yeah, I was just thinking about some stuff. Is it all right to sit here?"

"Not a problem. Let me guess what you're thinking about. Have something to do with the potentate rising again?"

Judd nodded. "That's part of it."

The Peacekeeper chuckled and sat. "I've wanted to work for the Global Community ever since I heard about His Excellency. Winding up here was a dream come true."

"Where are you from?"

"United North American States. Tallahassee, Florida, to be exact. The potentate made a point of hiring from every country so people would know this is truly a Global Community. Where are *you* from?"

Judd told him, being careful not to reveal too much. When the Peacekeeper asked where he was staying, Judd said, "Right now a friend and I are with this musician from the States. He's a singer with The Four Horsemen."

The Peacekeeper's mouth dropped open. "Not Z-Van! You're staying with him?"

Judd shrugged. "We kind of helped him out in Israel."

The Peacekeeper slapped Judd on the back. "That's awesome. I heard some teenagers had rescued him, but I didn't believe it. What's he like?"

"Works alone in his room a lot. He can be kind of annoying, especially at two in the morning."

The Peacekeeper stuck out a hand. "Roy Donaldson."

"I'm Judd . . . er . . . Wayne Judson." They shook hands and Judd sighed. He couldn't believe he'd almost given his real name to the Peacekeeper.

"I suppose you'll stay here and take the mark of loyalty in New Babylon," Donaldson said. "A lot of people are doing that. What kind of identifier are you going to get, Wayne?"

"I . . . uh . . . haven't been able to make up my mind. What about you?"

"I'm going for the big one, you know, the one that covers the whole left side of the forehead. I want to really show them how loyal I am."

"That'll do it," Judd said. "They'll be able to see that a block away."

Judd waited for a chance to talk with Roy about the truth, but the more they talked, the more it became clear that Roy had chosen the wrong path. Unless something happened to lift Carpathia's trance over him, the boy would take the mark and his eternal destiny would be sealed.

Roy stood to leave. "I have to say, I envy you, Wayne.

To be in the same hotel room with a star like Z-Van and listen to the songs he's writing about the potentate must be something." He edged closer and handed Judd a piece of paper. "Do you think you might be able to get me an autograph?"

Judd asked Roy to write his name and address on the paper and said he would have Z-Van send him something.

"Awesome!" Roy said.

When Roy was gone, Judd sat back and ran a hand through his hair. He was about to stand when he heard a rustling behind him. He turned to see a teenage boy in some bushes. He was shorter than Judd, dark hair, clearly Asian. On his forehead was the mark of the believer. He put out his hand. "Are you Judd Thompson?"

"Are you C. W.?"

The boy smiled. "Chang Wong. It's nice to meet you."

Mark held the map in the front seat of Colin Dial's van and watched for the shortcut to Route 12. As soon as Vicki's phone had gone dead, Mark awakened the other kids and asked them to pray. He and Colin had set out immediately for the roadblock, not knowing how much Vicki heard of their instructions.

"If they're following Vicki's car with the satellite, we have another problem," Colin said. "They'll follow our van too."

"Is there any way to block it?"

"If you can come up with some kind of energy shield

before we get there," Colin said, smiling. "If not, our only hope is that God strikes them blind or some clouds roll in."

They passed a small lake and Colin slowed. He turned left onto a dirt road that led past more farmland. "This comes out just inside the old Illinois state line. Let's hope we're in time."

Looking at the road, Vicki knew it would be impossible to drive back up the embankment. But a few yards farther was a more gradual hill. Vicki backed out, the car screeching against a fence by the road, and roared onto the highway. Without the tailpipe, the car sounded like a tank, but it didn't seem to bother anyone but Phoenix.

Vicki hated not having contact with anyone in the Young Trib Force, but with Maggie's cell phone dead and no other means of communication, they were on their own.

The road narrowed to a stretch of rebuilt road. The blacktop was smooth, and the yellow lines in the center seemed to glow in the moonlight. The car crested a small hill and Darrion pointed at a road sign. They were two miles from Wisconsin and probably even closer to the roadblock. Vicki stopped in the middle of the road and rolled down her window.

"What now?" Darrion said.

"Let's get a little closer and look for a place to ditch the car. We can walk into one of those fields and find Mark on the other side."

Darrion frowned. "If he's really on the other side."

"He'll be there," Vicki said.

Darrion scooted closer and covered her mouth with a hand. "We've got another problem. How are we going to get bowser back there to keep quiet while we're tiptoeing through the countryside?"

"You want to leave him?"

"No way," Charlie said from the back. "I know what you're talking about, and we're not leaving Phoenix."

Vicki smiled. "You think you can keep him quiet?"

"I know I can," Charlie said.

Darrion held up a hand and looked behind them. "You hear that?"

"What?" Vicki said, sticking her head out the window.

A whirring sound rose above the noise of the crickets and frogs and the car. Vicki caught the flash of headlights coming over a hill. She glanced in the rearview mirror. A second set of headlights crested a hill behind her.

Phoenix whimpered, and Charlie cradled him in his lap as the car sped down the hill. One half mile later they came to another hill. Vicki noticed something shining at the bottom of the incline. "Quick, everybody out!"

Darrion gathered their things and Charlie picked up Phoenix. Vicki put the car in neutral and wedged a stick against the accelerator, revving the engine.

"What are you doing?" Darrion said.

"Run!" Vicki said as she jammed the car into drive and jumped out of the way.

Tires screeched as the car picked up speed. Vicki watched it cross the center line into the next lane. The roadway dipped, causing the car to swerve right. Just before the bridge, it veered toward an embankment.

Vicki ran into the nearby field and joined Darrion and Charlie. They heard a terrific crash in the distance and rushed into the night.

Natalie craned her neck to see the flashing lights of two GC cruisers ahead. Henderson pulled up to the bridge. Natalie followed him and the other Peacekeeper down the embankment on foot. Maggie's car had smashed against a tree and both doors had flown open. The air bags had deployed. Natalie imagined Vicki and the others lying dead alongside the car.

"Happened a few minutes ago," a Peacekeeper near the car said.

"Anybody in it?" Henderson shouted.

"No. And there doesn't appear to be any blood around."

Henderson inspected the debris, then leaned into the car. "It's in neutral. They must have let it roll from up there." He turned to Natalie and handed her the cell phone. "Get satellite on the line now. We need to know which way they went."

Natalie took the phone, dialed the number, and asked for the satellite operator Henderson had been working with. She had helped the kids escape, but now, by pinpointing their location on the ground, she was helping capture them again.

Henderson took the phone. "Yeah, we've found their

car but the kids are gone. Can you locate anyone on foot? .
. . What? That can't be!" Henderson looked up.

"I can see the moon as clear as day!" He gave the coordinates again. "I don't believe this. All right, I'm going to stay
on the line and let me know when you make contact."

"What's wrong?" Natalie said.

"New guy took over. He says there's some interference, but it can't be the clouds. Must be a glitch in the
system." Henderson gathered the other Peacekeepers.
"You three go west along this creek bank. The three of us
will go east. Radio me the second you spot anything."

———————————

Vicki ran as quickly and quietly as she could through the
tall grass, leading Darrion and Charlie away from the
road, then north. Three cars had passed on the road and
stopped near the bridge, so she was sure they had found
Maggie's car. Would the GC come looking for them away
from the road or stay with their cars?

Vicki was exhausted, and she could tell that Darrion
and Charlie were tired and scared. Phoenix whimpered
and Charlie clamped his mouth shut.

As they neared the creek, the three knelt by the
stream. There was movement near the road, but Vicki
couldn't see how far away the GC were.

Phoenix suddenly put his paws on the ground and
wriggled free. Charlie lunged, but the dog was gone,
scampering along the creek toward the road. Darrion
grabbed Charlie's arm when he started after the dog.

"I'm sorry, I—"

"Shh," Vicki said. "Let's just get away from here."

"But what about—?"

"Phoenix will take care of himself," Vicki said. "Come on."

———————————

Natalie saw Phoenix first. He was coming from the east, trotting along, sniffing at the creek bank.

"Look!" Natalie shouted. "That's the dog!"

Phoenix barked and Henderson unholstered his gun.

"I saw him just loop around us," Natalie continued. "It looked like he came from back toward the road."

"Our cars!" Henderson said. He looked at Natalie. "Get that dog and meet us at the road."

Natalie ran after Phoenix, but the dog dodged her and followed Henderson. She looked into the darkness and prayed for her friends.

———————————

Vicki's legs ached as she ran up a knoll and through a cluster of trees. She was sure the satellite would locate them. She stopped and heard a radio crackle from their left, so the kids ran east a few hundred yards, then north.

"I see a road," Darrion whispered a few minutes later.

They ran beside the road until Darrion held up a hand. "I'm turned around. We could be running right toward them."

Two headlights blinded them as a huge vehicle pulled out of the brush. It skidded to a stop in the gravel and a door opened.

"Need a ride?" Mark said.

29

JUDD shook hands with his new friend, Chang Wong, and Chang suggested they move to a gazebo that was more private. As they walked, Chang talked about the Peacekeeper Donaldson.

"I feel bad for the guy," Judd said. "He seemed so blind."

"From what my sister says, there aren't many Global Community workers left who are open to the truth."

"What does your sister do?"

"Her name is Ming. She has been working at a women's facility in Belgium. The Global Community sent her on assignment here last week."

"She's older than you?"

"Yes, she is twenty-two. Do you have family left?"

Judd shook his head and told Chang the story of his family's disappearance.

"As difficult as it must be to lose your parents and a

brother and sister, I wish your story were mine. My mother and father do not know God personally. My father is a devoted follower of Nicolae Carpathia, and I'm afraid of what will happen if my parents find out my sister and I are both believers."

"How did you and your sister discover the truth?"

Chang smiled. "We grew up in China and didn't have much religious training. I studied computers and electronics and different languages."

"Your English is perfect."

"I had a good teacher. Anyway, my sister's story is tragic. She was married two months when the disappearances occurred. Her husband was riding a commuter train that crashed when some of the men controlling it vanished. A short while after Carpathia signed the peace treaty protecting Israel, she joined the Global Community and was assigned to what used to be the Philippines.

"At the same time, I was watching the world fall apart from home. When school resumed, many in my high school were gone. There were rumors that they had been involved in the underground church that had become so big in my country."

"Did you figure it out on your own?"

"I tried to watch Dr. Ben-Judah on television, but my father turned it off. That made me more curious.

"Some friends stumbled onto a meeting place of one of the former underground churches. One whole family that owned a restaurant in our area had disappeared. These boys decided to investigate.

"At the rear of the kitchen they found a false wall.

Behind it was a room that would hold as many as one hundred people. Tucked away in a secret compartment were hand-copied Bibles and song sheets. We also found a schedule of meetings. These believers came at all hours of the day and night, one hundred at a time, to pray and study God's Word."

"Incredible," Judd said.

"Yes. Each week hundreds passed through that room and learned the truth of the Bible. Even more incredible is the letter my friends discovered. An envelope was tacked on the wall next to the secret opening. On the outside it read 'If we disappear.' It was as if they knew what was going to happen."

Judd rubbed his arms and felt a chill. He thought about Pastor Bruce Barnes and the video he had found explaining the Rapture. The letter from these Chinese Christians wasn't as high-tech, but it contained the same message.

"What did the letter say?" Judd said.

"I'll show you a copy sometime. Basically it said that if people had disappeared and no one knew where they were, it was because Jesus had come back for his followers. The Rapture happened during the day in China, so many people were injured and even killed because of absent drivers and accidents. The father of my friend Chu Ling was washing windows on a tall building with a man who had talked to him about God for many months. Chu's father looked away for a moment, and when he turned around, the other man was gone. Only his clothes and his squeegee remained."

"What did your friends think of the letter?"

"Some believed right away and prayed the prayer the pastor had written. Chu prayed that day and came to my house immediately. He took me upstairs and locked the door because he was afraid of my father. I read the pastor's letter and it all made sense. For things in the Bible to come true like that was too much of a coincidence.

"Of course, I downloaded a Bible from the Internet almost immediately and started studying and reading Dr. Ben-Judah's Web site. That's when I started writing Ming."

"How did she react?"

"At first, I could tell she didn't want to listen, but we had been good friends through the years and I made her promise that no matter what she decided, she would not tell Mother and Father. I reprinted the letter the pastor had written and included the prayer. I also copied verses from the Bible and sent them to her. Ming finally wrote that she had become a follower of Jesus. It was one of the happiest days of my life."

"And she stayed in the Global Community?"

Chang nodded. "She has tried to help fellow believers."

Chang asked to hear more about the Young Tribulation Force and hung on Judd's every word, from news of the underground newspaper in their high school to the recent satellite transmission from the kids in Illinois.

"You know this Vicki B.?" Chang said.

Judd smiled. "She's one of my best friends. Did you see her?"

"My father required me to go to the meeting. When the Vicki B. segment came on, I noticed her mark and prayed she would be able to continue. The authorities at our site were able to shut off the satellite feed, but only after many had heard and believed the message."

Judd checked his watch. "I should get in touch with my friends and tell them I'm okay."

"Call from my apartment," Chang said.

As they walked, Judd showed Chang the buildings he had visited during his previous trip to New Babylon. He briefly told Chang of Pavel and Pavel's father, Nada, and her brother, Kasim. Chang showed an identification card at the front door, and the guard let them inside.

"So your dad's pushing you to do the same as your sister?"

Chang nodded as they entered a glass elevator and pushed the button to the fourth floor. The Wongs' apartment was number 4054. Chang's mother was small with dark hair and didn't speak English as well as Chang, but Judd understood her enough to carry on a polite conversation. Judd called Lionel and told him what had happened and said he would be back in an hour or two.

"No, you have dinner with us," Mrs. Wong said.

"I really shouldn't—"

"I insist. You meet husband too."

Judd looked at Chang, who shrugged and cocked his head. "Looks like you're staying for dinner."

Chang took Judd to his room. "We have to be careful, especially during dinner. My father will ask you many questions about your allegiance to the potentate and what you plan to do in service to the GC."

"I understand. Now tell me what's going on."

"I know I might help the cause if I work for the GC," Chang said, "but we already have someone inside the communications center. Plus, I'm not sure I can stomach being close to Carpathia. The things I saw at the resurrection nearly made me want to jump up and shout my trust in God."

"Where were you sitting?"

"In the VIP area near the main stage. When Fortunato called down fire on the three rebel potentates, we were so close I could smell the smoke. My father was in tears when Nicolae pushed that Plexiglas coffin lid off and stood up. I don't even want to think about that day. A lot of believers were killed by the lightning."

"So why can't you just tell your dad the truth? He'd understand, wouldn't he?"

"You don't know my father," Chang said. "The other reason I can't work for the Global Community is Carpathia's mark. All employees are required to receive the biochip injection and the mark within a few weeks, but I have heard rumors that new hires will be first in line."

Judd nodded. "Makes sense. That way they hire you knowing you're loyal."

"Exactly. And I will die before I take Carpathia's mark."

"If you told your dad that, he'd never make you work for the guy."

"If I admit I am a follower of Christ and an enemy of Nicolae, Father will report me. That's how loyal he is to the potentate. But it's not only my life that's at stake. I am afraid he will demand to know the truth about Ming."

"What does she say about all this?"

"She thinks I should remain quiet, but I don't know how I can."

"Come with us," Judd said. "The Young Trib Force will hide you."

Chang smiled. "Thank you. I've thought about that. I'm afraid the GC would catch me and that would kill my father."

The front door opened, and a man spoke loudly in the next room. "That's him," Chang said as he led Judd to the kitchen area. The man's English was slightly better than his wife's, and he spoke rapidly and forcefully. Judd noticed Chang's shoulders droop when his father talked.

"I visit Personnel Department today. Show your grades, letters of recommendation, whole thing. They like it and say they will take your information straight to top. What do you think?"

Mr. Wong slapped Chang on the back and beamed. Chang grabbed Judd's shoulder and pulled him forward. "I'd like you to meet my new friend from the former United States."

"United North American States now," Mr. Wong said. He eyed Judd and thrust out his hand. "You applying to work with Global Community too?"

Judd smiled and nearly laughed, but he composed himself, crossing his arms over his chest. "Uh, no sir, I'm just visiting."

"He's staying with Z-Van, the famous singer," Chang said.

Mr. Wong nodded. "Much talent. Very loyal to His Excellency. Music too loud, but I can plug my ears."

"Dinner in one hour," Mrs. Wong said, and Chang led Judd back to his room.

Vicki kept looking behind the van, sure that the GC would find them using the satellite. Mark filled her in on what had happened to the kids since they had separated. She couldn't believe the danger the kids had encountered or the way God had moved among the people at the shelter.

When Mark pulled the van into the parking area of the underground hideout in Wisconsin, Vicki finally felt safe. She couldn't wait to see the others. Shelly was the first to hug her, and Janie brought food for them.

"I'm too tired to eat," Vicki said.

The others wouldn't let her go until they had heard what had happened in Des Plaines. Darrion helped tell the story. When they finished, Conrad opened the van door and looked around. "Where's Phoenix?"

Vicki explained what had happened. Charlie apologized and everyone assured him it wasn't his fault. The kids asked about the Shairtons' farm, but Charlie was too emotional to talk. "I'll tell you in the morning."

"I think we ought to pray and thank God," Shelly said after Vicki had finished her story.

The kids joined hands and thanked God for keeping them safe and providing food and shelter. After a few minutes, Charlie said, "And, God, I want to thank you for giving me friends that would risk their lives for me. And I ask you to take care of Bo and Ginny in that jail. Help them get out of there. And for Mr. Zeke too. Be with them every step of the way."

"And for Maggie and Natalie," Vicki prayed. "Help them to not get in trouble for helping us."

"And Phoenix," Janie said. "I know he's just a dog, but he's been a big part of this group from the start. Protect him and bring him back to us."

Shelly showed Vicki to a shower, and a few minutes later Vicki crawled into bed between fresh sheets.

As the sun came up on the Wisconsin hideout, Vicki was twenty feet underground in darkness, dreaming of her friend Ryan Daley. He was laughing and playing with Phoenix, just like the day they had first met.

30

JUDD prayed with Chang about the GC job and his parents. He asked God to give Chang clear direction. Chang prayed for Judd, Lionel, and their new friend, Westin.

Mrs. Wong called them to dinner. When everyone was seated, Mr. Wong folded his hands and closed his eyes. He said a few words in Chinese, then began eating.

Chang glanced at Judd. "My father just gave thanks to Carpathia for the apartment and the food."

Mr. Wong slammed down his fork and scowled. "You not call him that. You say His Excellency or Lord Carpathia. Never use only last name, understand?"

"Yes, Father."

Mrs. Wong passed Judd a full plate. He tried to avoid eye contact with Mr. Wong, but the man kept looking at him.

"How you meet my son?"

Judd carefully wiped his mouth with a napkin, thinking quickly how much information he wanted to share. "We were on a Web site a bunch of friends and I put together."

Chang kicked Judd under the table.

"What Web site?"

"It's harmless, really. We talk about things going on in the world and try to figure out what will happen next."

"What you think of Carpathia coming back to life?"

Judd took a mouthful of food and sat back. He swallowed and leaned forward. "We actually nailed that one."

Mr. Wong frowned. "Nailed? What is nailed?"

"They predicted it before it happened," Chang said. "Father, why do you have to interrogate my friends?"

"I ask question. What so wrong with that?"

"I don't mind," Judd said.

Chang's mother said something in Chinese that angered Mr. Wong. The two sat in silence. Finally, Mr. Wong started a conversation about the new Nicolae. "I hear today that potentate not need sleep. He stay up twenty-four hours every day."

Judd knew this was because Carpathia was inhabited by Satan. Judd didn't want to think of all the wicked things Nicolae had prepared for the world. He knew the man would eventually rise up against Jewish people and believers, but most would blindly follow him.

"You say you not here to work for Global Community," Mr. Wong said. "Why you here?"

Judd didn't want to lie to the man. Mr. Wong needed to know God just like everyone else. But if he was loyal enough to pray to Carpathia, he was surely under the spell of the evil one.

"I'm actually here against my will," Judd said.

Mr. Wong frowned. "You kidnapped?"

"Not exactly." Judd told the story of finding Z-Van in the rubble of the earthquake in Israel and how they had been promised a flight home. "We changed course and headed for New Babylon. Z-Van wanted to attend the funeral and that's why I'm here."

"You see the man rise from the dead in person?"

Judd nodded.

"Most incredible thing ever."

Judd kept nodding. "I can't think of the right words to describe it."

Mr. Wong looked at Chang and said something in Chinese. "Very soon I have two children working for Global Community. Our daughter, Ming, she is Peace-keeper."

"Chang told me you were all together during the . . . funeral service."

"What a day. And soon my own son work for most wonderful leader world has ever seen."

"Father, I haven't even graduated high school."

"So? You could teach high school. They have tutors here. I talk with leader few minute ago. Very high up in Global Community. He say they want you."

"For what? You know they're not going to—"

"He say they let you complete school here."

"But what department would take a—"

Mr. Wong smacked the table. "You genius! No question. You program any computer, fix any electronic in house. You the future of Global Community."

Chang rolled his eyes. "If I'm the future, the Global Community is in big trouble."

"No!" Mrs. Wong said. "Husband right. After paperwork through, you work for Mr. Fortunato—"

"Supreme Commander!" Mr. Wong yelled.

"Yes, sorry," Mrs. Wong said.

Chang dropped his fork noisily. "What paperwork?" A pause as Mr. Wong eyed his son. "Father, what have you done?"

"I give documents to Personnel Department. Application and transcripts already through."

Chang rose and pushed his chair back from the table. "You had no right to do that. I told you I can't work for them. Stop pushing me!"

"You get used to being away from your mother and—"

"That's not it!" Chang yelled. "I'm not working for the GC, and that's final."

Chang stomped from the room and slammed his door. Mr. Wong shook his head and kept eating. Judd looked at his food and tried to think of a way out of the apartment.

Mr. Wong leaned toward Judd and smiled. "He afraid to leave home, but this an opportunity of lifetime."

"Maybe it's more than being away from you. Maybe he's not GC material."

"He perfect GC material. He change mind when he find out about mark."

"What do you mean?"

"You promise not to tell?" Mr. Wong looked toward Chang's door and chuckled. "Man on phone is named Akbar. Big in Global Community government. He say Chang's résumé already get to His Excellency. Potentate actually talk about Chang." Mr. Wong rubbed his hands together with delight. "Only a matter of time before he is processed. Then he sign more papers, the Global Community make offer, and Chang take mark of loyalty."

"But if Chang doesn't want to—"

"It settled. Chang will be among first to take mark, and I be there to watch."

Judd's heart sank. He knew Chang would die before he took the mark of Carpathia. He excused himself from the table and headed toward Chang's bedroom.

Mr. Wong stood. "You go now. Chang upset. We leave him alone."

Judd nodded. "Okay, maybe I'll call him later tonight."

"Not good idea. You go."

Judd thanked Mrs. Wong for dinner, and Mr. Wong walked him to the elevator. Judd asked if he would have any trouble getting out of the building, and Mr. Wong shook his head and stared at Judd.

"I have bad feeling about you."

"I don't understand," Judd said.

"All through dinner you never talk about Potentate. Not say anything good or bad, except that you predict his coming back to life."

"What do you want me to say?"

The elevator dinged and the door opened. A young

couple in Peacekeeper uniforms stood at the back. Mr. Wong bowed to them slightly and ushered Judd into the car. "You no call my son."

As Judd walked to the hotel, he tried to think of a plan to get Chang out of New Babylon. No matter what, he had to do it before the GC tried to give him Carpathia's mark.

———————————

Vicki awakened in a darkened room and couldn't remember where she was. A clock by the bed glowed 2:17, but since there were no windows she couldn't tell whether it was morning or afternoon. She lay back, closed her eyes, and thought of Natalie and Maggie. She wondered if Deputy Commander Henderson had pieced the plot together.

A mechanical whir sounded through the air ducts overhead. She heard muffled conversation through the vents and recognized Charlie's voice.

When Vicki emerged from the small bedroom, Shelly gave her something to eat and ushered her into a living area complete with a television monitor that doubled as a computer screen.

"We were wondering when you'd wake up," Shelly said.

Mark introduced Colin Dial's wife, Becky. She was tall with blonde hair and Vicki guessed about forty. Becky smiled. "If you need anything, all you have to do is ask."

"I could use a toothbrush," Vicki said.

"Ready for a tour?" Mark said as Becky went to the supply cabinet.

"I need to talk with Charlie first."

Vicki found Charlie with Conrad and Janie. Charlie was clearly sad about losing Phoenix, and the others tried to console him.

When he saw her, Charlie stood and hugged Vicki. "I didn't get to tell you last night how glad I was to see you. You and Darrion risked your lives for me."

"Nothing you wouldn't have done for us."

They all sat as Charlie began his story. "After you guys left Bo and Ginny's farm, we settled in. I was so worried about you guys the first night I couldn't sleep. Then we read the e-mail that said you'd made it and I felt better.

"These GC guys came back a couple of days later. They had found the satellite truck where you guys hid it and wanted to ask Bo more questions. The guy said he knew the satellite truck had been in the barn."

"He must have noticed that first day," Mark said. "Why didn't you get out of there?"

"We thought everything was going to be okay. Bo said they'd leave us alone, but they didn't. We heard clicks on the phone line, and Ginny said they were listening." Charlie stared off, thinking.

"What is it?" Vicki said.

"Remember when I asked you if we were going to die before Jesus came back?"

Vicki nodded, recalling their long talk the night the kids left for Wisconsin.

"Well, you said a lot of believers were going to be killed in the next couple of years. When the GC came for us, all I could think of was whether we would be some of the first to die, and it scared me."

Mark put a hand on Charlie's shoulder. "I don't blame you. It scares me just to hear your story."

"What happened the night I called?" Vicki said.

"Bo saw some GC cars from the barn loft, so he knew they were watching us. He pulled his car to the back of the house, and we loaded up a bunch of stuff."

"Why didn't you e-mail us?" Vicki said. "We would have helped."

"I told Ginny it would be okay, but she wanted to be careful."

"That was smart," Mark said.

"Bo and Ginny fought about what to do. She wanted to just drive away right then, but Bo said we should wait and leave after dark. We were going to drive through one of the fields to get to the road."

"But they came for you," Vicki said.

Charlie nodded. "We turned all the lights off so they'd think we were asleep. Ginny wrapped some of her stuff in a blanket so it wouldn't break and took down all her picture albums. That's when she freaked."

"Why?" Vicki said.

"One of her big albums was missing. Bo said they were only three and a half years from seeing Jesus and not to get upset over a bunch of faded pictures, but she got really mad. She said if the GC had that album there wouldn't be any pictures of me. They'd know I wasn't their son."

"So that's how they pieced it together," Mark said.

"Ginny took the rest of her stuff to the car and came running back inside. Said somebody was moving around outside."

"Creepy," Janie said.

"We locked the doors, and I helped Bo move some stuff to block the front door. Then we went into the cellar. We could hear radios outside and Bo said just to keep quiet. That's when you called, Vicki."

"If I'd known you were in that much trouble, I wouldn't have called."

"They started banging on the doors, trying to get inside. Ginny told me not to talk, so I put the phone down. That's when they crashed through the windows. We could hear them walking around upstairs, so we kept quiet. For a while we thought we were going to be okay, but then something bumped the cellar door and stuff started dripping through the boards."

"Gasoline," Mark said.

Charlie nodded. "Bo and I flew up the stairs and tried to open the cellar, but they had it blocked."

"I can't believe they tried to burn you alive," Janie said.

"They use fire against believers everywhere," Mark said.

"How did you get out of the cellar?" Vicki said.

"I told Bo to move and I kicked the doorknob off. It took about three good hits to get it open, but I finally did it. The fire started at the back of the house." Charlie's lip quivered. "I really thought we were going to die."

Vicki closed her eyes and imagined the fire spreading

through the farmhouse. Everything the Shairtons owned was gone in minutes.

Charlie held up his left arm, and Vicki noticed a five-inch-long gash. "I helped Ginny through the window and got this. Bo's clothes caught on fire and we had to roll him on the ground, but he was okay."

"And they took you into custody?" Mark said.

"They weren't real happy we made it out, but they put us in different cars and brought us all the way back to Des Plaines. The guy in the front kept asking if I knew where Ben-Judah was, and I told him I didn't have any idea."

"I'm glad we got you out of there," Vicki said.

"Me too," Charlie said. "But I keep thinking about Ginny and Bo. If we don't get them out, they'll die."

31

NATALIE sat at a desk near Deputy Commander Henderson's office with a blank yellow legal pad before her. She listened to the talk around the office, the whispers at the watercooler, the hushed conversation behind partially closed office doors that Henderson might be reassigned.

Natalie had spent the hours after the chase in Wisconsin in fear for her life, wondering if Henderson would piece together the facts and blame her. But a strange turn of events caused Henderson and his companions to trust her again.

After searching for Vicki and the others until early in the morning, Henderson had left the area and driven to Maggie Carlson's home in Des Plaines. Natalie rode along, apologizing for her part in letting the kids get away. Henderson didn't say much, clearly upset that they weren't able to track the kids by satellite.

At Maggie's house, things quickly fell apart. Henderson accused the woman of giving false information about her vehicle to throw them off. Maggie listened quietly and ran her hand across the tablecloth. "I knew you'd figure it out sooner or later," she said. "I helped those girls escape and I'm glad I did."

"You're one of them, aren't you?" Henderson scowled.

"I serve the true, risen Savior, Jesus Christ," Maggie said. "I'll do anything to give that message. I'll protect anyone who is a fellow believer. Helping those kids escape is one of the best things I've done in my life."

"It will be one of the last things you do," Henderson said as he handcuffed the woman and led her to the car.

After arriving at the jail and helping process the woman, Natalie walked back to her apartment, wondering about Maggie's future and why the satellite hadn't worked the night before. Had God blinded the operators somehow?

The next day Natalie sat at her desk and filled out forms explaining her story, but something still wasn't right. She phoned the satellite operations number, and a woman flipped through the logbook. "Looks like Brad was on until late. Then Jim Dekker relieved him."

Natalie explained why she was calling, and the woman reluctantly gave Dekker's home phone number. Natalie called and left a message.

She scribbled on the yellow legal pad, feeling alone. This was one way of talking to someone, even if it was only a sheet of paper staring at her.

1. Leave and find V. and others.
2. Stay and keep out of Henderson's way.
3. Stay and help Maggie, Ginny, Bo, and Zeke.

The first option seemed the safest. She could simply contact Vicki, find a ride north, and meet up with the Young Tribulation Force in Wisconsin. She crossed out option 1.

The second option was a good one. Natalie could do her job, blend into the surroundings, and keep the Young Trib Force alerted to the GC's movements. If a new leader came in, which was almost sure to happen, she could make herself almost invisible.

She crossed out option 2 and studied option 3. *If I don't try to help, I'll never forgive myself,* Natalie thought.

She tore the page off the pad and shredded it in a nearby machine. Something blipped on the computer in Henderson's office and Natalie pulled up the network e-mail. A system-wide message marked "urgent" had just been sent by GC headquarters to "all United North American States personnel."

All jails, prisons, and reeducation centers will receive shipment of the first loyalty enforcement facilitators within seven to ten days.

Why don't they just call them neck and head separators? Natalie thought.

The biochip injectors will ship separately directly from New Babylon. All Global Community personnel should

303

*refer to the machines with the exact terminology used
above. The loyalty enforcement facilitators should not be
called guillotines, and their use will not be referred to as
a beheading. We will not use language that causes the
public to think of violence or causes followers to think we
are forcing people against their will.*

Natalie sighed. *So we shouldn't say, "Take Carpathia's
mark or we'll chop off your head!"*

*On the contrary, the Global Community has been
forced to implement this needed equipment to maintain
peace and harmony for the people of the world. In fact,
we hope we never need the loyalty enforcement facilitators and believe only a few enemies who see themselves as
martyrs will even consider not taking the mark of loyalty.*

The message listed sites around the country and
added that the first United North American States location to apply the mark would be the former DuPage
County Jail in Illinois. Natalie checked a calendar. She
had to save her friends or they would prove the Global
Community wrong. There were many who wouldn't take
Carpathia's mark, and she was one of them.

Judd met with Lionel and Westin about Chang's situation. They agreed the only safe plan was to get Chang
away from his father, which meant having him hide or
even return with Judd and Lionel to the States.

"How about Israel?" Lionel said. "He could stay with Mr. Stein."

"I don't think Z-Van's up for more company," Westin said. "He talked about you two this morning and asked what I thought about ditching you."

Judd's mouth dropped open. "What did you say?"

"Didn't say anything. He floats stuff like this a lot just to see how you react. I think he thinks I'm kind of attached to you guys."

"Maybe we shouldn't go to Israel after all," Lionel said.

Westin held up a hand. "Z-Van's kept you around this long. Don't bail yet."

"What about Chang?" Judd said.

"Keep in touch with him. They'll have to give him a date when they want him to start work. We'll get him out before he takes the mark."

Vicki asked Mark to show her around outside the underground shelter. Mark took her through a series of doors that led out. The hideout was well hidden, and Mark explained why Colin had built the shelter.

Vicki looked out on the Wisconsin countryside. "I think I could live here."

Mark took her inside the small house where Colin and Becky lived. "There's another level to the underground. Come on."

Beneath the living area, even farther underground, was storage for food, water, and an emergency generator in case of a power outage. Mark opened another door into a darkened room and Vicki stepped inside.

"You ready for this?" Mark said.

Vicki nodded and Mark turned on the lights. On the length of the back wall was a map of the world with pins placed in various cities. Around the room were different types of computers and printers, most of them turned off. There were three smaller rooms to the side with recording equipment, cameras, and other high-tech gear.

"What's all this for?" Vicki said.

"Colin and his wife were just going to use this as living space, but he really wanted to use this place to reach more people. They have a friend who's a computer whiz, and he found a lot of this at churches and Christian ministries. The rest of it Colin bought."

"What's the map for?"

"The red pins are GC outposts," Mark said, pointing at Des Plaines. "If there's a yellow pin, it means he knows there's somebody on the inside who's a believer."

Vicki saw at least fifty yellow pins in North America alone. "But what's all this for?"

Mark shrugged. "Colin doesn't know yet."

"Do you think it has something to do with us?"

Mark sat at one of the working computers and pulled up the kids' Web site. "If we could get everybody working on something, pulling together all these resources, there's no telling what we could do. We could hack into GC mainframes with the right passwords and change information. We could send e-mails, help Chloe Williams's co-op, communicate with all of these believers at the different GC sites—"

"You have to remember that they won't be working there much longer. Once they make them take Carpathia's mark they'll have to run or die."

Mark turned to the computer and pulled up a drawing. "This is a mock-up of Carpathia's mark. Colin's friend figured out a way to make it into a fake tattoo."

"And fool the GC?"

"Right. We hack into the GC records and make them think the believers already have the mark. Of course, we have to find out if it looks enough like the real thing, but it could be done."

Vicki sat and stared at the floor. She thought of Bo, Ginny, Zeke, and Maggie. *What about them?* She thanked God for bringing them to Colin and Becky's place. "And please," she prayed silently, "show us what to do next."

When Natalie saw her chance, she grabbed a file folder from a stack near Deputy Commander Henderson's office and went downstairs to the holding area. Women's cells were on the north side of the building, and the men were on the south.

Natalie showed her identification and looked in the folder. "Just a couple of questions Henderson wants answered of the Judah-ite."

The guard nodded and buzzed the door. Natalie walked through confidently and heard the lock click behind her. She passed several women sleeping in the dimly lit cellblock and heard someone whispering down the corridor. Maggie Carlson was talking with a woman in the cell next to her. Maggie glanced at Natalie and winked. Natalie walked to the end of the row and heard verses of an old hymn. "Are you Ginny?"

The woman glanced at the mark on Natalie's forehead and nodded. "When I was little, I learned a lot of songs at a country church. I thought they were old-fashioned at the time, but the words stuck with me."

"It sounds beautiful."

Ginny took Natalie's hand. "Do you know anything about my husband?"

Natalie shook her head. "I haven't been in the men's side and don't know if they'll let me in, but I came to tell you that Charlie is safe."

Ginny put a hand to her mouth and whispered, "Praise God."

Natalie briefly told her what had happened and that Vicki and Darrion were safe too. "I'm trying to get you and your husband out of here before they start giving people the mark."

Ginny shook her head. "It's too dangerous."

Natalie's lip quivered. "If you stay here, they're going to make you take Carpathia's mark, and the only option—"

The door opened at the end of the hall, and the female guard yelled, "You okay?"

"Yeah, almost through."

When the door closed, Ginny reached through the cell bars, took Natalie by the shoulders, and locked eyes with the girl. "Listen to me. It does my heart good to know Charlie and the others are safe. You risked your life to do that, and I'm sure you wouldn't hesitate to risk it again for us. But you have to understand that we're ready to go."

"What do you mean?"

"I've had one thing on my prayer list since I became a believer, and that's my husband, Bo. Charlie and the others told him the truth and somehow God opened his eyes. I'm forever grateful for that."

"But you don't understand. They're going to kill you if—"

"I do understand. Bo and I talked about what we'd do if the GC caught us and made us swear loyalty to Carpathia. I don't look forward to it, but from what Dr. Ben-Judah wrote, we know God will give us the strength we need at just the right time."

Natalie wiped away a tear. "I'm still going to try."

Ginny smiled and slipped a piece of paper in the girl's hand. "If you can, pass this along to my husband. And don't blame yourself if you can't get us out of here. Just make sure you're safe."

Natalie nodded and slowly turned down the hallway. Behind her came the words, "He is risen!"

She turned, looked back at Ginny, and with tears in her eyes repeated the words meant not for Carpathia, but for Jesus Christ. "He is risen indeed!"

32

NATALIE wiped away a tear and straightened her uniform. She held her cell phone to her ear and waved at the guard through a small window.

"That's what the woman told me," she said as the guard opened the door. "You want me to talk with the husband?"

The guard sat at a small desk, leafing through a magazine. Natalie put her hand over the mouthpiece and said, "The deputy commander wants me to speak with the husband."

The guard looked up and winced. "We don't usually allow females—"

"You want to talk with my boss?" Natalie said, holding out the phone.

"No, that's okay. If he wants you in there, go ahead."

While the women's side had seemed subdued, the

men's side was noisy. The guard walked a few feet inside the cellblock. "Stay in the middle, miss."

Natalie slowly walked down the corridor. She had heard of the arrest of several gang members only days before, and as she walked, she sensed the eyes of the inmates on her.

An older man spoke over the hoots of other prisoners. Some yelled for him to shut up while others wanted to hear him.

"You think you know the truth and the rest of us are idiots!" one prisoner said.

"Yeah, old man, what makes you an expert on religion?" another said. "Owning a gas station?"

Some laughed and made jokes about pumping gas for God, but the older man wouldn't quit. "I never said I was an expert, but you don't have to have a degree to see what's happening. Everything that's going on in the world was predicted in the Bible thousands of years ago. Pretty soon, they're going to come in here and lead us out one by one and tell us we have to take Carpathia's mark. I'm warning you, if you take that mark, your eternal destiny will be sealed."

"What happens if we don't take it?" a man yelled.

"They'll kill you."

Several men groaned loudly. One said, "I'll take my chances with the mark. I don't want to die."

A thin man behind Natalie called out, "Carpathia's a monster. I don't trust somebody who kills people who disagree with him. I won't take the mark either."

"But it won't do any good to refuse the mark without

receiving the forgiveness God offers," the older man said. "Accept it now, before it's too late."

"Listen to him!" a man said near Natalie. He had a higher voice and spoke with a slight accent. "My wife tried to tell me the truth for a long time, but I wouldn't listen. It took a kid showing me the Bible to make me believe."

"Are you Bo?" Natalie said.

The man nodded.

Natalie held out the piece of paper. "It's from your wife."

Bo took the paper and thanked Natalie, recognizing the mark of the believer on her forehead. "What are you doing in here, sister?"

"I wanted to talk with you and Zeke about getting out of here," Natalie whispered.

Bo smiled. "I don't think you could get Zeke out if you tried. He's got a captive audience."

As Natalie approached his cell, Zeke turned to a younger Hispanic man with tattoos on his face, neck, and arms. "You remind me of my son."

"Mister, I don't understand the prophecies you talked about, but I used to hear about God in my mother's church. The priest said Jesus died for each of us, but I never did more than look at him up on that cross."

"What's your name?"

"Manny."

"Manny, Jesus did die on that cross for you. He lived a perfect life, no sin at all. But you've sinned, haven't you?"

Manny lowered his head and nodded. "I've done bad things."

"We all have," Zeke said.

"There is no way he could forgive me."

Zeke stared at the boy. "God loved you so much that he sent his only Son into the world so that anyone who believes in him, or puts his trust in him, won't be separated from God after they die, but they'll have eternal life."

"But you don't know. I would have to spend a lifetime trying to make it up to God."

"Once you sin, you're guilty, no matter how big or how small that sin. You can't go back and change that. That's why Jesus took your place. He lived a perfect life, and God accepted his sacrifice on your behalf. All you have to do is reach out in faith and ask him to come into your life."

The cellblock hushed as Manny sat on his cot. Natalie needed to speak with Zeke, but she waited, standing in the shadows by his cell.

"I have to warn you that if you go through with this, you won't be able to accept Carpathia's mark."

"What do you mean?"

"When you ask God to come into your life and forgive you, he seals you with a mark on your forehead. We can't see it yet, but we will once you've prayed."

A man hurled insults at Zeke and told him he was crazy. Others quieted him as Zeke stared at Manny.

"God won't let you take the evil one's mark because you're his," Zeke continued. "You see, the world is taking sides. Either you're on God's side, or you're on the side of evil. There's no straddling the fence."

"I want to pray," Manny whispered. "I want to be on God's side, no matter what happens."

"All right, then go ahead and tell God you're sorry."

Manny took a deep breath. "God, I'm sorry for killing that guy. And for all the stuff I stole and for the drugs . . ." Manny kept praying, whispering sin after sin until he was finished.

"Now pray with me," Zeke said. "God, I believe you sent your Son to die in my place and that he rose from the dead, and right now I want to accept the gift you're offering me. I ask you to forgive me of all of those sins I've committed, wash me clean, and be my Lord from now on, amen."

Manny prayed along with Zeke and looked up with tears in his eyes. "I feel like I've just had a hundred pounds taken off my back."

A prisoner laughed and others mocked Manny. "God, forgive him for kicking his dog!" one yelled.

Natalie heard a noise and saw a man with a mustache looking through the window at the end of the hall. She glanced away. When she looked back, the man was gone.

Manny stood and wiped his eyes, ignoring the jeers. His face lit up when he saw Zeke's forehead. Then he pointed at Natalie. "She has one too!"

Zeke turned. "Is there something I can help you with?"

"I'm trying to find a way for you to escape," Natalie whispered. "Manny too."

Zeke smiled. "I appreciate you risking your life. But there comes a time when a man has to take a stand."

"I can't let them—"

"You don't understand. I'm a trophy for the GC.

They've charged me with selling fuel oil on the black market, but they know I'm a rebel. Anybody who tries to help me will be in the same boat. I've made peace with God. The only thing bothering me now is getting the rest of these guys to see the truth and to find out about my son. I'd like to know he's all right."

Natalie told Zeke about Vicki and the other kids in the Young Tribulation Force and that there had been a fire at the gas station. "The GC never found any bodies, so I'm sure your son made it out."

Zeke bowed his head and shook with emotion. "I've been praying God would send somebody to tell me about him. I know he'd get a message to me if he could, but that would only put him and the people of the Tribulation Force in danger."

The door at the end of the hall opened and the guard stepped inside. Zeke yelled, "Why'd you send a girl down here to do a man's job? I told you I'd never tell you what you want to know!"

The guard quickly walked toward Natalie.

"This might be the last time I get to come here," Natalie whispered.

"Then remember this," Zeke whispered. "Forget about getting me out of here and get yourself to safety. They'll be making you take that mark pretty soon."

"Miss Bishop?" the guard said. "It's time."

Natalie turned and walked away. She glanced at Bo, who was sitting on his cot, reading his wife's letter. He mouthed, "Thank you," as she passed. Behind her she heard Zeke say, "He is risen!"

Natalie whispered, "He is risen indeed."

Natalie thanked the guard and told her she hadn't learned as much as she wanted. She sprinted up the back stairway and hurried to her desk. She wanted to quickly e-mail Vicki and the others in Wisconsin but knew she had to wait. Her phone rang and she picked it up.

"This is Jim Dekker of satellite operations. You called my house?"

"Yes, Mr. Dekker, I'm sorry to bother you. I just wanted to ask about the other night."

"Is this from you or Deputy Commander Henderson?"

"Well, he may want to talk again, but I'm curious about the conditions during our chase. When we got out of Des Plaines, it seemed like the sky cleared, so I don't understand—"

"How many times do I have to tell you people? You can look at the record for yourself."

"But how do you explain it? If it's clear from the ground, doesn't that mean you should have been able to see?"

"Unless there was some kind of interference. I can't explain it."

Natalie smiled. "Well, thanks for the information. . . ."

"Before you hang up, I have a couple of questions for you."

"Shoot."

"Is the reason you're asking because you think this whole thing might have been caused by God?"

Natalie forced a laugh. "Why would you think that?"

"Just a hunch. And another thing, what's a Morale Monitor doing in the jail area asking questions of prisoners?"

Natalie looked at the caller ID on the phone. It read "Private." "I don't know what you're talking about."

"I think you do. And if you have the right to ask me questions, I think I deserve some answers."

Natalie didn't know what Jim Dekker was up to, but she felt like slamming down the phone and running out of the building. By the time he could call the GC, perhaps she could be far enough away that they wouldn't catch her. She took a breath. "I was delivering something for my boss."

"Right," Dekker laughed. "Okay, how about this one. Why didn't you handcuff that kid in the backseat? You know, the one who was supposed to have maced you?"

"You want to check my eyes, buddy? They're still red from that stuff."

"I believe it. I also believe you sprayed yourself to make it look like one of them did it."

"Look, if you're going to accuse me of something, you'd better have proof!"

"All right, I accuse you. Ready for the charge?"

"Just say it!"

"Natalie Bishop is a Morale Monitor gone bad. You're a follower of Tsion Ben-Judah. You're employed by the Global Community, but you're really working against it. You have no loyalty to Nicolae Carpathia and you think his rising from the dead proves he's evil. For some reason you're visiting prisoners. Maybe you're trying to help them escape like you helped those kids last night."

Natalie sat down hard, her mouth open. She couldn't speak for a moment.

"You want me to continue?"

"No, I mean . . . that's crazy. Who are you?"

"I told you who I am. Now why don't you tell me who you really are, you Judah-ite."

Natalie looked at the nearest exit. If she grabbed the keys to Deputy Commander Henderson's car, she could be in the parking lot in seconds.

"I'll tell you another thing," Dekker said. "You're wondering how you're going to avoid taking the mark of Carpathia and still work for the GC."

"I have to go," Natalie said.

"Hang on—"

"I'm not talking to you anymore!"

She slammed the phone down and looked around the corner. There was no way to get past Deputy Commander Henderson's secretary without her seeing.

Natalie walked past a row of empty desks and looked for car keys. Nothing. Leaving on foot wasn't the best idea, but she had to get to an exit.

The stairwell door was only a few feet away when an office door on her left opened and a tall man with a mustache stepped out. "Going somewhere, Natalie?"

33

NATALIE caught her breath and stepped back. She put a hand on her chest and smiled. "You scared me!"

The man wore a flak jacket and dark clothing. He was tall—Natalie guessed over six feet—thin, wore glasses, black boots, and a baseball cap with the letters GCSD. "Didn't mean to frighten you, Natalie. Why don't you step in the office?"

"This is Peacekeeper Vesario's office. What are you—?"

The man grabbed her arm. Natalie wanted to scream but in a flash she was pulled inside, the door closed. She gritted her teeth and rubbed her arm. "Who are you? What do you want with me?"

The man sat on the edge of Vesario's desk and crossed his arms. "I'd like some answers to my questions."

"What are you talking about? I've never met you."

The man took out an identification card from his shirt

pocket. It read "Jim Dekker, Global Community Satellite Division."

Natalie finally figured it out. Dekker was the man who had looked inside the cellblock earlier. How long had he been watching her? Did he just suspect she was a Judah-ite or did he have evidence?

"Look, I can explain about going into the jail."

"Can you? How about the part about being a follower of Tsion Ben-Judah?"

Natalie put a hand in her pocket and felt for her key ring.

"I'll bet when you hear the phrase 'He is risen,' you don't think about Nicolae at all." Dekker raised his eyebrows and smiled. "Am I right?"

"You have no proof," Natalie said. "I've been a faithful employee—"

"Until you made a couple of mistakes with those kids. I went back in the files and saw you were at the youth event where the satellite truck was stolen. Care to explain that?"

Natalie slowly twisted the top on the Mace dispenser inside her pocket. This man knew exactly who she was. She had to get out of Vesario's office, out of the building, and out of the Morale Monitors forever.

Dekker stood and took a few steps toward the door, turning his back to her. Natalie pulled the Mace dispenser from her pocket and aimed.

"The truth is, you don't need to explain anything," Dekker said, slipping his identification card in his pocket. "I'm the one who should explain."

He put a hand to his head and turned. Natalie aimed at the man's eyes but stopped when he took off his hat. On his forehead was the mark of the believer!

Natalie fell to her knees, shaken. "Why did you do that?"

Jim Dekker knelt beside her. "Wanted to see how you'd react to a little pressure. And I came down here to make sure my hunch was right."

"How did you know?"

Dekker shrugged. "That car chase was strange. Seemed like a setup. I found the report and wondered if this Maggie lady was the only believer involved. I spotted your mark when you were in the men's cellblock."

"So the satellite did see everything."

Dekker nodded. "I watched one of the operators handle it. He had those kids nailed. There was no way they were going to get away."

"What did you do?"

"The guy wanted to keep going until we caught them, even though his shift was over. I convinced him to leave, told him I'd make sure everything worked out. He hung around for another fifteen minutes, the longest fifteen minutes of my life. When he was gone, I programmed a glitch, then covered it up so they couldn't find it."

"I thought it was something God did to blind the operators."

"Well, I think God had something to do with it. He put me there, and I wasn't even supposed to be working. Something told me I needed to be there."

Natalie shook her head. God's protection astounded her. "How did I do with the pressure?"

Jim smiled. "Fine. I need you to keep your cool for a few more days. If we're going to get your friends out before they start applying the mark, I'll need you right here."

"How are you—?"

"Trust me." Jim pulled a plastic case from a pocket and gave it to Natalie. "I'm assuming you have contact with the Young Tribulation Force?"

Natalie nodded.

"When you get home tonight, send them this file. They might be interested in it."

"I want to hear your story," Natalie said.

"Yeah, and I want to hear yours, but not now." Jim sat in front of Peacekeeper Vesario's computer and worked at the keyboard. "Watch the door."

After a few minutes Dekker jotted some notes and stood. "I won't be able to key in the orders from my computer. You'll have to do it from here."

"And we'll be able to get all of them out?"

"Who's down there?"

Natalie listed the four believers she knew. Jim frowned when she mentioned Zeke. "The Zuckermandel guy is off-limits. The others are low enough priority that it might work, but we'll have to work together."

"That means Zeke will have to choose between taking the mark or facing the guillotine."

Jim nodded. "You talked with him. He say anything about it?"

"He said he was ready to take a stand." Natalie looked at the floor. "You should have seen him down there. He was telling people about God, and they were mocking him and laughing. But he didn't care."

Jim put a hand on Natalie's shoulder. "I know it's hard to lose somebody like this. I hate it. But we have to understand that God is in control and he sees the whole picture."

They heard the elevator ding and the voices of several people in the hallway. Jim opened the office door, shoved Natalie out, and closed it quickly behind them. He whispered, "I'll be in touch soon. Find a way into one of these offices and get the password to the computer." Jim turned and headed for the stairwell as Peacekeeper Vesario came toward them.

Natalie went back to her desk and slipped the computer disk Jim had given her into her purse. She couldn't wait to send the file to the kids in Wisconsin and tell them they had a new friend.

Judd found an e-mail from Chang early one morning and shared it with Lionel and Westin.

> Judd,
> So far nothing has changed about my position with the GC. Perhaps I can hack into their computers and give myself a deadly disease so they won't want me. (My sister is worried, but I am hopeful.)
> I'm very sorry about my father's actions toward you.

I continue to pray that he will understand the truth soon.
I won't give up on him or my mother until they actually
take the mark.
C. W.

"He'd better hurry," Westin said.

"Why?" Judd said.

Westin sighed. "Z-Van talked with one of the GC heavyweights last night about his Israel performances."

"There's going to be more than one?" Lionel said.

Westin nodded. "His contact told him the loyalty contraptions—I call them head choppers—are already being sent around the world. They're going to start applying the marks on prisoners to make sure there are no glitches. Then GC employees get a chance. New hires are first in line."

Judd rubbed his forehead. Their time to give the message to people was running out.

Vicki was thrilled when Natalie told her about Jim Dekker. She put her head on the desk and thanked God for his mercy and provision for their safety. When Vicki tried to download the file Natalie sent, the computer seemed to lock up.

"No, it's retrieving it," Mark said, watching the progress. "It's huge. Wonder what's on it."

Vicki composed a message to Natalie as she waited. Mark went to another room and pulled the file up on a different computer.

The kids had settled into a routine in Wisconsin, helping Colin and his wife, Becky. They all slept in the underground hideout, girls in beds in one room, boys in sleeping bags in another. Everyone seemed to be adjusting well except Charlie, who took long walks in the countryside each morning and evening. Vicki tried to assure him that the kids would do everything possible for Bo and Ginny, but Charlie didn't seem to believe her.

When Vicki relayed the information Natalie had sent about Jim Dekker and the plan for Bo and Ginny, Charlie's face lit up. "Do you think they'll be able to come here?"

Vicki smiled. "If Natalie and Jim think it's best, they'll be sleeping in the next room."

Mark seemed out of breath as his voice sounded over the intercom. "Could everybody come to the first-floor computer room?"

Mark stood in front of the screen, his hands in his pockets, as the kids gathered. Colin and Becky were there as well. Charlie scooted close to the monitor and tried to look around Mark.

"I suppose it was enough that this Jim Dekker altered the satellite record and saved us all," Mark said. "But he didn't stop there. He's been working on this program for a while. First, take a look at the note he sent."

Mark dragged the letter from the smaller screen to the larger one at the front of the room.

To: The Young Trib Force
Fr: Jim Dekker, GC Satellite Department, Illinois
Re: The Cube

I've been watching you guys for a while and have admired your work. That stunt with Damosa and the satellite school was priceless.

You might wonder what a guy like me has to do in his spare time. Well, this is it. I've been working on it since I came to know God and started reading Tsion Ben-Judah's Web site.

I thought we could use a simple way to explain the truth about God that used more than words. This may be too late, but I think God wants me to give this to you guys and let you go wild with it.

If you don't think it's a good idea or if there's something wrong with the presentation, trash it. I don't want to give bad information.

If you like it, feel free to send it out and duplicate it any way you'd like. You can print it, put it on a digital assistant, even load it to your watch. I call it The Cube because of the Dynamic Hologram Projection.

God bless you all.

J. D.

"Let's see it!" Charlie said.

Mark clicked a small icon of a cross with a 3 over the upper right quadrant and the program spun to life. The screen went blank, then projected a 3-D image of a cube in midair. A man floated to the bottom of the cube and Scripture appeared underneath.

"The program runs with or without the text," Mark said. "If you e-mail it to someone, you can leave the text on or off."

The man clutched his chest, and thorns grew around him. The scene represented sin and its hold on every person. The text of Romans 3:23 scrolled into view, "For all have sinned; all fall short of God's glorious standard."

A white shape hovered over the man's body. "For the wages of sin is death, . . ." The image dissolved into a bright light. Then a hand reaching out filled the cube. ". . . but the free gift of God is eternal life through Christ Jesus our Lord."

The hand turned and Vicki gasped as a nail pierced the flesh. The image enlarged and pulled back, revealing a man on a cross at the top of a hill. The image rotated, giving the kids the entire scope of the scene. "For God so loved the world that he gave his only Son, so that everyone who believes in him will not perish but have eternal life."

The cube went dark, then slowly lightened to show the entrance to a tomb. The murdered man on the cross appeared in the opening and stretched out a hand, which grew larger until the nail print became visible.

Finally, images of judgments the earth had suffered since the disappearances flashed. The earthquake, locust-demons, fiery hail, a meteor crashing into the ocean, and people dying.

"These judgments have been given by God so that each person might find the truth that is Jesus Christ," the text said. "Without him, we perish. With him, we have eternal life."

More verses were listed along with a prayer to receive the gift of God. The 3-D image of the cross swirled and came to rest on a lonely hill, and the cube went blank.

The room fell silent and Vicki wiped away a tear. Everyone seemed moved by the presentation.

"What do you think?" Mark said.

"How soon can we send it?" Conrad said.

34

VICKI and the others began work immediately with The Cube. They set up an e-mail database of every person who had ever contacted their Web site. Vicki helped separate believers from unbelievers and e-mailed an explanation and the file to the believers first.

This is a tool to use with your family, friends, and anyone you think needs to understand the message, Vicki wrote.

Shelly was in charge of finding any angry or threatening e-mails. They would eventually send The Cube to everyone, but they didn't want to contact loyal Global Community followers and have them post warnings.

By the next day, response was pouring in. One girl in Greece wrote, *I've been trying to explain what I believe to my family for so long. The Cube helped show them God's love. My family hasn't prayed yet, but I'm not giving up. Thanks for your work.*

A teenage boy from California reported that he

showed The Cube to a few friends and they were blown away by the holographics. *I kept the text off when I played it and they had no idea what it meant. When I read the verses, a couple of them understood and prayed. I'm still working on the others.*

Colin Dial walked in smiling. "I just talked with my friend who helped me find this equipment. I told him what Dekker created, and he's found a truckload of some personal digital organizers. You could give one of those to a person on the street if you want, or pull it out and use it as you're talking with someone."

"I just saw a report about the satellite schools," Conrad said. "They're starting up again. We could pass those gadgets out to people going inside."

Mark talked with Natalie by phone late one night and worked throughout the day to hack into the Global Community's computers. With Conrad's help, he finally made it inside and found important information, including a drawing of Carpathia's mark.

Vicki spent most of her time at the computer answering e-mails. She was excited to open a note from Tsion Ben-Judah. He wrote that the adult Tribulation Force had found a safe hiding place, and he was busy teaching converts around the world.

I would especially appreciate your prayers about a sensitive matter in the Force. Things happen when you young people pray, I know it, so please ask God to give us wisdom in the coming days.

If I am right, Antichrist will pour out his wrath

against my believing countrymen soon. Someone will need to lead them to safety. This person will be a modern-day Moses, fleeing an evil ruler and taking his people to a safe haven.

Pray this person will have confidence that God can work in him and communicate through him far beyond any ability he ever had before. He will have to oppose Antichrist himself and rally the masses to do what is right.

Thank you for praying. I ask that each of you will be strengthened inwardly for the difficult days ahead.

Vicki posted the letter in different rooms of the hideout. Charlie asked what Vicki thought was going to happen in Israel.

"What do you think?" Vicki said.

Charlie scratched his head. "I've been trying to figure it out. I think Nicolae is going to break his promise about protecting Israel and do something in the Jewish temple." He scowled. "What does *defile* mean?"

"It means you take something good, something holy, and mess it up really bad."

"How do you know big words like that?"

Vicki smiled. "I had to look that one up myself. What else do you think's going to happen?"

"Nicolae is really mad at Jewish people. God doesn't want him to hurt them, so he's got a hiding place. This person Dr. Ben-Judah wrote about is going to lead them to it, and I think I know who it is."

"Who?"

"Well, he has to be Jewish, and he has to be a believer. I'd expect he'd have to be able to speak well enough to get people to follow him. Sounds like Dr. Ben-Judah to me."

"You might be right," Vicki said. "Tsion teaches that God's people will be supernaturally protected."

"What does that mean?"

"Do you remember back before the disappearances when Israel was attacked?"

"You mean all the bombs that fell but didn't kill anybody?"

Vicki nodded. "I think God and his angels will protect them."

Charlie looked at the floor and sighed. "I wish Phoenix was supernaturally protected."

"Is that why you've been so down?"

Charlie nodded. "You promised Ryan you'd take care of his dog, and I took that seriously."

Vicki put a hand on Charlie's shoulder. "It's not that I don't take it seriously. I know Ryan wouldn't have wanted us to put ourselves in danger. I actually think Phoenix was trying to save us in some way. He must have sensed the danger."

Charlie nodded. "I wish I knew what happened to him."

———

Natalie Bishop watched the communication between Deputy Commander Henderson and his superiors. The man seemed in a frenzy meeting with high-level officials.

Natalie wondered if Henderson's job was on the line, but she didn't dare ask.

One afternoon Henderson called her into his office. "Is something wrong, sir?" she said.

"No, I just thought I'd let you in on your new assignment. Command asked me to ID people from different levels to participate in an upcoming exercise."

"You're moving me?"

"No, I recommended you represent Morale Monitors at the processing of the first group taking the mark of loyalty. You'll observe at the GC compound in Wheaton."

Natalie felt faint. She put a hand to her head and gasped.

Henderson put a hand on her shoulder. "I know it's an honor, Bishop. And you've earned it."

"When does it begin?"

"Only a couple more days and you'll be able to wear the mark of your lord and your god."

I already do, Natalie thought.

Judd didn't hear more from Chang for a few days and worried that something might have gone wrong. Finally, Chang wrote that he had been able to avoid meeting with the GC, but that his father continued to insist he work for Carpathia.

Judd outlined a plan for Chang to get away from his parents' apartment and hide on Z-Van's plane. Westin would meet him at the airport and make sure he made it safely. He would hide there until the trip to Israel. Mr.

Stein and Sam Goldberg had agreed to help find Chang a place to stay.

Chang agreed but asked that Judd and his friends wait. Chang said he had spoken with another believer on the inside of the Global Community who was also trying to help.

Z-Van called everyone in the suite together, which now included more members of his band and his agent, Cyril Bernard. The man had rushed to New Babylon after seeing Z-Van's surprise press conference, but Z-Van had refused to see him until now. Cyril dressed in colorful clothes and huge glasses. His shoes sparkled and he smelled of too much cologne.

"This project is going to be, without a doubt, the greatest album in the history of modern recording," Cyril said in his heavy British accent. "It represents the two greatest comebacks—"

Z-Van rolled his eyes and said, "Shut up!"

"I was speaking of yours and His Excellency's, of course."

Z-Van slurred his words and appeared to sway as he talked. He stood between Judd and Lionel, put an arm around each, and introduced them as the reason for his miraculous comeback. "If my music brings joy or causes people to worship the true and risen lord, you can thank these two young people."

Judd glanced at Lionel, and it was all the two of them could do not to run from the room. Z-Van's breath smelled terrible, and he hung on the boys like an old coat.

"I'm sure these two have wondered why I've let them

stay so long. The truth is, they tried to convince me their religion was right and I didn't buy it. Now I'm trying to convince them that the potentate is lord."

"As if anyone would need convincing of that," Cyril muttered.

"If they haven't been persuaded yet, perhaps being in the audience today when the second in command speaks will convince them."

"You mean we're going to meet Reverend Fortunato?" Cyril interrupted.

"Not Reverend," Z-Van said. "Most High Reverend."

Later, Judd and Lionel looked for a way out as the group walked along together. It was noon in New Babylon and the temperature felt a lot like the day of Nicolae's resurrection. Tourists still walked the grounds near the palace with cameras, gawking and pointing at anyone they thought might be famous.

Two GC Peacekeepers ushered the group inside the vast church of Carpathianism. Judd and the others were seated near the front, at the right of the podium that seemed to hover high above the audience. When the time came, a velvet curtain parted and Fortunato emerged, wearing a long red-and-blue robe.

The Most High Reverend reported on the race to complete duplicates of Carpathia's image. Live interviews with people at different locations around the globe showed the progress, but none had as many as the United Carpathian States.

Some statues were black, many made of gold, some crystal. When the screen showed an orange replica of

Carpathia, Lionel leaned over to Judd. "I wonder if that
one comes without pulp."

Judd snickered and Cyril elbowed him.

Fortunato relayed the sad news that Jerusalem had
failed to begin the building process of their statue. He
looked into the camera and scowled. "Speaking under the
authority of the risen potentate, I say woe! Woe and
beware to the enemies of the lord of this globe who
would thumb their noses in the face of the most high!"

Just as quickly, he was back in his gentle mode, speaking as if he were tucking them all in bed for a bedtime
story. He reminded everyone that he had been given
power to call down fire from heaven on the unfaithful,
but that Carpathia was full of love and forgiveness.

"Yeah, right," Lionel whispered.

"One week from today, the object of our adoration
shall personally visit his children in Jerusalem. He will be
there not only to deal with those who oppose him—for
he is, besides being a loving god, a just god—but also to
bless and accept worship and praise from the citizens
otherwise without voice.

"As your global pastor, let me urge those in Jerusalem
who are loyal to their lord and king to bravely show your
support to the one worthy of all honor and glory when
he arrives in your home city. May it be a triumphal entry
like none before it."

Fortunato promised safety for anyone who would
worship Carpathia in the presence of Judah-ites and
Orthodox Jews. "Unless they see the error of their ways
and come on bent knee to beg forgiveness of their lord,

new leadership will be in place before His Excellency leaves that great city.

"And to those who swear that the temple is off-limits to the potentate himself, I say, dare not come against the army of the lord of hosts. He is a god of peace and reconciliation, but thou shalt have no other gods before him. There shall not be erected or allowed to stand any house of worship anywhere on this planet that does not recognize His Excellency as its sole object of devotion. Nicolae Carpathia, the potentate, is risen!"

The crowd assembled rose with a cry of "He is risen indeed," but Judd and Lionel half stood, half sat.

"All statues must be completed within two days and should be open for worship. And, as you know, the first one hundred cities with finished and approved units will be the first to be awarded loyalty mark application centers."

Fortunato showed a replay of his calling fire from heaven and Carpathia's rising from the dead. Judd shuddered. This, along with recorded messages from Carpathia and Fortunato, would be shown at each mark application facility.

Fortunato addressed the possibility of counterfeit marks. "While it may be impossible for any but highly skilled and trained observers to tell a fake mark from the real, biochip scanners cannot be fooled."

Judd glanced at Lionel and winced. The screen switched to a shot of a guillotine, and Fortunato laughed. "I can't imagine any citizen of the Global Community having to worry about such a device, unless he or she is still in the cult of the Judah-ites or Orthodox Judaism."

The Most High Reverend showed the world a stack of applications from people who wanted to be first to show their loyalty to Carpathia. Judd noticed Z-Van squirm in his chair like a child grasping at a new toy.

"Does the application hurt? It does not. With technology so advanced and local anesthesia so effective, you will feel only the pressure of the biochip inserter. By the time any discomfort would have passed, the anesthetic will still be working.

"Bless you, my friends, in the name of our risen lord and master, His Excellency the Potentate, Nicolae Carpathia."

As the crowd rose and applauded Fortunato, Lionel leaned over to Judd. "Chang doesn't have much time."

35

NATALIE frantically worked with Jim Dekker to get the believers out of jail, but she became discouraged when she discovered that Zeke Sr. had been moved to the facility in Wheaton. Jim Dekker helped her stay focused on the Shairtons, Maggie, and the newest believer, Manny.

Jim invented a Commander Regis Blakely, who was stationed in Joliet. He e-mailed Deputy Commander Henderson a list of four prisoners he wanted to interrogate before the mark of loyalty was given. If Henderson bought it, Colin Dial would become Commander Blakely and retrieve the four.

Natalie sat outside Henderson's office, waiting for the man's reaction to the e-mail. She heard him curse and slam his fist on the desk.

"Is anything wrong, sir?" Natalie said, sticking her head in the door.

"A commander thinks we're not doing our job," Henderson said. "He wants to interrogate some prisoners."

"Can I help?"

Henderson looked out the window as a document printed. He handed her the page. "Make sure we actually have all four of these people. We'll transport them tomorrow to a holding facility in Joliet."

Vicki and the others in Wisconsin helped clean the Dials' van. They wanted it to look like an official GC vehicle, so the kids scrubbed it clean, inside and out.

Next, Becky Dial brought a printout of the Global Community's insignia and began painting it on both sides of the van. Becky had studied art in college, and when they were finished, Vicki compared the picture with the painting and couldn't tell the difference.

Mark took an emergency call from Natalie, who gave directions to Jim Dekker's home. Dekker had a GC uniform for Colin and instructions for the rescue.

Mark told the others Natalie's plan. Everyone had been excited about The Cube and its success on the Internet, but now they had to concentrate on helping their friends.

"I don't think anyone should go with me," Colin said.

"At least let me tag along in case you need help," Mark said.

"I know how these guys operate," Conrad said. "Let me go."

Mark and Conrad argued until Vicki suggested they flip a coin. Conrad won. The kids circled around and prayed for safety. Vicki turned away as Colin kissed his wife and whispered something to her.

A noise in the distance startled Vicki. Charlie heard it too and ran to the front of the house. When Vicki caught up, she saw something running through a field toward them.

Ears flopping, jaws bouncing, a dog lumbered toward the house.

"Phoenix!" Charlie yelled as he ran toward the animal.

"How could he have found this place?" Mark said.

Vicki smiled. "I've heard of things like this, but I've never seen it happen."

The dog bowled Charlie over, and the two rolled in the grass fifty yards away. When Phoenix made it to the house, everyone took turns petting and hugging him.

Mark and Conrad inspected the dog's collar for a homing device, but found nothing. "From the looks of him, he hasn't eaten in days," Mark said.

Becky ran for some food, and Charlie said he was going to give Phoenix a bath.

"That's a happy ending," Melinda said to Vicki.

Vicki nodded and watched Colin and Conrad get into the van. "We need one more happy ending before this is over."

Conrad stayed out of sight in the back of Colin's van until they found Jim Dekker's address. The farmhouse was in McHenry, a small town in Illinois just south of the Wisconsin border. The earthquake had damaged a grain silo and the barn in the back, but the white house still stood. The porch was screened in just like Conrad remembered from his grandparents' house.

Jim Dekker greeted the two and had them park in the back. The house smelled musty and white sheets covered the furniture. Conrad noticed a rickety piano with yellow keys in the living room. A GC uniform hung from a dusty chandelier in the dining room. Jim took Colin's picture and loaded it into his computer for his new ID badge.

"Where did you get the uniform?" Colin said.

"Satellite operations has its own dry cleaning in the basement. I made a master key that gives me access. While I was on my coffee break last night I borrowed it. We'll need to return it before tomorrow morning."

Colin smiled. "I suppose you made a nameplate for me?"

Jim nodded and pulled off the plastic wrapping. "Believe me, when you meet any Global Community personnel, they'll stop in their tracks and salute."

Conrad explained that he had been a Morale Monitor before becoming a believer. "I've been teaching Colin the correct way to salute."

"Good," Jim said. "Have you had any military experience, Colin?"

Colin shook his head, and Jim gave him a crash course on GC protocol—when to salute, how to talk, and how to treat those lower in rank. "You walk like a top dog, like you're superior. It's all in the attitude."

"I didn't think I was actually going into the building."

"You won't, unless you have to. Natalie says Henderson leaves around 5 P.M. You'll call him just before he leaves and tell him you're in the area with a GC vehicle and would like the prisoners you requested."

"Won't they be suspicious when I don't have a driver?"

Jim pointed at his head and said, "Attitude." He stood, threw out his chest, and said, "Try me."

"Okay, uh, Commander, why are you driving around without a—"

"What business is that of yours, Deputy!" Jim interrupted. "If I want to ride in here on a motor scooter and take these prisoners to the North Pole, you'll salute and go back to your office. Understand?"

Conrad laughed.

"What are you smiling at, kid? Wipe that grin off your face."

Conrad shook his head. "You act like that and we'll be able to bring the whole jail home."

Colin asked why they had to leave Zeke Sr. behind, and Jim explained that the GC wanted to make an example of him. "Natalie says they've even separated him from the rest of the inmates and have a separate guard."

"They think he's going to try and escape?" Conrad said.

"No, Zeke's been telling all the prisoners about God, and the GC is afraid he's having too much influence on them."

Jim brought some food and asked about The Cube.

"Some kids are writing and saying they've been 'cubed' and are going to 'cube' others. It's wild."

While they waited, Conrad asked to hear Jim's story.

Jim said he would try to give the short version. Jim had grown up in Glen Ellyn, a suburb west of Chicago. "My mom and dad were Christians and took us kids to church every week. I have three older sisters.

"I was into computers, biology, and read a lot of science fiction. Big horror fan. Any movie that was supposed to scare you and I was there. I wanted to go to Northwestern, had the grades too, but it was just too much money for my parents, so I settled for a state school."

"Did your parents know you weren't a Christian?" Conrad said.

Jim nodded. "I'm sure. I'd argue with them about evolution and creation. They sat me down one night and said they were concerned about the direction I was headed, but I blew them off. I wasn't a bad kid. I didn't do drugs or run around. In fact, that was what kept me from really knowing God."

"What do you mean?"

"I never really thought I was that bad a person. I didn't need God. I didn't even believe he existed. I went to church, sat in the Sunday school classes, closed my eyes when people prayed. I even took notes during the sermon sometimes. Other kids played the good-Christian routine, then went out and partied, but I didn't. I figured if there was a God, he'd be okay with me if I just did what my parents told me.

"I signed up for the military after college and they put me into a specialized unit that used satellite technology. I had a blast. When I got out, I was hired by a computer company developing advanced search-and-destroy technology. Stuff in fighter jets and helicopters."

"That's how you knew how to make The Cube!"

Jim smiled and nodded. "I had talked with my dad one evening about his health. He wasn't feeling well and my mom was worried. He said he was proud of me for all I had accomplished, but that the most important thing was whether I truly knew Jesus. He told me the Lord was coming back and that I needed to be ready."

"What did you say?"

"I didn't want to upset him so I just told him he didn't have to worry, that I'd made my peace with God." Jim leaned forward, elbows on knees, and shook his head. "That night it happened. People I'd known all my life disappeared. I heard about it the next morning and drove over to my parents' house. There were people in the streets, confused, crying, looking for their babies. I walked inside the house and a sound scared me to death."

"What was it?"

"Silence. In all my years growing up, Mom and Dad had played a Christian radio station. It was on all through the night. You couldn't walk into that living room without hearing a Christian song or some teaching from the Bible. That morning it was like somebody had sucked the life right out of that place.

"I found their nightclothes in bed and a bunch of medication on the nightstand next to my dad's side, along with his Bible. Dad had a little notebook underneath that he used to write out prayers for his kids. Before he fell asleep that night, he had written something about me."

Jim went out of the room and returned with a dog-eared spiral notebook. He opened it and handed it to Conrad. Colin leaned in close to see. The handwriting was scrawled across the page and hard to read:

> *Father, I pray again for Jimmy tonight and ask that you would open the eyes of his heart so that he would know the hope you want him to have. He doesn't know about the riches of the inheritance he could have or the great power of your strength that can work so mightily in him. I pray that you would take off the blinders and help him see how much you love him. Jimmy could do such great things for you if he would only give his heart to you. Show him the truth. In Jesus' name, amen.*

Jim looked out the window to the back of the farm. "I found about a dozen of those notebooks on the shelf in his closet. Every one of them had pages and pages of prayers for me. That one was taken from Ephesians. He didn't know it, but his prayers were answered that morning by his bed. I called out to God and prayed I wasn't too late."

"What about your sisters?" Colin said.

Jim shook his head. "All three of them were gone, with their families. I was alone. For a long time I thought it was hopeless, that I'd just missed out. Then I started reading the Bible and trying to understand the things I had heard all my life. You can't believe how relieved I was when I started reading about others who had prayed and had been forgiven. Then Tsion Ben-Judah came out with his findings about prophecy, and I knew I had to work on the inside of the Global Community to help people."

Jim asked them to follow him, and the three descended the musty stairs to the basement. "Over the past few months I've been able to set up a bunch of names for made-up GC soldiers and workers. I knew I'd have to have more than just names to make them look real."

Jim switched on the light and Conrad gasped. Racks of GC uniforms lined the walls. He had everything from Morale Monitor to Peacekeeper outfits, both male and female.

"We should be able to find something for you, if you want to be the commander's driver," Jim said to Conrad.

"How did you get all these?"

"I got the idea right after the earthquake. I knew there would be a lot of GC bodies with the coming judgments, so I found a believer at a funeral home who was handling the bodies. He agreed to get me as many uniforms as he could sneak out. I don't own any higher rank than a deputy commander."

After Jim had given final instructions, he handed Colin a cell phone. "This is yours, Commander."

Conrad drove the van and followed Jim toward Des Plaines.

Colin sat in the passenger seat buttoning his commander's uniform. "You ready for this, Morale Monitor?" he said in a deep voice.

"Yes, sir."

36

NATALIE watched the clock at the jail and prayed that Colin would arrive soon. From her access to the GC computer she saw that Deputy Commander Henderson had approved the transfer of the prisoners for early the next morning.

Henderson approached his secretary and asked her to contact Commander Blakely's office in Joliet. Natalie's heart sank. "Is there anything I can help you with, sir?"

Henderson shook his head. "Something's weird about this Blakely. I'd never heard of him before yesterday, and neither has anybody else around here."

Henderson's secretary buzzed him. "I've found Commander Blakely in the database, but no one can tell me how to reach him in Joliet."

"Odd," Henderson said.

"Check the message he sent with the transfer order," Natalie said.

Henderson pulled the message up, and Natalie pointed to a phone number at the bottom of the screen. Henderson punched his speakerphone and dialed. The phone rang twice, and then a man with a deep voice answered gruffly, "Blakely."

Henderson sat up straight. "Uh, Commander, sir, this is Deputy Commander Henderson in Des Plaines."

"Yeah, glad you called. You get my transfer order processed?"

"Yes, sir, we'll transport them tomorrow."

"Don't bother. I'm headed your way now. I'll pick them up myself."

"But, sir, I thought we were supposed to—"

"Hey, tough break with those Judah-ites who got away. I'm hoping one of these will break and tell us what we want to know."

"Well, sir, the Hispanic prisoner, Aguilara, isn't charged with sedition. He's here on a gang charge—"

"Yeah, but I understand you had him in proximity to the gas station owner, was it Zuckermandel?"

"Yes, but he is in solitary now and—"

"We're pulling up to your place now. You bring 'em out and I'll wait here."

Henderson looked at Natalie and mouthed, "He's here."

"You want me to have the guards bring the prisoners outside?" Natalie said.

"You got that, Henderson?" the deep-voiced man said.

"Yes, sir, we'll be right out."

Henderson phoned the guard station and asked that

the four be brought to the front parking lot immediately. Natalie tagged along, not wanting to miss the exchange.

Henderson walked through sliding doors into the sunshine. A GC van was parked near the entrance. Commander Blakely stepped out and Henderson saluted. The commander returned the salute and handed him official-looking papers.

Henderson scanned the documents. "We had planned to bring the prisoners to you in Joliet tomorrow."

"I appreciate that. Truth is, I'm part of a covert division looking into the Judah-ites. I'm hoping for new information from these prisoners."

"You don't think we've been lax in our questioning, do you?"

The commander held up a hand. "This has nothing to do with your hard work, Henderson. As a matter of fact, your name came up in a joint conference we held the other day."

"Me, sir?"

"Nobody envies where you are. It's a real hotbed of rebel activity."

Henderson nodded. "I had wondered what the upper brass thought of my situation."

Commander Blakely hesitated as the prisoners were led outside. The guard handed a key to the Morale Monitor driving the van.

"When will you begin applying the mark of loyalty?" Blakely said.

"I'm headed to observe another facility in the morning. We hope to start here tomorrow afternoon."

"Good," Blakely said. "Now, if you'll excuse us, we'll

take care of these prisoners. And I'll put in a good word for you at command. You've been very helpful."

As the commander drove away, he tipped his hat to Natalie, showing the mark of the true believer. She smiled and saluted.

When Conrad had driven a few minutes from Des Plaines, he sighed and pulled to the side of the road. Colin released their new friends from their shackles.

"That was quite a performance back there," Maggie Carlson said, slapping Colin on the shoulder.

Jim Dekker pulled in behind them and climbed in. He greeted the four former prisoners and took his cell phone from Colin. Everyone agreed to meet at Jim's house in McHenry before heading to Wisconsin. "Stay in character, Commander, and keep going."

Vicki and the others whooped and yelled when they heard the news from Conrad. Becky Dial quickly brought some new cots and sleeping bags out of the storage area and prepared for the new arrivals.

After Fortunato's speech, Judd and Lionel had kept their distance from Z-Van's crowd and slipped back to the hotel with Westin. After conferring, they decided they would call Chang that evening and tell him of the escape plan.

Judd dialed Chang's number and Mrs. Wong answered. "He not talk now."

"Please, I really need to talk with him."

The phone clunked on the table, and the woman said something in Chinese. Mr. Wong picked up. "You the one have dinner with us?"

"Yes, sir, I just wanted—"

"You not good influence on my son. You stop calling. No more. Understand?"

Mr. Wong slammed the phone down and Judd hung up. He turned to Lionel and Westin. "I don't like the sound of that. Mr. Wong's really angry."

"You think he knows Chang's a believer?" Lionel said.

Judd shook his head and tried e-mailing Chang again, but there was no response.

"Okay, that's enough for me," Westin said. "New plan. The plane's ready. All we have to do is contact Chang and take him there. The question is, how?"

"We could just go in and get him," Lionel said.

"Too much security," Judd said. "Only way in is through the front door and GC guards check IDs."

"They can't keep him inside forever," Lionel said.

"Good thinking," Judd said. "We'll set up watch outside the building and if Chang comes out alone, we'll grab him and head for the plane. If he's with his parents, we can follow them and wait until he goes into a bathroom or something."

Lionel and Westin agreed, and Judd described Chang to them. Lionel volunteered for the first watch, and Judd walked him to the GC building. It was getting late and most of the lights were out in the apartments above them. Lionel found a spot behind some shrubbery where he could see the front door.

"That's the only door I've seen anybody coming through," Judd said. "I think they have to check in and out with the guard."

A new guard for the next shift walked past. When the man had gone into the building, Judd patted Lionel on the back and told him to call if he saw anything. "I'll be back at about five in the morning."

Natalie's joy at the release of the four believers was short-lived. The next morning she accompanied an excited Deputy Commander Henderson and a number of other Peacekeepers to the former DuPage County Jail. It was now the main holding area for criminals in the Midwest.

The jail buzzed with activity as workers prepared for the application of Carpathia's mark. The group was led to a room specially created at the entrance to the cellblock. Prisoners were to be taken one by one to the "loyalty application room" and given their biochip injection and identifying mark.

Natalie asked a woman she knew where the guillotine was and the woman frowned. "You're not supposed to use that word. It's 'loyalty enforcement facilitator.' "

"Right," Natalie said. "Where is it?"

"They won't need it. I mean, who in their right mind would choose death instead of a little injection and a tattoo?"

Natalie wanted to tell the woman the truth. This was more than simply numbering people for identification. Any person who willingly took the mark of Carpathia would seal their eternal destiny. "In case there is somebody who's that stupid, where would they do it?" Natalie said instead.

The woman pointed to the top of the stairs. "They're putting it together in one of the interrogation rooms. But don't get your hopes up."

Deputy Commander Henderson had seemed happier since meeting Commander Blakely. He spoke with a friend he knew at the facility and assured the man his job wasn't in jeopardy.

When they completed the tour, Henderson adjusted his dress uniform and motioned everyone outside. "It's show time, people."

Cameras and microphones covered the lawn outside the jail. A slight breeze swept through as GC employees gathered in a semicircle behind the cameras. The head of the facility introduced himself and made a short statement.

A reporter asked, "Sir, do you expect any executions today?"

The man smiled. "We have seen the leader of our world rise from the dead. Who could say no to this man? All he asks is that we identify ourselves with his cause, the cause of peace."

When the press conference was over, Natalie and the others returned to the loyalty application room. The crowd was so large at first that she had to stand at the top

357

of the stairs to watch prisoners being led in. Two women were shown in first, surprised at all the onlookers. After what seemed like only a minute, the procedure was over. The crowd applauded and gawked at the insignia both women had chosen.

Natalie was able to move closer after the first few prisoners were processed. One man held the injection device for the biochip and two other officers were in charge of the tattoo. They worked like machines, turning out followers of Carpathia like sausages.

Each person was asked a simple question when they entered the room. "Are you ready to show your loyalty to His Excellency?"

Most simply said, "Yes," but one man muttered, "What choice do I have?"

It was after noon and Natalie still hadn't seen Zeke Sr. Her heart leapt when she heard one worker say, "That's the last of them."

Deputy Commander Henderson checked the list and said, "What about Zuckermandel?"

Natalie climbed halfway up the stairs and listened to the echo of footsteps down the corridor. Zeke Sr. stood tall as he walked the length of the hall. Natalie wondered if she would have the strength to watch.

"Are you ready to show your loyalty to His Excellency?" a guard said.

"I sure am," Zeke said.

"Where do you want the mark, on the forehead or the hand?"

"You can keep it. I'm showing loyalty to the real

Potentate—God. And I'm not taking your mark or your injection."

Silence. Deputy Commander Henderson stepped forward. "You know what this means, you old fool?"

"I'm not the fool. People who take this mark are because—"

A slap, then Zeke crumpled to the floor. Natalie wanted to cry out, but she held her tongue. A guard hustled Zeke upstairs and Henderson followed close behind. Natalie couldn't move as Zeke was pushed past her. A door closed around the corner.

Natalie managed to climb to the top of the stairs. She slipped inside a nearby observation room, where she could see what was happening through the one-way glass. Zeke stood by the guillotine, blood trickling from his mouth.

Henderson pointed at the guillotine. "You will not make a mockery of this process. Will you take the mark?!"

Zeke spoke slowly through gritted teeth. "I . . . will . . . not."

Two guards pulled him to his knees while Henderson raised the blade to its full height. Zeke's lips moved in silent prayer as the guards cuffed him. The old man leaned forward until his head fit through the opening.

"You have one final chance," Henderson said.

Natalie put a hand to her face and trembled. She wanted to rush into the room, mace all the guards, and release Zeke. Everything in her screamed out to help, but there was nothing she could do.

"Father," Zeke said, "I pray you'd forgive these people for what they're about to do. Help them see the truth. Jesus Christ is the true Lord of the universe. He alone deserves to be worshiped."

Deputy Commander Henderson raised a hand, and the guard beside the machine reached for a lever. Zeke whispered, "Into your hands I commit my spirit."

Natalie turned away at the sound of the falling blade. She crumpled onto the floor of the darkened room and wept. As workers removed the lifeless body, she cried for Zeke. She cried for the other believers around the world who would have to endure the same punishment. And she cried for herself.

ABOUT THE AUTHORS

Jerry B. Jenkins (www.jerryjenkins.com) is the writer of the Left Behind series. He owns the Jerry B. Jenkins Christian Writers Guild, an organization dedicated to mentoring aspiring authors. Former vice president for publishing for the Moody Bible Institute of Chicago, he also served many years as editor of *Moody* magazine and is now Moody's writer-at-large.

His writing has appeared in publications as varied as *Reader's Digest, Parade, Guideposts,* in-flight magazines, and dozens of other periodicals. Jenkins's biographies include books with Billy Graham, Hank Aaron, Bill Gaither, Luis Palau, Walter Payton, Orel Hershiser, and Nolan Ryan, among many others. His books appear regularly on the *New York Times, USA Today, Wall Street Journal,* and *Publishers Weekly* best-seller lists.

Jerry is also the writer of the nationally syndicated sports story comic strip *Gil Thorp,* distributed to newspapers across the United States by Tribune Media Services.

Jerry and his wife, Dianna, live in Colorado and have three grown sons.

Dr. Tim LaHaye (www.timlahaye.com), who conceived the idea of fictionalizing an account of the Rapture and the Tribulation, is a noted author, minister, and nationally recognized speaker on Bible prophecy. He is the founder of both Tim LaHaye Ministries and The PreTrib Research Center. He also recently cofounded the Tim LaHaye School of Prophecy at Liberty University. Presently Dr. LaHaye speaks at many of the major Bible prophecy conferences in the U.S. and Canada, where his current prophecy books are very popular.

Dr. LaHaye holds a doctor of ministry degree from Western Theological Seminary and a doctor of literature degree from Liberty University. For twenty-five years he pastored one of the nation's outstanding churches in San Diego, which grew to three locations. It was during that time that he founded two accredited Christian high schools, a Christian school system of ten schools, and Christian Heritage College.

Dr. LaHaye has written over forty books that have been published in more than thirty languages. He has written books on a wide variety of subjects, such as family life, temperaments, and Bible prophecy. His current fiction works, the Left Behind series, written with Jerry B. Jenkins, continue to appear on the best-seller lists of the Christian Booksellers Association, *Publishers Weekly*, *Wall Street Journal*, *USA Today*, and the *New York Times*.

He is the father of four grown children and grandfather of nine. Snow skiing, waterskiing, motorcycling, golfing, vacationing with family, and jogging are among his leisure activities.